THE NAUGHTY CORNER

BY MARK TOWSE

A THREE NOVELLA COLLECTION

EERIE RIVER PUBLISHING
www.EerieRiverPublishing.com

Eerie River Publishing
www.EerieRiverPublishing.com
Hamilton, Ontario Canada

This book is a work of fiction. Names, characters, places, events, organizations and incidents are either part of the author's imagination or
are used fictitiously. Any resemblance to actual persons, living or dead, or actual events is purely coincidental. Except all the details about Hell, that is real.

Paperback ISBN: 978-1-998112-17-3
Digital ISBN: 978-1-998112-18-0
Edited by David-Jack Fletcher

Cover design by Don Nobel
Book Formatting by Michelle River of Eerie River Publishing

ALSO BY MARK TOWSE

Nana
Crows
3:33
Gone to the Dogs
There's Something Wrong with Aunty Beth
Nature's Perfume
You Only Live Once
The Bucket List
Mischief Night
ARCRANIUM

COMING SOON

Chasing the Dragon (March 2024)

STORIES

THE GENERATION GAMES 7

MY NAME IS BRIAN 105

THE NAUGHTY CORNER 151

ABOUT THE AUTHOR 263

SNEAK PEEK - CHASING THE DRAGON 264

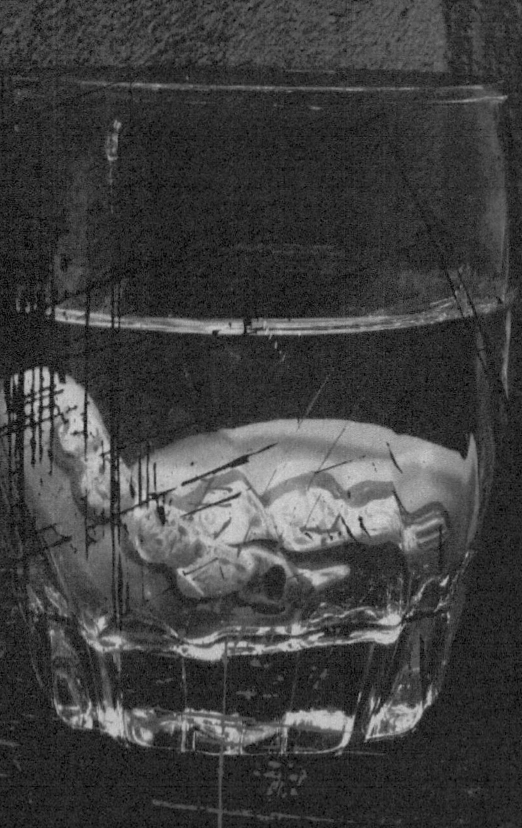

As usual, I'm dedicating this collection to my greatest fan. Thanks for all your help and support, Mum. That said, I also want to give a massive shout-out to all who have taken a chance on me, including the countless reviewers, podcasters, and "bookstagrammers" who have helped spread the word.
From the bottom of my heart, thank you.
X

THE GENERATION GAMES

Jenny and Patrick

"Run, Jen!"

"Patrick, it's gaining on us!"

He turns his head to see the snapping teeth just behind his wife's mass of hair; the once expensive just-stepped-out-of-a-salon bouffant now resembling a smashed-in haystack. "We're nearly there, Jen. Dig in!"

"I am!" Skin the colour of beetroot, her feet falling heavy into the soft ground, Jenny feels like her heart might explode. Beyond her husband's pale and taut face, she sees the drones ahead, hovering over the finishing line fifty yards away, perhaps less. "Patrick!"

"Don't think, just run." As his left foot catches an exposed root, Patrick snaps his head back around, momentum doing just enough to save his life. He sees his wife struggling. "Jen, you have to dig in! You have to—"

"You're pulling too hard, Patrick," she cries, tears cutting their way down her reddened cheeks. She can smell the foulness behind her, hear the rattly breathing of the thing with only feeding on its mind. Twenty yards back, she made the mistake of looking over her shoulder, catching its stare—predatory, beyond animalistic. And she swears it was wearing a smile.

As her husband glances over his shoulder again, Jenny reads in his eyes how close the thing is. Hope fades. Even the threat of becoming a zombie platter couldn't keep her away from the one-health-star aisle. The salads her husband carefully prepared, the precise measuring of ice cream portions, even limiting her cookie intake to two per day, all for nothing. His inevitable snoring being the trigger for her to sneak downstairs and gorge on her secret bounty. The operational planning was so intricate and detailed: the multiple hiding spaces, the stashing of empty wrappers in the spare duvet cover, waiting until the eve of bin collection and sneaking out in dark clothes to dispose of the evidence. But her magnum opus being the dresses from the back of the wardrobe, the ones she used to wear at her largest.

"Run!" her husband screams.

But each breath is like swallowing fire. She's lightheaded. The world spins, her husband's face caught in a swirl of pistachio and chocolate. "I can't."

It's like dead weight. Patrick grits his teeth and plants his feet into the damp earth, but he can't do it alone. "Fucking run, lard-ass!"

It's a last-ditch effort to inspire something—aggression, adrenaline—but he can't deny the inkling of anger that she would put his life at risk for a Twinkie. He turns, eyes on the finish line, unable to believe they could come this far only to fail. "Run, you fat fuck!" He had his suspicions, but if questioned, she'd turn on the waterworks, deny everything, and accuse him of shaming. It's time for hard truths. "Run, fatty, run!"

Her husband's comments land without a sting. It's a passage of time where words carry no value or consequence, a window between life and death where nothing means anything. As she continues going through the motions with leaden legs, gasping for air, she can feel its hot breath against her neck, tasting its last meal. "Patrick!"

And as he turns, she sees the hopelessness in his eyes. No further words of encouragement emerge, no more insults, just an open-mouthed appreciation of finality.

She feels its hand on her shoulder, her husband now leading a chain of three. With a raspy growl, it's on her back, riding her as though she's a knackered workhorse on its last legs. It sinks its teeth into her neck. She lets out a cry and goes to the ground, her clammy hand slipping from her husband's.

Patrick stops dead, watching the thing pushing his wife's head into the mud, muting her watery cries. It lets out a growl and plunges its teeth into her back fat, ripping into the now exposed doughy white flesh as though it's freshly baked bread. Willing himself from his temporary trance, Patrick rushes towards it, flailing his exhausted arms at the grotesque face now dripping with his wife's blood. Before he can get a decent shot off, its grey hand snaps around his left ankle, taking his leg away and sending him to the ground with a soft thud that does no justice to the searing pain exploding across the back of his head.

"Patrick!"

It's a sickening cry, full of pain and knowing. He tries to move, but only manages to roll to his side, body overrun with pain, every part of him screaming to stay the fuck still. Helpless, he watches the thing spin his wife around like a rag doll and rain down a barrage of punches that sends her head this way and that. For a moment, he thinks he sees it smile.

"Get off her!" he screams, wincing as his leg crunches but holds underneath him. Offering an alien cry, he hobbles towards the *thing* again. Even as he unthreads his belt and wraps it around the thickness of its neck and pulls, the creature continues to pound his wife's head, her face an unrecognisable canvas of slop. Continuing to yank at the thing, he screams, giving it all his might, but his wife is already gone, and he knows it. As more roars emerge from behind, he turns.

Too many to count.

The thought of going the same way terrifies him, but before he can even make a move, pain rips through him like fire. He looks down to see the thing's teeth lodged in his calf, magnificent red spilling across his white ReGenevate sneakers. With a garbled scream, he rips his leg away and runs, albeit with the parting gift from his wife's murderer, and an already-twisted knee. He makes it ten yards before he goes to the ground, pants around his ankles, the smell of mud filling his nostrils.

Those Underpants Are Wearing Him

Trudy turns ninety-four next week but doesn't look a day over fifty. Look at those cheeks, plush lips, eyes as clear as crystals, and neck muscles as tight as cable cords. What use is money in the bank when you're expired?

Don't let age define you.

Together, we can turn back time.

ReGenevate – your passport to youth.

The advert fades, giving way to a horrendous composure of otherworldly groans from the monitor and Malcolm's relentless chewing—mouth open for maximum acoustics, chin glistening with an unholy cocktail of sauce, milkshake, and liquefied meat. He looks like a big fat baby in the first stages of learning how to eat. Even before he made a vile pass at Fiona at the Christmas party, she hated him. She finds herself praying he'll one day— *Please be today*—choke on a mouthful of the shit they sell at Fat Tony's.

"You really are a sadistic little bastard, aren't you?"

It's not the first time someone's called him that or thereabouts. Self-reflection not being his strong point, he shrugs, and drops the drone in closer. "It's what they want, Fi. You heard Frank in the briefing this morning; we have to 'up the stakes, give the viewers all the meat and gristle.'"

"It's sick, though." She winces as blood sprays across the lens.

"Only if you let it get to you." Malcolm shoves the burger into his mouth, cursing as red sauce spatters the already-stained ReGenevate sweater. "It's just a job, Fi."

A shudder runs down her spine as she watches the carnage unfolding on screen, white bone becoming exposed as the poor woman's flesh is ripped and stretched, blackened teeth chomping into rawness. *Just a job.* "That's someone's mum. Someone's *grandma* getting her insides gnawed."

"Should be grateful at her age."

Face screwed up, Fiona watches as the thing on the screen lets out a feral roar and begins bathing in the lady's intestines. *What a way to go for poor Jenny,* Fiona thinks. *The thimble collector and keen gardener from Margate.* She feels sick, but she can't peel her eyes away.

Another *thing* joins in the feeding frenzy, but it only gets one bite in before it's sent on its way by the murderer. In contrast to the ensuing carnage, the corner of each screen depicts the ever-changing image of an older woman to young, the youthful version with skin so smooth, shiny like a pebble, and eyes as clear and innocent as a sunny day. Underneath the transitioning image is the wording, *"ReGenevate – your passport to youth."*

"It's beyond sick," Fiona says as her eyes draw across to Malcolm's half-eaten burger, its innards glistening, red chilli sauce oozing down the middle. Her stomach flutters, the smell of meat and stale fart adding sensory overload to the nastiness continuing to unfold on the screen. "I didn't sign up for this."

Malcolm swivels his chair around, giving her an eyeful of ingredients. "We all had to sign that contract, darl. And I bet you didn't complain when that bonus landed in your account on Tuesday."

"But it's gotten so much worse." The screen shows the thing scooping a hole in the old lady's insides, her ReGenevate sweater now just a canvas of meat and blood. "I can't believe people want to see this. It's depraved, it's—"

"Bringing in the numbers." Exhaling as he takes a break from chewing, Malcolm reaches for his milkshake. "We've gone up ten spots since last week. And look at the viewer numbers today!"

It's just a blur in the corner of the screen, each count adding further validation to the hopelessness she feels. She notices four more of the things flocking—a small herd—keen to take their place at the feeding table. All the channels available, all the options for the viewers, her stomach churns at how savage humanity has become, obsessed with beauty, money, death.

She opens her mouth to speak, but Malcolm beats her to it, a rip-roaring belch filling her nostrils with the essence of fatty meat and a side-serve of strawberries. "It's just the way it is," he says, bringing a fat arm across his chin. "What's the name of your kid?"

"Christ's sake, Malcolm, we've been working together for almost bang on a year now. It's Jasmine."

"Whatever. You're a single mum, Fi. Only the rich get to choose. The rest of us toe the line and do as we're told." He swivels the chair back around, homing in on the old lady's head as the thing fingers out her eyeballs. "Besides, they all know what they're getting into. Once they sign that waiver, they're fair game."

"Not like they have much of a choice."

"But they do have a choice, Fi, that's the whole point."

Screen four shows the husband still alive, barely. Another drone tracks him carving a slow and muddy path across an empty field, shirt ripped open, and jeans—once up past his nipples—now around his ankles, giant bloodied underpants on display.

Malcolm brings the drone in closer. "This fella got close. Shame, but rules are rules."

"His name is Patrick Adams. And on screen one, Jenny—the lady he brought breakfast to every day with a rose between his teeth, now no longer recognisable—was his wife of over forty years."

"Tell me about it! I had a fifty on these two to make it all the way. So close."

She watches Malcolm hover his wet finger over the red button. What a fight the poor old man gave, trying to rescue his wife from the clutches of that filth. She wants to tell Malcolm to leave him be, but she knows it's futile; rules for this game state both need to cross the finishing line. Besides, she noted how the man's eyes clouded each time the couple embraced. "Always and forever," he had whispered into her ear at the start of the show. It brought a tear to her eye, and she hasn't stopped thinking about it since.

Malcolm swings the drone around, focussing on the man's watery eyes for the sake of trying to milk every ounce of emotion. But only a moist and desolate landscape awaits as Patrick lets his head fall to the ground. Fiona knows the man's fight is over, the muddy, zombie-laden field being the final resting place of what's left of him and his wife. *Rest in pieces.* Knowing the couple has a son who is likely watching, she fights back the tears, unable to imagine the pain their kin will be going through.

Screen three shows even more of the things lurching towards the now stationary meal, a series of grunts filling the room that sets Fiona's skin crawling. She notices the count continuing to climb, word no doubt getting around that there's something more interesting to watch than *The Serial Killer Wants a Wife*. She's never seen numbers like it, and it shows no signs of easing. The comments feeding through, too, dozens for every blink, further portraying just how depraved the world is.

I can't watch, but I can't not watch.

So I guess there are some people that zombies can outrun.

What the fuck should we call those flappy-skinned fuckers anyway? And I'm not talking about the contestants. Zombies? Grey skins? Flesh eaters? Angry raisins?

Bet she tastes like jerky!

Those underpants are wearing him.

Did anyone order the open-faced crusty to go?

"Besides," Malcolm says, "if we carry on like this, we won't need a marketing manager anymore, and you'll be free to spend all day with—with—"

"Jasmine!"

She had no idea how far production had started to take things, only ever working on the marketing campaigns and intros. It makes her feel dirty, and there's an instinctive need to shower and brush her teeth.

"Tell Nick I'll give him that fifty tomorrow," Malcolm shouts. "Or we can go double—"

She slams the door behind, the familiar smell of coffee, ass, and sweaty feet providing odd relief. She can't escape it, though, the name "ReGenevate" plastered across every wall, every cup, even across the compulsory shirt she begrudgingly wears. It's stifling, even more so after what she's just witnessed. Her stomach flutters as she tries to maintain decorum across the marble floor, the click-clacking upping in tempo as she nears the far wall.

The toilet is empty and clinical, but the sights and sounds are in her head, and she knows they always will be. Curiosity has left her with blood on her hands. She splashes her face with water, but the mirror only portrays the mangled face of Jenny, one lip remaining and a single tuft of wispy grey emerging from the bloodied scalp. Even up to an hour before her death, Jenny was so proud of her latest "do", asking hair and make-up to give it a quick spray to hold it in place. She reminded Fiona of her mum, April, proud and resolute, even throughout the cancer scare, always with unimportant questions like: "Is my make-up okay?", "My head isn't too shiny, is it?"

Goosebumps prickle her skin. She grasps the basin with both hands, a shudder working its way to the floor. She tries to slow her breathing but feels her heart rate picking up. More visions fill her head—grey skin flapping as *they* run, eyes projecting only animalistic hunger, teeth snapping at the air. The first retch is dry, but the second one produces a spray of greyish liquid and a series of shivers, forcing her to clasp to the metal even tighter. Mucus swings like a pendulum from her right nostril as she begins to cry, sucking in as much of the clinical air as possible. But the scraping of teeth against bone won't let her be, and it's no longer Jenny Adams in her head but her own mother. Her leg buckles, but she forces herself to stay up, knowing her mum would tell her to get a grip.

With a final exhale, she wipes the tears away, and pushes from the sink. Nobody notices her smudged make-up on the way back to her desk, everyone too engrossed in their quest for over-stimulation, alternating between devices, faces framed in tractor beams of blue light. She flops into her seat, studying the hologram of April and Jasmine, both faces overwhelmed by gums and teeth. In six months, her mum turns seventy. Six months to that next life. She bites her lip to stem further tears, thinking back to the day she got the job at the network and the relief of a regular income. It was all short-lived, though, lie after lie to her mother and daughter about what the job entailed and the ever-expanding limits of acceptable viewing material. Today's show was next level, though.

She sniffs back tears as her eyes fall on her display, the immersive font of the ReGenevate graphic twisting her stomach. If it weren't for Jasmine—a parting gift from Rick just before he took the rest of her savings on a drug-fuelled sayonara—she would consider volunteering herself for termination. She fantasises about it sometimes, imagines herself inching into oblivion. This world has become too cold, too savage, unapologetic, apathetic. The usual wave of guilt washes over her as she closes her eyes, picturing her daughter's smile.

She alters her glance to the glass office wall at the end of the corridor. Frank Turk, the CEO, is hunched across the desk, all smiles, and Jake McGrath, MD, is leaning back with his hands behind his head, rocking in his chair. From Fiona's angle, it looks like Jake is giving him head. *Hardly an ounce of real emotion between them.* Frank lost his sister on Tuesday but didn't even take the afternoon off. Took a whole week when the family Chihuahua, Popsicle, died. "Just part of life," he had said when addressing the office in the Wednesday morning meeting. "At least the ones on the show have a chance."

Debriefing

"Did you see the size of the guy's underpants?"

"Jeez, Frank, I've seen smaller parachutes."

"What a show." Frank pounds his fists against the desk, prompting Jake to recoil, almost sending his chair toppling over. "What a show. What a fucking show!"

Jake studies the man before him, the one he's known for over twenty years, the one who looks younger with each passing day, regardless of the boozy nights and endless hookers. "Yes, numbers were great." Nothing left behind the man's eyes but greed—desensitised to everything that isn't a number. He hates the fucker with a passion.

"They loved it, Jake, lapped it up. Folks at ReGenevate are euphoric!"

Jake brings the chair down on all four legs, a craving for stability as he chews the question trying to force itself from his head. "Can I ask you something without you getting mad, Frank?"

"Spit it out, Jake. Get me while I'm moist."

"We've known each other for a long time, yeah? Ever since—"

"Jake, give me some credit and stop blowing hot air up my ass. What's on your mind?"

"I've always been behind you, Frank, always—"

"Trying to slip one up me, you horny little bastard." He flashes teeth whiter than white. "Hit me with it."

"Do you think we went too far today? I mean, I know this is—"

"Fuck, no!" Frank eases into his chair, the purely-for-show projected scene of his wife and kids fussing around Popsicle the rat dog, playing to his left. He blows out a dramatic exhale, letting his shoulders drop as if trying to re-enact what he remembers empathy to be. "These are the lucky ones, Jake. Chance, fate, a lottery, call it whatever you like—if the computer picks their social security number when they hit sixty-nine, we offer hope, a way out. A passport. Ten million big ones, and a lifetime's supply of ReGenevate serum for the winners. We're the good guys here, Jake. Those that choose to pass up the opportunity, that's on them."

"She was only sixty-four, though, the man's partner—Jenny, was it?" There's a twinge in his stomach for already almost forgetting her name. "Such a sweet lady. It just seems so—"

"And Patrick had four months until he turned seventy, until lights out time. At least this way, they went out fighting together. Surely that's better than withering away in mourning until it's her turn for the needle?" Frank sighed, following up with a hateful grin. "Your problem is you think too much, Jake."

"I know, but—"

"Were you in that global leaders meeting discussing how to solve the population crisis?"

With his stare aimed at the floor, Jake shrugs, resigning himself to one of Frank's little pep talks, the kind of speech that would make the Devil blush.

"Were you one of the members that voted on population legislation, including setting termination age at seventy?"

"No."

"Were you involved in setting the cost of the passports or negotiating the cost of the serum?"

"No."

"All we're doing is providing a little light relief, adding entertainment value to a taboo subject." Pressing his hands together, Frank leans forward across his desk as though on the verge of delivering something quite profound. "We spend our first months trying to escape from the vagina, yeah? When we finally do, kicking and screaming, we spend our next years wondering what the fuck is going on. And the next few after that are spent trying to climb into every vagina we see, perhaps a subconscious admission that we preferred it in there in the first place. And then we die, simple as that. That's life, so you've got to grab it while you can."

"Those things, though. Detestable, evil—"

"Death row prisoners, also given a choice just like the oldies: the needle, or a drop of the other stuff from ReGenevate. They get to do what they do, serve their purpose. Everyone's a winner here, Jake."

Jake stares into Frank's eyes, knowing the man believes every bit of bile emerging from his own lips. "I just think—"

"I told you, Jake, that's your problem right there. No room for thinking in this world, just doing. Thinking loses you time, puts you behind, weakens you. Is my hair shiny?"

"Eh?"

"My hair; is it shiny?" He runs his hand through the glossiness and gives his head a quick flick.

"Yeah, I guess."

"Any circles under my eyes?"

"No."

"Any lines on my forehead?"

"No."

Thrusting himself to his feet, Frank begins working at his fly. "Any wrinkles on my foreskin?"

"Fuck's sake, Frank!"

"Just kidding. But you should see it, Jake. It's like the dick of a twenty year old, shaped like a rocket. The missus is over the moon." He plops back into the seat again. "Do you get it?" He runs a hand through his sleek, black mane again. "Back to the point, do I look seventy-three?"

"No, Frank."

"That's right. Because money talks, Jake, and we're making a shit load of it. It's this or the waiting list for Mars, and I ain't one for long-haul flights." He performs another exhale, dropping his shoulders even lower. "Listen, my friend. Your Judy... I know that's where all your money goes, and I respect you to Hell and back for it. But the biggest companies in the world have spent billions trying to cure cancer. You need to let her go, enjoy your years while you can. She might as well be dead for all the moping around you do. Imagine what you can do with all that money as a single man. And hell, with a bit of hard work and few more bonuses like the last one, you might even be able to scrape enough for a passport."

A million responses entering his head, Jake opens his mouth to retort, but he knows they'd all be wasted on the wide-eyed monster sitting across from him. The guy is the wealthiest person in his circle, but the greedy fucker wouldn't even buy a passport for his own sister. "You have to earn your place in this world," he had said. "Stacey was as good as gold but dumb as dogshit. Used to think Fleetwood Mac was a hamburger, for Christ's sake!"

Jake knows there's no reasoning with the man. Every moral fibre in him screamed for him to quit in the run up to this week's show, but as Frank pointed out, money talks, and it's the only thing keeping his wife alive.

"No disrespect meant, friend," Franks says, leaning in closer, "but I worry about you. We were unstoppable once, a freight train of destruction, and now you've developed all these feelings and things that cloud your judgement."

Jake's mum was seventy-five when the legislation came into effect. Like millions of others, she was given a few days to say her farewells before the dose of lethal injection, involuntary euthanasia as a means of easing the strain on Earth's resources. Only the rich get a pass, buying themselves a ticket of immunity, blending in with the crowd with the help of the ReGenevate serum. Unable to afford both, it was an agonising choice: keep his wife alive in the hope they finally find a cure for cancer or buy his mother a passport to live out the rest of her life. His mum made it an easier decision.

"You need to let her go, my friend," Frank utters softly, reaching for his hand. "It's making you too weak."

Jake's instinct is to recoil, but he nods instead, wishing the man in front of him with the perfect smile would curl up and die. The thought lingers, stepping into Frank's shoes as CEO and all the things he'd change. Christ, with Frank's salary, he'd be able to buy a passport and triple the amount he sends to cancer research.

"Jake, are you still with me on this train, or do you need to get off at the next stop?"

But hospital bills are through the roof, and he needs this job as much as he needs to hold his wife's hand. If he let Judy go now, his mother would have died for nothing.

There's no going back. "With you all the way, Frank."

"Excellent," Frank says, strutting behind Jake. He clamps his hands around his employee's shoulders and begins a gentle massage. "Okay, emotional stuff put to bed—who do we have lined up for next week's show?"

Jake fumbles in his pocket for his phone and issues his voice command. "Who are the contestants for next week's show?"

James and Charlotte Valencourt. They live in Bexley. James is an ex-investment banker. Charlotte is sixty-six and still working as a criminal lawyer. Their financial situation took a turn for the worse after a few bad personal investments made by James, thus the need for Charlotte to continue working. They have no children.

Bryan and Steph Taylor. They live in Gloucester. Bryan is a retired builder. Steph is sixty-seven and works from home, making candles. They have one daughter, no grandchildren, and a cat called Puddy Tat.

Doug and Cass Murano. Doug is a retired IT Director. They live in Yorkshire. Cass is sixty-six, a retired kinder teacher who runs a small business as a cake-maker. They have no children, no pets.

Sam and Helen Hicks. They live in Leicester. Sam is a nurse and a part-time writer. Helen is sixty-six and a part-time florist with a fondness for Sudoku and word searches. They have a daughter and a German Shepherd called Groucho Barks.

"Excellent," Franks mutters. "Let's see if we can up the ads this week, anywhere and everywhere—buy what space we can. We have to stay ahead of the pack on this."

"Yes, Frank."

"Who's the girl in marketing?"

"Fiona."

"Make sure she lays it on thick this week, okay? As close to the line as we can take it."

"Frank—"

"Get to it, Jake. Let's make this next one even more of a doozy."

Jonathan and Teresa Adams

The holographic image displays a montage of the best clips from the show, mostly involving the terror-stricken faces of his parents. Even with the volume turned low, Jonathan can hear the screaming and the chewing. He eyes his wife, Teresa, on the couch, head in her hands, shoulders shuddering as they rise and fall.

"Thanks, Viv... Yeah, I'm beside myself, to be honest, Teresa, too... Yeah, we might put a few sandwiches out down the pub and invite our nearest and dearest... I guess we'll sell it... No, haven't thought about that yet... Yes, she doted on her grandma... For sure... Yeah, not looking forward to that conversation... Thanks so much... Give my best to Pete, by the way... We appreciate your thoughts... You too."

Avoiding the launched phone by a smidge, the cat offers a hiss as it shuttles through the flap into the light rain. It turns, getting ready to shit in the flowerbeds, fur already matted as it eyes Jonathan with a look equating to the middle finger.

"Fuck! Fuck! Fuck! Useless fucking bastards!" Stiff with anger, Jonathan takes his seat next to Teresa, watching the replay of the fatal moment. "It's her fault, look. Dad was home and dry, but she fucked it."

The voiceover confirms Jonathan's thoughts, casting speculation on whether Jenny did enough training leading up to the big day, one of the female leads suggesting a few extra squats wouldn't have gone amiss.

"Kept telling me she was losing weight, but I think she just wore bigger dresses. Last week when I dropped off those fish oil tablets, I found two empty packets of cookie dough shoved down the side of the couch. Looked like they'd been licked clean."

Teresa isn't ready to lift her head yet. She loved Jon's parents to bits, but the prize money would have been enough for passports for all, including her parents, and one in reserve for the child she's sure she could have convinced Jon to have. All she can think about of late is the fact her father turns sixty-nine next week. Jon's right: Jenny fucked it.

"Turn volume to forty-two," Jonathan says, leaning in towards the image. "Stop. Rewind ten seconds. Play in slow motion."

"Leave it, Jon. It's done now. There's only so many times I can watch your mother's face being eaten."

"There. You can see it. She slowed down! Rewind ten seconds."

"Perhaps once we sell their house, we can talk about having children?"

"All she had to do was keep at the same pace." He pushes himself from the couch and makes his way to the opposite side of the image. "This one coming from the side distracted her. We prepared her for this, though."

"Jon."

"The money was as good as ours. Now we're left with a shitty two-bed terrace and all those fucking thumb hats."

"They're thimbles, Jon. Perhaps with the proceeds from the—"

"Not happening, Teresa. This world is for the rich, not for people like us. And besides, the money from their little house will hardly touch our mortgage."

She concedes. "I'll make a cup of tea." The drink for any occasion, extending to having your mother-in-law eaten live on air. "I'm truly sorry about your parents, Jon."

"Should have gone harder in training. Mum burst into tears when I put that training playlist on, but I should have persisted.

Had that bloody great big log dropped off for nothing, too." Jonathan stands, wiping the moisture from his eyes. He makes his way towards the patio doors and gives the glass a firm knock, startling the cat over next door's fence. As the commentators talk through the final scenes once more from an overhead point of view this time, he eyes the small obstacle course he set up in the garden for after morning tea. More tears begin to fall as he recalls his mum getting wrapped up in one of the tyres and rolling into the hedgerow.

"Do you want a biscuit, love?" Teresa shouts from the room opposite.

"No, I think I'm going to cut down."

Bryan and Steph Taylor

"Bryan."

"Don't talk to me mid push-up, woman."

"That tap's dripping again."

Veins popping in his saggy neck, face as red as a cherry, he gives up, letting his cheek come to rest against the coarseness of the wood.

"And I think we're getting a sinkhole in the garden."

"Fuck's sake, Steph!"

"You'll do yourself an injury before we even get there, Bry. And do you ever throw any leg work in there, Mister chicken legs?"

"What the hell are you bringing up sinkholes and dripping taps for anyway?"

"I just don't want our Bec coming in, having to get that looked at when her dad's a retired plumber."

He pushes himself from the ground, reaching for the wall as the grey floaters rush in. "Have you done your ten minutes on the treadmill today? Cost us a bloody fortune, that new-fangled reality simulator, and you hardly use it."

"I can't, Bry." She feels her lips starting to go, pressure building behind her eyes. "Not today. I just—"

"Oh, love." Bryan brings her in close, kissing her on the forehead. They sway in each other's arms, Puddy Tat brushing herself against their legs, alert to their moroseness and taking full advantage.

"I'll sort the bloody tap," Bryan whispers. The same kitchen for thirty years, Steph threatens him by sending the contact details for overpriced designers each time the tap starts dripping. Faster than a speeding bullet, he's under the sink with his wrench. No such threat today, though, and it puts a big old rock in his chest. They stay like that for a while—Bryan, Steph, and Puddy Tat—only two of them aware the union could be one of their last.

"Love you, Steph," Bryan mutters as they break, wiping the moisture from his eyes. He studies his wife, noticing the single tear making its way down her right cheek, and how her thin lips tremble. He wants to say something profound like in the books she listens to when she's making her candles, words of comfort to hang onto if things don't go as planned. Words she can take to the next life. "I'd give it ten minutes on woodland setting if I were you. Incline of two."

She looks him in the eyes and tries to smile, but Bryan knows a break down is looming. "The new upgrade's great," he says. "You can even see the birds in the trees, feel the breeze as they cut in front. Swear to God one of 'em shat on my shoulder yesterday." Humour is his go-to, but his timing isn't always great. Sometimes even when she's fuming at him, he can make her crack, but he concludes his potentially-last-night-alive material is limited at best.

It's no good, she can't hold it back. The tears come, her legs buckle, sending her sliding down the wall. Bryan reaches for her, but it's too late. He's left watching as she wraps her arms around her legs as though trying to make herself small enough to slip through a gap in the floorboards. As she begins a violent sob, he stands over her, helpless, opening and closing his mouth, searching for his next golden nugget. "I'll put the kettle on." It's weak but lends order to things. Whether happy, sad, scared, angry, stressed, or even on the eve of getting eaten by zombies, Bryan figures you can't go wrong with a cup of tea.

Guilt washes over him; all those days on the couch, watching his remastered classic movies, ignoring requests from his wife to do stuff around the house. He walks through to the kitchen, leaving Puddy Tat to console his wife. Even little things would have made her so much happier, her being at home all day. He was always so exhausted when he got in from work, though, just needing his dose of nostalgia, his fix of better times, when movies were movies, and when the cloud of death wasn't constantly hovering over their heads.

As he flicks on the kettle, an action he once thought an almost infinite process, the lump in his throat grows. He eyes the blue and pink pill organisers on the counter, individual sections marked with letters, tablets ready for subsequent days that may never come. It's the photograph of their daughter, Bec, on the refrigerator that breaks him, though, inducing the tears. She refused to come tonight. She said it would be "too much." He knows she blames him. But it was Steph who insisted they take part, saying she would rather die with him than spend the next couple of years alone with only the cat and dripping tap for company.

James and Charlotte Valencourt

"You see how they're not making full use of the space, James? They're both too open, too exposed. The woman—Jenny—she had the agility of a fridge, but if she'd have just used the trees, she might have had a chance."

"More champagne, dear?"

Charlotte flicks him a scowl. "I wish you'd stop referring to that sparkling toilet water as champagne! And no more for you, either— we need to be sharp for tomorrow."

He fills the glass anyway. "We've been through this a million times, Charlie. We've done the prep. We're in the best shape we've been in for ages. It's as good as ours."

She snatches his glass from the table and throws the contents into the Monstera pot. "I'm not fooling, James. I'm sick of living like a normal. Done it for longer than I can bear. Suburbia's not good for my skin, and as for that piece of shit vehicle that takes me to work every day... It's all so embarrassing."

It's been over two years, but not a day goes by without her rubbing his face in it. It's as if she thinks he enjoys drinking cheap liquor and being seen in the glorified go-kart he's forced to travel in. They've stopped getting invited to all the cool shindigs, too, the highlight of the last few weeks being Charlotte's sister's birthday bash at The Dirty Duck, sticky tables full of pork pies, sandwiches with the crusts trimmed off, and jellied eels in place of caviar.

"Are you listening, James?"

He cried when he had to sell his Rolex. His mother used to say to him, "You can tell a lot of a man by the watch he wears." He misses the reflection of the successful version of himself—the shiny Italian shoes, the tailored suit that hugged his shoulders, making him look slimmer than he was. It's like staring at a stranger these days, what with the ill-fitting clothes, dark circles under the eyes, and the defeated softness in a face that inspires self-hatred. "A normal," as Charlotte so eloquently puts it. The belly made things even worse, but at least he's back in some shape now. *Stage two tomorrow.* Once they get their hands on the prize and the serum, he'll be able to take flight again, back to near his prime and shitting on the underlings.

"James!"

"Yes, dear."

"Good. One more time then. Rewind twenty and play at quarter speed."

James huddles in, careful not to invade his wife's space. She likes a minimum of two feet of air between them these days. No coincidence, he suspects, this little request developed after he blew their entire life savings by investing in one of ReGenevate's competitors. It never used to be like that; she couldn't keep her hands off him when he carried the smell of money. Bit of a nymphomaniac in the day, too. Sometimes three times a night, with a little help from the blue pill—role play, dirty talk, porn, food, nothing was off limits. Now they're down to once a month, lights off, and she refuses to use her tongue or call him Sinbad.

"Is your sister still sniffing around?" he says.

She curls her lips into a snarl and nods. "Hardly wanted anything to do with us when you lost our house, but she's got the scent again. As subtle as a fart at a funeral."

Picking up on the tremor in her last few words, he studies the well-worn lines in his wife's face as they soften. Her eyes, too, filling with moisture to project a rarely seen vulnerability. "Charlie, darling." He's seen the look only once before, the day he told her they were broke, the day before they had to sell both their passports. "Charlie, it will—"

"I'm fine."

The tear rolling down her left cheek tells him otherwise. He reaches for her, but as he approaches her invisible forcefield, she recoils. "I'm going to bed. Don't wake me when you come up."

He waits until she reaches the top of the stairs before taking a swig of the Super Saver special. The horrible aftertaste is second only to that of failure, but he knows both could be washed away with exuberant decadence. "Cheers, love," he says as he brings the bottle to his lips. Not once has he contemplated not making it to the finishing line, the thought of failing again impossible to bear. His attention turns to the looping replay of the couple's demise, watery gurgles, and the sound of ripping flesh filling the small living room. If truth be told, he'd prefer death anyway to living through another day in the shoes of the man he's become.

Sam and Helen Hicks

"I love you, Groucho," Sam mutters into the German shepherd's fur. Watery eyes reflect Sam's sadness as the dog nuzzles its wet nose into his open palms, less melancholy and more patting on its mind. "Janie will take good care of you if we don't come back." The dog usually isn't allowed on the couch, but tonight is no ordinary night, Helen's usual rules out the window. She even let Groucho eat her untouched dinner straight from the plate, his grateful eyes flicking between her and the food as though it might be a trap.

They decided yesterday there would be no further mention of their imminent ordeal until absolutely necessary. Regardless, Helen's evening continues to be monopolised by thoughts of what happened to the previous contestants, and she suspects, by how sloppy Sam is with the dog, her husband's night is panning out the same. She thinks about Janie, her daughter, and how their morning coffee became an inconsolable episode of dampness and wails. If there was an opportunity to back out there and then, she would have taken it, hands down. Everything about tonight feels different; Sam in here instead of his study, and the time after eleven. Most nights they retired well before ten, but they're playing by different rules this evening, the concept of sleep a distant memory.

Her stare falls on the flickering image in the corner of the room intended to distract; a young family with sparkling white teeth enjoying breakfast in a brand new kitchen. She hears words, but they don't mean anything, as though a different language. Blood pulses in her ears, and she feels like she's burning up.

"Helen."

The scene gives way to the image of a grey-haired lady with a kind face, albeit punctured with deep lines and watery eyes underlined with dark circles. The head begins to rotate as if on a rotisserie. By the time it's done a full revolution, the lines are all but gone and the hair a vibrant auburn. The face looks wrong to her, though—too harsh, lacking human nuance and softness. The room begins to spin, a slow shift at first but picking up speed.

...age define you...

All she can see are teeth now, everywhere, spiralling above her, chattering across the carpet, but these are blackened and have bits of pink flesh hanging from the gaps. Another voice floats across, one she recognises as her husband's soft tone, but again, it isn't right, as though he's developed a different dialect. She feels hot, burning up, and begins to sway, grey floaters swimming from the outside in. She imagines her own head rotating, but this time on a spike held by one of those monstrous creatures.

ReGenevate – your passport to youth.

There's sudden pressure on her shoulders, and the grey is being shaken away. Wetness presses against her arm, and she hears Groucho's heavy breathing.

"Helen."

She blinks everything back into place, but it still doesn't look right. Normality is dead, chaos taking its place. "I don't think I can do this, Sam."

Doug and Cass Murano

"Doug, do I look presentable?"

Lifting his stare from his belly to his wife, the knot in his stomach grows larger as he takes in her offered smile. A little bit of blush and a touch of lipstick, that's all, and the hair—the bane of her life—only a little less fuzzy than it was before.

"Perfect," he replies. Patches of skin begin to prickle, and he feels that now-familiar pressure behind his eyes.

Cass perches on the end of the bed next to him, reaching for his age-spot speckled hand. "A good cup of tea that, love, thanks."

"I love you, Cass."

"Don't you dare cry on me again, Doug."

He pushes himself from the softness, swallows hard, and gets back to pacing the room, hands painfully clasped behind his back. "How do you do it? Remain so bloody composed, I mean."

"I was a kinder teacher, remember." She offers a wink and begins patting down the ReGenevate emblem on her sweater. "Savage little bastards." But she can feel herself shaking, and it's all she can do to stop herself from running to the bathroom and locking the door. For Doug's sake, she widens her smile, pushes from the cream duvet she may never sleep in again, and makes her way towards the window. It's the only way she knows how to cope. It's what she does.

"Lovely day."

Not exactly what Bill Withers envisioned when he sang the song, Doug imagines, getting his insides scooped out by predatory mutants. He looks at his watch again, wanting nothing more than to go downstairs and spend the rest of the day listening to the vinyl collection his dad passed down to him, all from the safety of his favourite chair. "When music was music," his dad used to say. Less than five minutes to go. *Shit. Shit. Shit.*

"You had your tablets, love?"

Doug offers a little shake, a private joke to indicate them rattling around inside.

"When this is over, we'll book a little holiday, eh?" his wife says. "We could even go back to that nice hotel in Rimini, perhaps. Do you remember what you said that time, Doug?"

"I do, love." He knows she means well but thinks her chipperness is borderline psychotic, considering what they're about to experience and considering that not one couple made it out alive in last week's show. A rather horrible few days, all in all, relentless calls and messages offering support, even from people they'd not heard from in years. He wanted to tell them all to fuck off, but Cass remained stoic to the end—annoyingly so—quashing concerns with tried and tested jibber-jabber.

"Such a lovely day."

It's just how she copes; he knows that. Situations that made her feel nervous always induced a barrage of nonsense and endless baking frenzies. What limited training they'd been doing had almost certainly been cancelled out by her signatory cream puffs. She's gotten worse over time, Doug thinks, the world taking its mental toll. They used to sit for hours debating politics and the arts, but it's as if positivity is displacing her sharpness. All the times he's skipped invitations at work just to avoid such awkwardness. But he loves her and wouldn't change her for the world, and he knows she loves him. It's why she insisted they go through with this.

"So what do you think about Rimini?"

"Sounds good, dear."

As conversation ebbs, Cass incessantly wipes her breath from the glass. At the same time, Doug treads multiple paths into the carpet, feeling light-headed yet heavy on his feet, a surreal but absolute experience. Nervous, he flicks his wrist to check the time on his retro watch. With less than two minutes to go, overwhelming relief at not having kids washes over him. Cass wanted a boy and a girl, but like many others with an eye on the world, they agreed to wait for things to improve.

He stops at the window next to his wife, remembering when the park across the road was full of fathers. They all stood proudly, watching their children squealing with fear and delight as the simulator put them in a boat on rough seas or on monkey bars, swinging across crocodile-infested waters that waited below. Most parks are gone, parents now gifting their children with the newest in the line of online toys mere days after they arrive in the world kicking and screaming. The field across from them has become an endless parade of joggers, all sporting the latest hi-tech gadgets and adorned in whatever fashion the malls brainwash them into wearing.

They waited. And waited.

But the world never got better.

Cass reaches for his hand, sensing her husband's melancholy. It's taking all she has to hold things together. "Such a lovely day." Feeling herself slipping, she swallows hard but is unable to dislodge the lump in her throat.

Winter sun bounces off the black paintwork as the driverless car turns into their street, bang on time. Her stomach flutters as she gives her husband's hand another squeeze.

Sizing up the Competition

After a two-hour journey, having to endure uncut repeats of previous shows, Doug and Cass are the last to arrive at the studio. As they draw close to the main entrance, where the other vehicles are already parked, they're further treated to a parade of previous winners who gush on and on about the effectiveness of ReGenevate. Before and after images come at them from all directions—vanishing bingo wings, once again visible cheekbones, butts with renewed elasticity. Marcus from Northampton even boasts about his all-night sex sessions in front of the log fire at his new ocean villa. He smiles towards the camera with perfect teeth. "ReGenevate puts lead back in your pencil."

Doug and Cass lock together, inhaling familiar smells and declaring their love. Only as the vehicle doors begin to slide open do they break with a kiss. "We've got this, Dougie," Cass whispers, but getting less sure of herself by the minute.

"Please leave all valuables in the compartment to your right." The voice is clinical as it feeds through the speakers. "Including wedding bands. We will return them, should you survive."

It's the last line that sends a shudder down Doug's spine, an apathetic affirmation they may not see tomorrow.

Fresh November wind wraps around them as they force themselves from the warmth. Hands held, pulses pounding against each other, they step through the sliding doors to see their elderly competitors waiting in the foyer, powdered faces tight with fear and extended anticipation. As Doug almost chokes on air tainted with the heavy, spicy tang of muscle spray, all heads turn to them. Machines go to work, projecting their X-ray images onto the air a few feet in front.

"Hello," Cass sings.

A short man with a winter tan pops his head from the bustle. Impossible to tell what age, anything from twenty to forty, the man flashes them a wide smile. "Welcome! Welcome!" he cries with matching enthusiasm. "My name is Tristan, but you can call me Trist. Can I get you anything? Coffee? Water? Come, come, follow." He snaps his head around. "Make-up, please!"

Even before Doug can open his mouth, the guy resembling a carrot with arms and legs disappears behind the others. "And will someone please sort their microphones?"

They nod and smile as they merge with the others, two of the couples mirroring their half-hearted greeting, but the thin-lipped athletic-looking pair who look like they shit gold offer nothing but a scowl. Doug scans the illuminated names on the front of their sweaters—James and Charlotte Valencourt—half-tempted to offer a bow.

"Jesus Christ," Doug mutters as a stocky guy emerges from the darkness, massive arms stretching the fabric of a ReGenevate T-shirt.

"Silas, actually." The man's voice is gruff and scratchy. He prods a giant finger into Doug's chest. "Microphone." He nods. "As soon as you step through those doors, everything you say will be broadcast live."

Doug looks down but sees nothing visible on the material. *Thirty years in IT, but the world is moving ever faster,* he thinks. He hears Cass let out a puff of air as she undergoes the same experience.

"Thank you, Silas," she says. She studies the man's lush carpet of hair covering the almost perfectly round head, thinking it not quite right. "Is that a perk of the job?"

"You're done," the guy says, stepping back into the darkness.

As Doug opens his mouth to check on his wife, a soft brush thrusts into his face. "Just a bit of powder for the cameras, love," the woman with lips like inflatable rafts says to him. Before he wonders where she came from, there's another almost identical one on Cass, boobs like rocks aimed towards him. On the far too-small ReGene-vate T-shirt, the two mounds come to a peak at the letters G and T.

If it weren't for Cass, he'd leave this world without a fight, slip into oblivion. Average age expectancy has shot up to over a hundred and ten years, and the thought of another forty plus years on this planet, the way things are going, scares the living bejesus out of him. "Stop the world, I want to get off" is a saying he throws about a lot, but Cass always has her optimism defibrillator on charge.

"Okay, ladies and gents." The shrill voice emerges from some-where close. "We're going live soon." And out he pops, Apricot Man, hands in the air and perfect teeth on display. "Listen, listen." Unnecessarily, he claps his tiny hands together, creating a surpris-ingly loud noise. "Through these doors is a corridor taking you to our newest game, 'Hell House'. Response to the ads on socials has been phe—nom—en—al, so we're expecting great things. Now, this one's a teaser designed to set the juices flowing and prepare you for the more challenging sections ahead. You'll need to work together as a team on this one, so I suggest putting any differences aside for now." There's a definite sparkle in his eyes as he rubs his tiny little hands together. "Phenomenal." Ushering them to follow, he begins making his way across to the large double doors, the group obliging, shuffling behind, taking part in another round of smiles and scowls. "As soon as these doors close behind you, we'll switch your microphones on, and from there on in, everything you do will be live streamed to our audience. Have you seen the numbers? Oh, my, you're all going to be famous. Dead or alive."

He leans in towards the scanner, prompting the doors to slide across, silent, efficient. "Sound check, visuals, all good to go?" He arches his neck and nods. "Right then. We'll see you on the other side." He runs his eyes across the group, treating them to his perfect smile. "Perhaps."

An Amble on the Cobbles

Railings run either side, forcing them to walk single file towards Hell House, Bryan finding himself in front and nervously leading the pack, hand clasped around his wife's. Charlotte and James trail close behind, followed by Sam and Helen, with Doug and Cass bringing up the rear.

Even with thoughts that these could be their last hours alive, a heavy blanket of paranoid pride falls across the group, all aware whatever they speak from here on in will be heard by family members and millions of other viewers. Fingers run against flaky paint as they use the railing and the simulated slither of a moon to help navigate the cobble-stoned path towards the grand but ominous house in the distance.

It all begins to feel too real, even the temperature dropping to what it was outside, a cold chill accentuating the nerves and playing havoc with their arthritis. From somewhere close, there's a flutter of wings and the hoot of an owl. As their bodies continue reacting to the manufactured breeze, a lightning bolt fills the sky, adding to their adrenaline, rolling thunder prompting the first few drops of rain and the smell of petrichor.

Cass studies the woman in front, thinking that the poor dear would be hugging cobble if it weren't for the railing. Hating herself for not knowing her name, Cass looks ahead to the others, noting only the almost identical-looking man and woman, third and fourth in line, showing no visible signs of fear. To Cass, they looked like the kind of people who thought themselves too good for anything, the type who bottled and labelled their piss—every year a vintage. With the situation tense enough already, the deafening silence adds to the unbearable heaviness, and she feels herself breaking. Her mother used to repeatedly tell her that every minute alive was a treat and that whatever the situation, you must make the best of things. *Exceptional circumstances, Mother.* Unable to hold on any longer, she finally cracks. "We'll all have to go for a bit of a shindig after this, eh?"

Doug glances back with a sympathetic smile, but the others in the group offer nothing.

"Where do the rest of you live, anyway?" Cass persists. "We're from Yorkshire, where the puddings come from, and the best cup of tea you could hope for."

"I could murder a cup of tea right now," Bryan says. "Gloucester, by the way. Barnwood, to be specific."

"And we're from Leicester," Helen announces, grateful to tag onto the small talk. "I could bore you to death with the history, but I don't think the viewers will be interested."

"Screw the viewers," Steph comments, surprising herself. "They can always—" She whips her hand back and offers a blood-curdling scream, one made even more dramatic by the lightning that wraps around them and the immediate roll of crackling thunder. As the line comes to a dead stop, it takes a moment for Steph to realise both her hands are clasped around the breasts of the tall, wiry athletic-looking woman with slicked-back hair. *Charlotte?* The woman has an eyebrow raised and four almost linear lines carved across her forehead. "You didn't even bring me flowers," she says.

"I'm so sorry," Steph comments. "My hand—"

"Is still on my tit."

"I'm so sorry," Steph repeats, feeling her cheeks getting hotter. "Sorry."

"It's not real, you silly old fool," James says, prodding at the lump of fur atop the gate. "It's just a prop."

"She wasn't to know," Bryan says, wrapping an arm around his wife's waist. "Looks real enough, unlike your wife's knockers. Look, its bloody tail is moving."

"If you're scared of a rat, what hope do you have?" Charlotte says. "You might as well bow out now and take the needle."

"Just worry about yourselves, will you?" Bryan brings his wife in closer still. "You alright, love?"

"No, Bry, I'm not."

"We'll get you a tetanus shot when we get home, love," Bryan says. "And I don't mean for the rat."

Helen's the next to go, unable to hold it together any longer. She doubles over in a series of sobs, her husband Sam doing his best to console but also drowning in hopelessness.

"Give me strength," Charlotte mumbles. "This will be easier than taking candy from a baby."

"Just shut the fuck up, will you?" Sam says, stroking his wife's back.

Only the voice in their ears instructing them to carry on moving prompts the line to shuffle forward again, all aware of what happened to the couple a few weeks ago who refused to budge.

There are no further scares en route, but the sense of escalating dread becomes almost palpable, a breathable toxin filling their bodies with icy rigidity. Cass continues trying to lighten the atmosphere, but the tiny slice of normality introduced by way of chit-chat has been all but consumed by darkness and the looming crumbling brickwork of Hell House.

They continue their approach, the building growing more menacing still, framed in mist and flickers of white, the ground beneath them shaking as the instantaneous thunderclaps echo through the makeshift alley. A crow perches atop the arched gates ahead, cawing loudly, feathers as glossy as the paintwork on the cars that brought them here. The bird fixes them with its stare, watching them in, on occasion performing an excitable hop from one foot to the next. Finally, it bows its head before taking off and merging with the surrounding darkness.

"So goddamn real," Bryan comments. He pushes his head through the gates, inspecting the broken shards of dirty, yellow light escaping through the splintered boards across the windows.

"I can't go in," Helen says. "I can't do it."

"Shh. It's okay, love." Sam does his best to console her but winces at the sound of his own voice. "It's just a warm-up, this one. Nothing's going to happen."

"It's not okay. It's not okay." She flails her hands at her husband as he continues doing his best to calm her down. "I can't do this. I want to go home. I want to see Janie! I want to see Groucho!"

Moisture in his eyes, his insides knotting, Sam looks to the others for support. He has nothing, his head full of redundant words running into each other and the same melancholic thoughts of being home. Sixty-nine years on the planet, yet nothing could prepare him for this.

"What's your favourite thing to do?" Cass asks.

Lifting his head towards the voice, Sam sees the lady with frizzy hair making her way towards them. It's an odd thing to think how well someone's hair suits them, but together with the constant shuffling and incessant chatter, he imagines electricity coursing through her veins. Wary and helpless, he steps back, allowing the lady some space.

"What's your wife's name?"

"Helen."

"Come on, Helen," Cass says, snapping her fingers in front of the woman's face. "Look at me."

Thunder rattles around them, and a scream rattles from beyond the gates.

"Ignore all that, Helen. Just you and me having a conversation." Cass clicks her fingers several times before she has the woman's attention. "When you're at home, what do you like to do, Helen? What makes you happy?"

The lady lifts her head, mascara running down both cheeks, heart pounding. She opens her mouth, closes it, and tries again.

"Flowers. I like to paint flowers."

"Excellent. What's your favourite flower?"

Helen blinks some of the moisture away. She has two—lilies and orchids. "Orchids."

"Beautiful flowers," Cass replies. "I think mine has to be the tulip."

Wiping more of the tears away, Helen stands, taking in a large mouthful of air. "They say they used to be more expensive than gold, you know. In Holland, a few centuries ago."

"Get away."

Helen nods. "It's true." She drags the sleeve of the sweater across her face, smudging her make-up further. "Orchids are my favourite because they get all they need from the air. No need for soil once the roots take hold. Isn't that something?"

"Sure is, petal. It sure is."

Sam watches the lady working her magic, extracting more facts from his wife that are familiar but, at the same time, new. He can't help but curse himself for that. Conversation in the early years used to be excitable and rushed. He wonders when they lost that spark, knowing he did nothing to salvage it, choosing to spend most of his time in the study, writing stories that few ever read. The knot in his stomach tightens as he watches the ladies peel themselves from each other.

"Thank you," Helen says, doing her best to rescue her dignity.

Cass shakes her head. "After all this is over, you'll have to show me some of your paintings."

"Nothing would make me happier."

As the gate begins to creak open, the talking carrot squeals in their ears for them to enter the house. "Coffee and tea-making facilities await. We'll give you some time in the lobby to make yourselves at home, so to speak. But not too much time, if you know what I mean. The writing's on the wall, people."

And so, to the sound of more rolling thunder, the group make their way towards the front door of Hell House, gargoyles and angry-looking garden gnomes watching them in from beyond both sides of the railings.

"Someone must have stolen their fishing rods," Cass says to her muted audience.

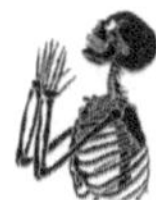

Frank is smoking a big fat one in his office, enjoying the crackle of ice in his glass. As anticipated, the numbers for the anniversary edition are through the roof, what with all the promises of blood, sweat, and tears. Malcolm's running a final test on the cameras spread throughout Hell House, chuckling at some of the comments feeding through on socials.

I'll have whatever Cass is drinking, please.

That Charlotte's a handful, isn't she? ☺

Demand for Yorkshire Puddings is going through the roof after this!

You have to feel for Sam; Helen's going to get them both killed.

Someone needs to fill out a crime report for those fishing rods. Even gnomes have rights!

My favourite thing to do is to watch old people get tenderised.

An Anxious Wait

The entrance is even colder than outside, each member of the group able to see their breath. As the door locks behind them, they begin to survey the room, eyes drawn to the enormous chandelier that monopolises the ceiling and sways from side to side, casting disorienting shadows on walls lined with black-and-white pictures. To their immediate left is a nondescript door with no handle. Beyond that, next to an ornate table in the corner of the room, packed to the brim with ornamental pieces and two small candles, an old grandfather clock ticks loudly, the giant pendulum swinging a slow and steady rhythm. Cobwebs stretch across every corner of coving, and the house carries an authentic staleness—a heavy concoction of mildew, must, and dancing dust.

"I think this might be one of those escape rooms," Steph says. "Christ, do you lot remember when these were all the rage—when people could bear to be in the same room as each other?"

"I miss those days," Bryan comments.

James releases a dramatic, pre-emptive sigh as he takes a step forward and pushes the metal door. "Locked." He turns to the group, ensuring all eyes are on him as he runs a hand through his hair. "Can I remind everyone this isn't the time for nostalgic trips down memory lane? Yes, we all know the world has gone to shite, but the grandfather clock is ticking, and we've done diddly squat.

Now, can we all start taking this a little bit more seriously?"

"Cup of tea, anyone?" Cass says. She lifts the steaming pot towards the first of the skull-shaped cups, thinking a slice of normality won't go amiss.

"Does a bear shit in the woods?" Bryan replies. "Two sugars, please."

Doug can't believe there's another one like his wife. He can imagine them both standing in front of a firing squad, lined up with others. "Any last requests?"— "Yes, a cup of tea would be smashing, thanks."

Only James and Charlotte opt out of a drink, preferring to get on with exploring and familiarising themselves with the surroundings. They start at the clock and move to the artefacts on the nearby table, lifting each piece individually and inspecting them from every angle.

"These morons are going to get us killed," James says.

"I fucking hate you for all of this," his wife replies.

Already shivering, Helen feels colder still as she studies the pictures lining the wall, the steam from the tea creating even further mystique. Each one has the subject in a death pose, arms crossed over their chests, but with eyelids open, beady black orbs tracking her every move and lending an eerie animation. Surrounding mourners in the picture appear faceless, just a grey blur where their features should be. She follows the wall all the way along, eyeing each of them, only stopping as she reaches her own deathbed portrait. "Sam," she mutters, studying the neighbouring pictures and picking out each other member of the group. "Sam!"

Sam makes to join her, stopping dead as a ghostly figure in a sleek, silver gown emerges from the left wall. The attractive lady turns, offers a wink, and blows a kiss from magnificent red lips before her transparent, ethereal form glides to the right, disappearing through the bookcase.

"That actually just happened, right?" Sam says.

"Sure did. But you can't trust that sort, Sam," Bryan replies. "You can see right through them."

"Fuck's sake!" Charlotte slams one of the fake artefacts back on the table, extinguishing one of the candles. "Why are you lot treating this like some trippy *Alice in Wonderland* tea party?"

"We all cope in different ways," Cass replies. "My mother always said—"

"I don't give a rat's ass what she said. How about looking for this bloody clue and—"

"Found it," Helen says.

Charlotte steps towards her, looking almost disappointed. "What? How?"

"It's written on the wall, just like the little guy said." Helen turns her attention to the framed writing at the centre of the deathly portraits, tracing a finger over the delicate calligraphy. "With the steam of the Devil, you'll have time. The more eyes on you, the better."

"Something to do with the grandfather clock," James says.

"No shit, Sherlock," Bryan comments. "Get this man a pipe."

James ignores him, tapping his right foot against the wooden board and stroking his chin. "The Devil. The Devil. The Devil."

"Good job it's not the Candyman," Bryan says.

James scowls, frustrated at the incessant breaking of his concentration. "Who?"

"Bloody classic." Bryan lets out a sigh and shakes his head. "Wasted on you lot."

"Can we please stop the bullshit?" Charlotte says.

"She's got it," Sam cries. "Look!"

The group turns to Helen, watching as she holds her cup under one of the photographs. A young girl on a stained mattress, seven adults, faceless, looming over her.

Charlotte marches to her side. "What are you doing?"

"The clue," Helen says. "Steam. Can you see the six in the bottom corner of the frame?"

"I'm listening," the stark lady says.

Helen moves her cup further along to the picture of a woman on a concrete slab, more faceless people standing around her. "Three of the pictures have the same thing."

"The mark of the Devil," Steph says. "Six, six, six. That's incredible, Helen."

"We're going to need more than luck in there," James says. "Besides, what does that even give us?"

"Fuck off and go look for your pipe," Bryan retorts. "I know too many people like you, all talk and no action. While you were knick-knack shopping with Medusa, this woman's cracked the bloody code."

Steph gives her husband an internal high-five as she turns the first of the photographs over. "Yes! A five. If there are three, I bet it's a time—for the clock. What are the others?"

"Brilliant work, Helen." Cass offers a little round of applause. "Just brilliant."

Helen offers a nervous smile, her cheeks beginning to flush. "It was your tea that did it, Cass. I've got a four here and"—she reaches for the third picture—"a two."

"Oh, this is so exciting," Cass says. "I'm so glad to have met you all."

Doug's already at the grandfather clock, opening the glass door. "There can only be six combinations."

"No, that can't be right," James says. "There could be thousands."

"For the love of god, no wonder you lost all our fucking money, James. The man's right, you halfwit." Charlotte marches past her husband to join Doug at the clock. "We have time to try them all."

"What if we only get one chance?" Helen says. She's running on adrenaline now, swept away with camaraderie and praise.

"Nonsense," Charlotte counters. "That's never been the case as far as I can recall, and as the guy said, this one's just a warm-up."

Helen shakes her head. "He didn't say that; Sam did. The guy actually said, 'this one's a teaser.'"

"Miss Marple's making a comeback," Bryan says. "She's only got four more feet to go."

"You're overthinking it." Charlotte leans in towards the clock, double-checking the face in case there's anything they might have missed. "Try the order of the pictures from right to left. Four fifty-two."

"Wait! Maybe Helen's right." Sam begins lifting the other pictures one by one. "Perhaps there's another clue we missed."

"You lot already wasted too much time playing house," James says. "Try it, Derek!"

"It's Doug!" The ex-IT director looks to his wife, who shrugs and offers her signature smile. He wonders how long they've already been in the room, the hands of the grandfather clock still pointing to midnight.

"Do it, Doug." Charlotte encourages from his left shoulder.

Hoping for feedback in his earpiece, Doug aims his stare at the chandelier. "How much time do we have left?"

Nothing.

"Shit." The tremor in his knobbly fingers is worse than ever as he works at the hour hand, dragging it around to the four. "I feel like I'm diffusing a bloody bomb." He places a finger to the left of the larger dial and begins nudging it around the face. He pauses just before he gets to the Roman numeral for ten, taking several shallow breaths.

"Go on," Charlotte says, breathing down his neck.

At last, he moves the hand in place, snapping his fingers away from the clock.

Nothing.

"Try the door," James says.

But before anyone can make a move, a loud mechanical moan from above has their heads turned towards the ceiling.

"Holy shit," Bryan mumbles.

They watch as the chandelier begins to turn—slow at first— but as the ominous groans become louder, so does the speed of its rotations. Faster and faster, the light spins, fizzing and buckling, a cacophonous screeching filling the group's ears as it threatens to fall. Metal twists, glass shatters, and revolutions become more aggressive until the chandelier explodes into flames, violently spinning like a horizontal Catherine Wheel, showering the group with sparks.

"It's coming loose. Move!" Sam shouts.

A loud thud and an ear-piercing scream from the next room add to the foreboding as the spinning light builds momentum, sending some of its jewels dancing across the wooden floor. The group hustles into the corner of the room, gathering around the grandfather clock, watching the ceiling begin to crack as the chandelier prises away from the plaster.

"Is it getting serious enough for you now, or shall I make another pot of tea?" James says.

"Shut up," the group—even Cass—yells in unison as they do their best to merge into one.

The impact is thunderous, bringing a ringing to their ears and crystal fragments exploding towards them like shrapnel. Only as the final spinning pendant comes to rest do they allow themselves to break.

Steph takes in the dimness, the tiny, already two-thirds down, flickering candle projecting their petrified shadows on the walls. "Crap. Crap. Crap." A shiver runs down her spine as she eyes the dark liquid cascading from the fresh opening in the ceiling.

"Such a shame," Cass says, inspecting the fallen chandelier. "Such a beautiful piece."

"What the hell is coming through the ceiling?" Helen asks, suspecting she might already know.

Steph takes a wary step forward and crouches down to examine the growing puddle on the floor. "Looks like—"

"Blood." Sam finishes.

"It's coming down quick, whatever it is," Doug says.

Steph grimaces as the liquid begins wrapping around her shoe. "We're going to drown in here."

"No. No, we're not." Helen studies the portraits once more only to find the mourners no longer faceless and their heads turned, their black, beady eyes on hers.

"What is it, Helen?" Doug asks.

"It's an order to things." She's counting in her head, moving from frame to frame and flipping the pictures. "The more eyes on you, the better." Sixteen black eyes find hers on the picture with a two on the back. Twelve for the one marked with a four. Six for the one with the five scrawled on the reverse. "Two forty-five. It's two forty-five!"

"You're a bloody godsend, Helen," Doug utters.

"Let's see if it works first," James says.

"We've been to the Red Sea, haven't we, Doug?" Cass inspects the liquid already well-past her ankles. "Oh, it was lovely and warm. You can float in it, too. Our favourite place has to be Rimini, though."

"You'll float, too," Bryan says in his best Pennywise voice. Nobody seems to get his reference, or at least care for it. Timing, he considers.

"If anything happens, it's on me," Helen says, already working at the clock and working at the first dial. "Can someone light the other candle before we're in total darkness?"

"A bloody good job you didn't extinguish both of them, Charlie," James mutters.

Charlotte tilts the flame towards the unlit wick. "Until we get out of here, James, you're not allowed to speak to me anymore."

"That goes for the rest of us, too, you floppy-haired fuck," Bryan says. "Unless you've got something useful to say, keep it zipped!"

Helen swallows, not a drop of saliva in her mouth. The harder she tries to stop the tremor in her hand, the worse it seems to get.

Sam places a hand on her shoulder. "You've got this, Hel."

She nods, biting at her lip as she works the minute hand around the face, warm red liquid pooling at her waist. "Okay, here we go."

As the dial slips into place, there's a satisfying click, but still, as the room continues to fill with red, the group's faces remain a collection of clenched teeth and sharp, entrenched lines.

"Congratulations!" The squeaky voice cries in their ears, causing a physical recoil in some. "The main door is now unlocked. Countdown will begin as soon as you enter the next room."

"Jesus Christ, he's like a talking mosquito," Bryan says.

"Fuck all of this to Hell and back." James shakes his head, wading his way across to the door.

"It's receding," Sam says. "You can see the red line on the walls. Well done, darling!"

"It has to be fake." Steph follows close behind, wincing as she wades through the viscosity. "It just has to be."

James stops at the door and turns to the group. "This is as real as it gets. We need to be on it as soon as we go through this door. No more—"

"Shove your pep talk up your tight little asshole," Bryan snaps. "And step aside, will you? If anyone's leading this group, I vote Helen."

The group murmurs their agreement, Cass even offering another ripple of applause. "I can't wait to see your paintings, Helen."

Reluctant, James shrinks back, lips pursed tight as though on the verge of crying.

Head bowed a little, Helen makes her way to the front. She turns, looking to Sam for encouragement, then continues running her eyes across the rest of the group. "I feel silly." She follows up with a cough to clear her throat.

"Can we hurry this along, please?" Charlotte says. "Before Bryan spits out anymore cheesy movie references."

Score, Bryan thinks. *A classic's a classic.*

Nodding towards the lady, Helen thinks she sees the flicker of a smile, one that threatens to break the resoluteness, but just as quickly, Charlotte's lips settle back into linearity. She tries to relax, imagining herself back at home, sitting in front of the bay window with her paints. "The most important thing is to drop any ego before we go in."

Heads turn towards James, who huffs, performing his signature move of running a hand through his hair.

"We need to work as a team," she says. "Any suggestion needs to be aired, no matter how silly you think they might be." She feels the need to honour James with another glance. "Don't try and solve things by yourself. If you find a clue, tell the group. And don't get disheartened. We all know what we're playing for."

"Bravo, Helen," Bryan says. "Anything else?"

"Something Charlotte said before about not overthinking things. She was wrong on that occasion, but there is logic to her words." Helen eyes the group again, feeling exponentially more confident than when she first stood before them. "If we get too worked up, too hot and bothered, our minds will melt. It's important to stay as relaxed as possible."

"Should we have a group hug?" Cass suggests.

"There might be such a thing as too relaxed," James mutters, now able to see his shoes again.

"On three," Helen says.

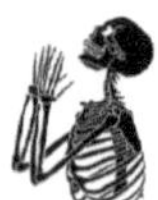

"How's it going over there?" Malcolm scoops up a handful of chocolate peanuts from his dirty cereal bowl as an ad plays on screen. "Excellent... Yep, they're all a big hit... Helen? Yeah, a proper dark horse, huh? Quiet as a mouse, but sharp as a razor... That one, a troublemaker for sure. Audiences love to hate the bad guy, though... Great... Yeah, Frank's ecstatic so far. Said he's got a boner the size of a baseball bat... Alright, let's do this... Talk soon."

As the ad comes to an end, screen one reverting to the group of eight coming to terms with their new environment, Malcolm crams another stash into his mouth and treats himself to a quick read of the latest feed.

Helen is on fire!

"Talking mosquito" had me in stitches.

Cass needs her own show. She's off her bloody rocker.

James is quite fit for his age. Shame he's such a bloody arse!

You'll float too—I remember that movie—what was it again?

I hope James and Charlotte make it to the last round so those zombies can tear them another asshole to speak out of.

Crystal Bloody Skulls

"Shit the bed." Bryan is the first to break the silence as the group takes in their new surroundings. He places his hand in an illuminated indent in the wall, inspecting his blue fingers.

Helen steps forward, trying to remain composed. However, the projected image of the timer ticking towards fifty-nine minutes lends an absolute finality to their situation. Blood begins pounding in her ears, each pulse as though a door in her mind is slamming shut. *Inhale. Exhale. Inhale. Exhale.* She surveys the oversized room—more of a large hall really—each wall covered in colourful charts or paintings. Taking centre stage is a large dining table adorned with a blood-red tablecloth, wares set out for eight people, and thick candles in the centre providing the only light source. A customary suit of armour stands halfway along the left wall next to a huge metal door with a numeric keypad. Opposite along the right side, a large bookcase stands inches from the ceiling, and just before it, a smaller table holding a draughts board, six crystal skulls of various colours, and a folded newspaper sporting a crossword puzzle.

"I love crystal skulls," Cass says.

James cuts a path down the middle of the room. "You do fucking surprise me."

Cass ignores him, inspecting the picture on the near wall.

"Look, Helen. Tulips. My absolute favourite. Red and yellow. Maybe you can paint some for me when we get out of here?"

Helen tries to speak, but no words emerge. She can feel herself beginning to sway. Clenching her teeth and curling her hands into fists, she tries to fight it. *Not now. Not now.*

"Where should we start, Helen?" Doug asks.

Oh god. Oh god. Helen clutches at her chest, reaching for the wall as her left leg buckles, the adrenaline from her poxy little speech giving way to paralysis of fear. She can feel muscles tightening, her skin crawling. The grey floaters are back, too, swimming around the rim of her vision and threatening to drown her consciousness in a single pool of nothingness. All the time, she's aware of the timer, possibly counting down their last minutes alive.

"Helen." Sam arrives at her shoulder, an arm around her waist. "Helen."

"Is she okay?" Cass asks.

"She has really bad attacks sometimes," Sam says, helping her to the floor, "especially when under stress. And I think this qualifies." Sam places a hand on her cheek. "Just breathe, Helen. We're back in the living room, Groucho nestled between us. Can you feel his wet nose? Breathe."

Charlotte crouches next to them and lifts Helen's feet from the ground. "I've heard it helps."

"It does, thanks," Sam says.

"Six numbers on this combination," Bryan hollers. "That's what we're looking for, people." He deletes the ones he's just plugged in, avoiding the enter button as though his life depended on it.

Head darting from one thing to the next, James is still busy adapting to their new surroundings. "Fuck. Fuck. Fuckity-fuck. We need a pointer, something to get us started." Lifting the visor of the armour reveals nothing but a long pipe. "Got to be something here."

"Remember what Helen said," Bryan says. "Stay calm."

"Stay calm? From the woman who just passed out?" James

begins inspecting the periodic table that hangs between a map of the world and an old Esso Petroleum poster. "I'm not sure I fully buy into her psychology." He draws in close, looking for any markings, any clues. "Fuck. Fuck. Fuck it all!" Finding nothing notable, he turns his attention to the smaller table, thinking himself silly for not noticing it before. "This draughts board has a hundred squares." He lifts the first of the pebbles. "A number one on the first, and…a hundred in the bottom right-hand corner. That must mean something!"

Bryan snaps the newspaper from the table, noting the blank and unnumbered grid, wondering how the hell you solve a crossword when you don't know where to put the answers. As he browses through the first few clues, he gets an idea.

"How are you doing, love?" Sam says, laying a hand across his wife's forehead.

"I've been better." She lets out a moan as she eases onto her elbows.

"Hey, there's a water cooler over there." Cass makes her way towards the far wall, collecting a wine glass from the table en route. "It isn't tea, but it will help."

"No, wait," Helen rasps, brushing away Sam's arm. "Tell her!" She tries to get up but feels like there's a heavy blanket lying across her.

"Cass, hang on!" Sam shouts.

Finger hovering inches above the plastic tap, the lady with the fuzzy hair turns. "What? What is it?"

"She's right," Bryan says. "Doesn't anyone else watch the trashy films from the twenties? There's an inch of water in that cooler, and I bet my saggy balls that's no accident."

"This is not acceptable," Cass cries towards the ceiling. "I had better conditions when I did my stint in telesales."

Bryan snickers. "Now you're stretching it."

Conscious of how much time they're losing, Charlotte rests a hand on Helen's shoulder. "You okay?"

Helen flashes a weak smile and nods. "We need to get cracking."

James has already moved on, feeling his way around the walls, looking for a secret room or the next clue. He's beginning to wonder if the fuzzy-haired loon called Cass has ever seen the live stream before, thinking she's perhaps expecting dancing girls, show tunes, and an after party. "Watch out for those candles, Charlie."

Not giving her husband anything, Charlotte continues running her finger over the softness of the tablecloth. The room reminds her of better times, incessant chatter and clinking glasses, a lovely little classical piece playing in the background. "There are some place cards here. They have our names on."

Cursing under his breath, Bryan removes the newspaper from the hole in the wall. For a moment, he thought he might be a hero, all too aware his contributions to date have been minimal at best, albeit for his untimely and vastly underappreciated movie references.

"These are nice plates," Cass says, making her way along the table's edge. "Reminds me of the ones we had in Rimini, Doug." She lifts one of the adjacent cards in the air to inspect. "Such pretty writing, too."

Biting at his tongue, James works his way around the bookshelf, running his fingers over the covers and noting the fading colours of the stickers on the wood. He picks one of the books at random and begins leafing through. "They've got Dickens and Mills and Boon on the same shelf. If Dickens saw this, he'd roll in his grave."

"Any that stand out?" Helen asks, scrambling to her feet with a little help from Sam.

"Not really. It's certainly an eclectic assortment. Shakespeare, Hemingway, and—who the hell is Mark Towse? We need a clue, something to get us going."

"This one has the number two on the bottom," Cass announces, tilting the card.

James sweeps his hair back as he rushes to the table. "How the hell did you miss that, Charlie?"

"Oh, I don't know, shit head," Charlotte responds. "I think you must have been distracting me with all the brilliant ideas you were reeling off."

"Can we please stop the bickering? It's not helping anyone." Sam squints and tilts the small card. "I've got four and five across here."

Steph holds up hers. "I've got seven."

"The names," Helen says. "All lowercase apart from one letter. Look!"

"Oh yeah," Cass says. "Rock and roll."

Back on form, adrenaline beginning to flow, Helen instructs the group to lay the cards on the table in number order. An instinctive glance at the timer tells her they've spent almost twenty minutes just trying to find the first clue, and god knows what will happen if it gets to zero.

Together they hover, waiting for inspiration to strike.

Sam

Cass

jAmes

heleN

charLotte

stEph

bryAn

Doug

"Scanlead," Doug orates. "Scan lead."

"Scan! There's a scanner at the entrance!" Bryan says.

"And lead!" James marches back to the periodic table.

Cass claps her hands together and performs a little jig that makes Doug want to cry. "Well done, team," she says. "Well done!"

"Pb. Pb. Pb. Here we go, atomic number eighty-two." James snaps his head towards the draughts board and grabs the second pebble from the ninth row. His hand trembles as he turns the stone over. "There's nothing on it."

"The scanner, dummy," Bryan says.

Feeling embarrassed, James marches to the hole in the wall and holds out the rock in the palm of his hand. "Nothing." He flips the pebble and tries again. "Yes! Letters—R and—J. R and J. R and J. What does that mean?"

"Thirty-nine minutes," Steph announces.

"Romeo and Juliet." Sam kisses his wife on the cheek and darts across to the bookshelf. "Come on! Come on! Where is—yes, here, here we go!" But as he opens the book and begins flicking through the blank pages, his heart sinks. "You have to be kidding."

"Try the scanner," James suggests.

Bryan performs a slow clap. "So, there is a brain cell under all that ego."

Excited, Sam marches over to the room's entrance. "What page?" The front of the book reveals nothing, the back cover, too. "Shit." He tries the first few pages but feels like he's clutching at straws. "We're missing something." Offering a defeated sigh, he throws the book on the table.

Cass inspects the crystal skulls, lifting one in the air. "What about these?" Its emerald-green translucency suggests importance, but she can't see anything obvious. "Fascinating."

"Likely a red herring," James says. "There to attract the low-brows like flies to shit."

Cass offers him a scowl, half-tempted to launch the skull towards his head.

Minutes pass as the group inspects every inch of the room, the escalating tension worn on their faces. Silence falls across them, a tacit admission of their lack of progress. They start over—repeatedly—the trail running cold each time, momentum beginning to crumble. Two on each wall, looking for anything that might help, frustration and fear are winning the battle, their eyes drawn towards the timer every few seconds.

"I don't suppose there's any chance of a clue?" Bryan yells. He groans as he futilely pushes at a wall.

"The shelves are marked," Steph shouts from beside the book-case. "The one it came from has red and yellow stickers underneath."

James raises his hand in the air, feeling like a halfwit for doing so. "I was just about to say that." His words feel weak, creating further inferiority.

"Come on, Helen," Charlotte says. "You've got this. You've got this!

"Red and yellow. Red and yellow. I don't know. I don't—" She breaks off, cursing herself for being so slow, but allowing herself a bit of slack, what with the threat of death hanging over her. "I love you, Cass."

Cass smiles a confused smile.

"The tulips," Helen says. "Red and yellow."

Sam's already inspecting the picture. "Seven yellow, twelve red."

I'm back, Helen thinks. *I'm doing this.* "Which sticker first—on the shelf—which colour?"

"Red," Steph replies before James can even open his mouth.

"That works. Page one hundred and twenty-seven." Helen affords a glance at the timer. 19:32. "Pass me the book. Pass me the book!"

"Can anyone else hear that?" Cass announces. "Like a hissing noise."

"Maybe it's Charlotte's tits deflating," Bryan replies. He begins hopping on his bad leg, regretting it almost straight away, but once a showman. "There's a snake in my boots."

"I know that one," Cass says. "It's Woody, isn't it?"

"Yeehah!" Bryan says.

"Page one hundred and twenty-seven. Here we go." It's like a sucker punch in Helen's chest, taking her breath, but also some of her hope. "Totally blank, just like the others."

"It's coming from the armour—the pipe." Charlotte moves towards the source. "I think it's—gas."

"We still have twenty minutes, though," Sam says.

"I guess that's how long they expect it to take," Charlotte responds.

"Fuck!" James slams the side of his fist on the dining table. "Get looking, trash the place if you have to." He marches towards the shelf and begins pulling at it, tearing at books, pages carpeting the floor.

"Do you guys get down to the local library much, Charlie?"

Bryan asks, unable to help himself, the words just hammering against his skill until he sets them free. *Nineteen minutes to live, that must be the toughest crowd ever,* he thinks.

Charlotte lets out a garbled moan as she runs a finger over the world map, adamant there's a clue within. "How do you do it, Bryan? And Cass? We're trapped in a room that's filling with gas, for Christ's sake."

"I'm used to that with Doug," Cass replies.

"And would you prefer us to react like your husband?" Bryan scrambles from under the table and dusts himself down. "Bloody King Kong over there. Look at the bloody state of him."

James is oblivious, face red raw, not helped by his current act of self-flagellation. "Think, you imbecile." He slaps himself across both cheeks. "Think!"

"As Helen so eloquently pointed out," Cass says, "we have to remain calm. Hel, pass me the book a tickety-boo, will you?"

A friend for life, at least what's left of it, Helen thinks of Cass as she hands her the book.

Cass pinches the page between her fingers and lifts it to the air. She knows they could have gone off course, mistaken a clue or two along the way. She flicks through the rest of the book but finds nothing. "Are there any other books corresponding to the letters R and J?"

"James has probably eaten them by now," Bryan says, heading over, back on the search. "Found anything on anger management yet, James?"

"Fuck off, we're all going to die!"

Bryan laughs. "Guess not.".

Once again thumbing through the book, Cass stops as she reaches page one hundred and twenty-seven. *Think, Cass, think. Must be something. Has to be!*

"Can't see anything." Bryan picks the books up one by one, flicking through each just in case. "*Robinson Crusoe*? *Jane Eyre*? Maybe we're supposed to be looking for two books?"

Helen recoils as Sam grabs her hand, her body an oversensitive composition of nerve endings. She tries a smile as he leans in close. "Whatever happens, Hel, I want you to know I'm grateful for every minute I've known you." They part with possibly their last ever kiss, Sam returning to searching areas already explored.

Doug eyes his wife with a combination of admiration and jealousy—looking death full-on in the face and refusing to curl up and let it take her quietly. As he glances towards the timer, dizziness washes over him, his legs offering a buckle. He suspects the poison might already be in their system, imagining it will take them out of action well before the counter reaches zero. He feels hopeless, a failure. His body begins to shake, and the more he tries to get it under wraps, the more violent its reaction. He reaches his arms out, but there's nothing to support him.

"Let me help you," Sam says, threading his arm under Doug's armpit.

"Fourteen minutes," Charlotte announces. "Have we got anything else? Anything we haven't shared?"

"We haven't used the crossword puzzle yet," Bryan replies. "I guess it could be a red herring, but I'm adamant it has something to do with it."

"What's the connection, though?" Charlotte says. "It's just a bunch of clues and a blank grid."

"And the world map. The poster. The water in the cooler." Sam escorts Doug towards the table. "We've got—thirteen bloody minutes—and we could still be so far away!"

As Helen flops into the chair, the wood creaks along with her bones. "I'm hoping it's just the stress, but I'm beginning to feel dizzy."

"Me, too," Doug mutters as Sam lowers him into another of the wooden chairs.

"Oh god. Oh god, no." James is in the corner, sliding down the wall. He begins to cry, wrapping his arms around his legs. "I don't want to die. Not like this. Not with—these people. I'm worth more than this, surely."

Bryan opens his mouth, but Steph flicks him a glance. *Timing.*

Charlotte drops into a chair, burying her head into her hands. "Twelve minutes."

"We can't give up," Sam says. "We can't!"

With the sight of their leader in distress and her husband unable to fake a smile, even Cass appears disheartened. "Come on, team." But they all look defeated, gone, preparing themselves for the big sleep. As a last resort, she places the book open-paged on the table and imagines herself back in the classroom, a blurry scene of finger paintings on the wall, children huddled on the floor, and coloured water in the used-to-be jam jars. "Hammer, hammer, hammer, shake, shake, shake, twiiiirrl, and clap!"

Charlotte lifts her head, unable to believe what she's hearing. "Have you lost your fucking mind?"

"Come on, you all have to do the actions. Follow me." Cass begins by slamming a clenched fist into her palm three times. "Hammer, hammer, hammer." She rattles her bony fingers at the air in front. "Shake, shake, shake." She spins her hands over each other. "Twiiiirrl." And finishes with a—"Clap!"

James burrows his head further between his legs. "This can't be happening. Ten minutes to live, and we're playing Simon fucking Says. Just kill me now."

Lifting his head from the table, Doug puts his arms out in front, managing a weak smile for his wife, albeit through watery eyes. He gestures for the others to do the same, amazed as some of them oblige. "The floor's yours, dear Cass."

And so, as the first digit on the counter disappears, six of the eight contestants take part in a classroom chant designed to get kids' attention and make them more alert. They hammer, they shake, they twirl, they clap. Cass becomes more animated with each round, eyes wide as she exaggerates every hammer and twirl. Doug's unsure if his wife is being swept away by the moment or if the one kite string keeping her grounded has finally snapped.

Only on the sixth round, as fake enthusiasm dies, does Cass cease, exhausted and scared to death, her hands falling against both open pages of the book.

Erik.

It's a subtle epiphany—no jolt, no internal fanfare, just a memory so lucid, so vivid that she could almost reach out and touch the boy's hair. Sweet boy, well-natured, kind with such a pleasant way. Almost totally blind. "It's braille. Here, feel it. It's only bloody braille!"

Helen leans across, running her palm across the page. "She's right; I can feel the bumps."

"What the fuck do we know about braille?" James says. And it dawns on him, the same time as it does for Bryan. They catch each other's stare as they scramble on the floor, looking for the book titled *Braille for Dummies.*

"Got it!" Bryan yells, holding it in the air.

Cass lowers herself in her seat, gliding her fingertips left to right. "I don't think we'll need it."

Doug forces himself not to look at the timer. "Come on, Cass, you beauty!"

Charlotte spins her chair around, ignoring the tightening in her chest and the pounding headache made all the worse as her husband begins smashing his fists into the iron door. She leans in, observing Cass as she goes to work, fingers tracing across the white page.

"The first letter is H, I'm sure of it."

"We need numbers, not letters!" James screams.

The vein in Bryan's head beats in perfect time to the thrashing of the metal door. "Charlotte, can you do something with that?"

"Don't worry. He'll curl up in a minute with his thumb in his mouth. Cass?"

"An E. It's an E." Cass sees her fingers trembling. "And this one's an A!"

"H-E-A," Bryan orates. "Head? Heavy?"

Cass's face crumples. "I'm not sure about this one."

Restless, Bryan shifts in the chair. "Come on, Cass, you've got this." It's too much, that noise—feels like someone has a pneumatic drill against his skull. "James, will you shut the fuck up? Just shut the fuck up, or I swear to God, you won't make the six minutes."

The thrashing of the door comes to an end as James flops to the floor, his subsequent raucous bout of tears almost as irritating.

Bryan flicks open *Braille for Dummies*. "Describe the shape, Cass."

"Four minutes," Charlotte says.

"It's a T or a W." She nods. "Heat! I think it's—heat. Yes, heat!"

"Holy shit." Helen almost throws herself across the table, reaching for the candle. "Cass, hold the page near the flame."

Bryan reaches his hand out towards Cass's chair and crouches in for the show. "Not too bloody close, mind."

Letting out an exhale, Cass pushes the book across the table. "My nerves are shot."

Sam's the first to scoop it up, and together, the group, minus James, watch the flicker of orange do its thing. It seems like an eternity until the first letters reveal themselves. Even before Sam has a chance to read out the word—*figurine*—Bryan's all over it. "It's an answer to a crossword clue! Figurine, the answer to three across. Next word, Sam."

"It's coming. It's coming. El—gar. Elgar."

Bryan runs his eyes over the clues, trying to get his head around the answer-first mentality. "Come on." *Think, Bryan. Think!* "Got it. It's an anagram of large—twelve across. That's three and twelve. Next!"

"Ample."

"I've seen that one. Four down. Too easy. Next."

"Geneva."

"Geneva. Geneva. Geneva. Where are you, Geneva?"

Charlotte moves to the door, skirting around her husband's feet. "What numbers have we got so far?"

"Across we have three and twelve, and down we have four," Helen replies.

The numbers on the display indicate progress as she taps them in, the task providing a well-received, albeit short-lived distraction. She offers her husband a glance, feeling a combination of pity and resentment, a man with ambition and dreams but the emotional intelligence of a child. All that's missing is the dummy. "Get up, for Christ's sake, James."

"Two minutes thirty-six," Sam announces.

The rest of the group joins James and Charlotte at the door, eager to escape the hissing suit of armour.

"Gen—knowledge, maybe?" The harder Bryan focuses, the smaller the font seems to get, and his head still echoes the beats from James's tantrum. He takes a deep breath and lets out a long exhale but feels even dizzier for doing so, the toxin likely already in his system. He sees the timer flickering from peripheral vision and the blur of all the faces pointing in his direction, their lives in his hands. *Come on, Bryan!* But it's as though there's a fog in his head, consuming any rational thoughts, his mind racing, but words running into each other in a nonsensical pileup.

"One minute, thirty-two," Sam says. "Come on, Bry."

James moans from the floor. "I don't feel well."

"Shut up," everyone yells.

The newspaper gripped impossibly tight, Bryan tries to focus, but the letters begin floating towards him. He tries to blink them back onto the page, but they spin and dance in the air. *We're all going to die,* James's voice cries in his head.

"One minute," Sam says.

Oh shit. Oh shit. Bryan closes his eyes, imagining himself in a movie, the cheesy hero tasked with saving the day, ready to tackle any nemesis apart from a dripping tap. An old British spy movie, perhaps. *Colin Firth. Yes, I'm Colin Firth!* "Let's do this. Rule Britannia and all that." Hunched over his special agent desk crammed with paperwork and full of code breaker books, Bryan pushes his non-existent glasses up the bridge of his nose.

Charlotte's face settles to her resting scowl. "What are you doing, Bryan?"

But he's not Bryan—he's Colin Firth, Colin Firth playing a British agent. He reaches for the turntable on his desk and engages the stylus, prompting a series of crackles. As the evocative music kicks in, he begins twirling a finger in the air.

Charlotte lets her head fall against the wall. "We're fucked."

"A girl who mixed with bad intelligence. Eva—a girl's name. Gen—eva. Fourteen down. It's fourteen down!" Bryan snaps his eyes open and does a little dance. "Eat your heart out, Colin Firth!"

"He still looks good for his age," Cass says. "Doesn't look a day over sixty."

Charlotte's already keyed in the numbers. 312414. She looks over her shoulder for approval, catching sight of the timer showing less than twenty seconds to go.

Bryan nods and shrugs. "Do it."

As soon as she hits the button, the hissing stops, and the door opens. The talking carrot awaits on the other side, the first to congratulate them. "What a team," he sings, bringing his little hands together.

Bryan doesn't know whether to kiss him or punch him. "I need the bathroom," he says, pushing past.

"Of course. Of course. We've got refreshments lined up, too. Come through, come through. You've earned a break." He ushers them through to a room with large tables lining both sides, an abundance of food and drinks spread across each. "Help yourselves. We've got thirty minutes before we go live again. Makeup, can we have a refresh, please? And bring their outfits." The hands come together once more, and that oh-so-white smile against the orange. "I must say, you are all putting on a wonderful show. How are you all feeling?"

"Knackered," Sam says. "And if you ask any more questions about our wellbeing, I'm likely to rip your little orange head off and shove it up your arse! We're here because we have to be, and no other reason, you little shit."

The giant security man, Silas, steps forward just as the little guy retreats. It's a perfect, smooth, synchronous move. "You are here because you chose to be, Sam." Tristan's voice squeaks from behind cover. "You could have opted to go quietly on your seventieth birthday."

Before Sam can react, Helen's at his shoulders, tugging on his arm. "Come on, pet, let's sit down and recharge."

After changing into the fresh clothes provided, using the bathroom for some well-needed solitary time, they sit at the tables and pick at the food, the inflatable twins dusting their faces with a brush. In the background, a montage of clips from the show plays on a loop. The best and the worst of them—the break-throughs, tears, nervous jokes. There's even an extended scene of James fighting with the door, an old heavy metal track playing in the background. Through it all, Tristan squeals and guffaws, tears of laughter streaming down his face.

"Will we have any aftereffects from the gas?" Doug asks. "I felt pretty shocking in there and only a little better now."

Offering another snicker, the little man spins around to the rest of the crew, who mirror his amusement. He looks so excited he might burst as he swivels back around on one foot. "I've got a secret."

"There was no gas, was there?" Helen suggests. "It was just a—"

"Sound effect." Orange man claps his hands and performs another revolution. "We had you going, though, didn't we?" He performs a little dance, hopping from one foot to the next. "Quite the experiment—often referred to as the nocebo effect."

"I swear to God, I'm going to—" An arm as thick as a tree trunk stops Sam's approach.

Silas narrows his eyes. "Sit."

"Relax. Eat the nice spread we put out for you," Tristan says. "Call that one an ice breaker, a chance to get to know each other—the competition. The numbers you guys are pulling in, I tell you. And some of you really excelled. I bet you even surprised yourselves, and now you're all warmed up there's no telling what you're capable of."

"What's next?" Cass asks. "Any chance it's a bake off?"

"My lips are sealed, but you only have twenty minutes to wait, petal." He about turns and offers a parting wave. "Maybe I'll see you; maybe I won't."

The group watches him out through the door, Silas two steps behind.

"I've got nothing against goblins, per se," Bryan mutters, "but that little fucker really gets my goat."

Opting to spend what could be their last moments together in a blatant declaration of war, James and Charlotte sit slightly apart, arms folded. The rest of the group also falls into a strained quiet, trying to process what they've been through and what else might be in store. Food goes untouched. Bathroom visits are frequent, surprising no one. Tears flow, eyes close with exhaustion, and bodies shudder with reflection and anticipation. At one stage, titbits of forced chatter threaten to build into a conversation until someone mentions family, and it all becomes too much, prompting them to revert to their bubbles and take comfort in each other's embrace. Albeit James and Charlotte, that is.

Nothing else for them to do, they wait. Wait for their cue. Wait for the next game.

Wait for their likely demise.

"Roger that. I wasn't sure we could top last week, but have you seen the stats?... Haha, yeah, that was some old-school magic... Shit, yeah, I didn't think they stood a chance... Me, too. I don't know how they got it together, not with King Kong shitting his nappy and the timer almost at zero... We sure fucked with them... Cass? Looks like she's on day release from the happy farm... Toughie, that one. For sheer entertainment value, I'd say it's between Bryan and James. The 'I've got nothing against goblins line' cracked me up... Yeah... Hey, we're just doing our jobs—it's as Frank says, at least we're giving them a chance... I know. Keep this hush, yeah, but my father's up next week for his... No. He's ready, said he 'ain't made for this world'... No pity, please. I'm just saying seventy is a fair old age when the world moves so quickly. He's seen a lot, too much as far as he's concerned... No, he's pleased his numbers didn't come up—took the decision away from him… Mum will be okay, she has good friends… No, I'm good, honest… Think of the bonus… Yeah, we best get on with it. Can't wait—the obstacle course is a fan favourite!"

The shake isn't as thick as Malcolm likes it, courtesy of the new skinny girl at Fat Tony's. He gives her five days tops, knowing being on the larger side is a major plus when you're serving that kind of food at that sort of establishment. Heavy on the fat, easy on the lettuce, and for Christ's sake, don't skimp on the ice cream. He lets out a loud and surprisingly long and satisfying belch as he wipes his greasy palm across the ReGenevate emblem.

Yeah, Mum will be okay, he thinks. But she was a different person last week when he visited, none of that fuss and fluff, not even a peck on the cheek. It's just the way it is, though. No point fretting. Besides, she only has two years on her own before it's her turn. Cursing himself for being so weak, he dabs at the tear with the bottom of his food-stained sweater and drags an arm under his nose. Four minutes until they go live again. He has high hopes, working through the company, putting in the years, and earning a passport. Doesn't need love or anyone else; he has something in the cupboard at home for that. Ignoring the pain in his chest, he shovels in another generous mouthful before unwrapping the next burger and removing the lettuce. As he sucks the shake through the straw, he casts his eyes over the latest comments.

That's some mean shit, man! Fake gas—way to get into their heads, though.

How do you stand on Elves and pixies, Bryan? We need to know! From one of Santa's little helpers.

Would you look at that? Helen and Cass stealing the show—who'd have thought?

After all that, the water was a red herring!

This looks like so much fun. If only I had some non-virtual friends.

Hammer, hammer, hammer. Shake, shake, shake. Twiiiirrl. And clap. How the fuck am I supposed to get any sleep tonight?

Beast Mode

Cass winces as she performs a stretch, muscles popping and bones crunching. She takes in the path ahead, noting the rope net and the wall halfway along that stands a touch smaller than her. And where the hell is that smoke coming from?

"I struggle to get out of bed sometimes because of my sciatica," she says. "And now I'm expected to climb up walls and swing on a bloody rope like Tarzan?"

"Breathe, Cass." Doug performs three star jumps, grateful he didn't stuff his face with all the pastries on offer. "I can't see a time limit anywhere, so I think as long as we make it, we're good. Where's all your airy-fairy positivity gone all of a sudden?"

"Fuck you, Mister this-fake-gas-is-killing-me."

"Cass!"

"And when all this is over, come hell or high water, you're taking me back to Rimini." Swapping legs, she eases herself down a couple of inches before letting out a pained groan. She glances either side over the barriers, sizing up the competition, noting James to her left punching at the air ahead and Charlotte's perfect yoga-style pose, her firm booty only a couple of inches from the rubber matting. To her right, Bryan jumps on the spot, trying to catch his backside with his heels. Steph's sitting on the ground, rocking back and forth, in hysteria or some understated meditation technique. Further along,

Sam and Helen stand beside each other, holding hands. She can hear a quiet whimpering coming from their direction.

"Going live in three minutes," Tristan calls from behind. "Bring on the flesh eaters."

"Oh no, Doug. Oh no."

"Oh god." Warmth spreads down Doug's right thigh as he glances behind to see the first metal cage, two burly guys on each side. His skin crawls as he studies it—the flesh eater—writhing and hammering at its metal fortress, being wheeled in like royalty.

Hammer, hammer, hammer. Shake, shake, shake. Twirl. And SNAP!

"Oh fuck. Oh fuck." He watches it clamp its jaws around the bars, pull its head back with animalistic curiosity, and let out a frustrated growl. It begins clawing at its own grey skin before fixing its stare ahead, Doug feeling like its eyes are on him and only him. It lets out a growl and pumps its fists against the cage.

Maybe they're just for show, Doug thinks—the gas trick all over again. But deep down, he knows things have taken a more serious turn.

The scream is piercing, catching Doug by surprise. For a second, he thinks the blood-curdling cry could have emerged from his own lips. As raucous sobbing follows, he snaps his head to the right to see Sam and Helen locked in an embrace. Sam offers another scream and doubles over, a string of thickness swinging from his chin.

"Cameras on lane four, quick! Stop the ads and put this out now," the tan man cries in their ears. "We've got a screamer! I repeat, we've got a screamer!"

"Oh no," Cass mutters. "This is too much."

It's the understatement of the year, but it is how it is, Doug figures. There's a fleeting, horrific thought in his head that competition would be slimmer if the couple bailed, but he shakes it off, surprised and appalled at the airspace it took up.

"Maybe we should just get the injection, Doug. I don't know about any of this anymore."

So meek and mild, Doug had a feeling it would be Helen to

crack first. It looked at one point as though they'd lose her in the first game, but she surprised him and came good. "I'm taking you to fucking Rimini, Cass."

"I can't do it, Helen," Sam screams. "I can't! I can't!"

As Sam pulls away and begins retching towards the ground, Doug watches security moving in. Helen desperately tries to spur her husband on, but Doug can see the man is already lost, face as white as a sheet, body trembling, sobs becoming more and more explosive.

"Stay away from me! Don't you fucking touch me!" Sam cries. "I want to go home. Take me home!"

"Sam, not like this," Bryan yells from Doug's right. "It's Helen's life on the line!"

"Bry, they won't do her as well, will they?" Steph asks. "Not really? It's just another hoax like the gas, yeah?"

"I think the jokes are over, Steph."

With mouth agape, Doug watches on, thinking the man seemed so solid, so reserved. How wrong he was about both. "Get up, Sam. Get up, you fool." Four guys approach, all built the same, shoulders like boulders sporting the "I should really be bald look" but a rug of thick hair cascading down the back of their necks. Doug finds himself wondering if they're all called Silas. For sure, he couldn't pick the one they met from the line-up. As the heavies form a circle around Sam and Helen, he loses sight of their new friends. *Come on, Sam. Come on!*

"You've got this, Sam," Cass cries. "Don't let them beat you!"

From within the ring of steel, Doug can still hear Sam's dampened protests. "I can't. I just can't. I'm so sorry, Helen. I'm so sorry."

"Bring them in," the orange man says from behind. "We've got what we need."

As the Silas clones roll in two more caged beasts, the reduced group helplessly observes the couple being escorted away. Sam continues kicking, screaming, and bawling, restrained by two grunts, while Helen walks with her head down, resigned to her fate, extending her hand for when Sam is ready to take it.

"I can't believe it," Cass mutters. "She was going to paint for me."

As Doug looks across, checking on the others, only to see James still bouncing up and down and punching at the air, the familiar clapping sound explodes from behind. "Okay, gang, we're up in sixty seconds." The tanned chipmunk squeaks. "Take your marks. Remember, automatic disqualification for a false start."

"Come on, Cass. We can grieve later. If we get through this."

"But Doug, I—"

"Stop that, right now! Think of that little balcony where we had breakfast, the water shimmering like emeralds, the warm breeze against your cheek. And speaking of cheeks, what about all those cute waiters with tight tushies?"

Cass rakes a sleeve across her face. "I like your saggy little ass." A short burst of tears explodes, but she manages to prevent a full breakdown, pinching some of the doughy skin on her inner thigh. "I'm going to need a new outfit, too."

"We've got this, yeah?" James says to his wife, finishing his workout with a right uppercut and popping his lips for effect. "Charlie!"

Charlotte's still blanking him, staring at the empty lane. "I've forgotten how nice real people can be," she says.

James huffs, readying himself on the starting line.

"Steph, you good?" Bryan asks, eyeing the rope net.

"That's probably the stupidest thing you've ever asked me." She takes her place, getting a flashback to her days as girls champion eight-hundred-metre-runner at school—before her skin suit began to inflate. "Love you, though." She blocks all thoughts of Sam and Helen from her mind, for now.

It sounds like a bomb going off, vibrations feeding up their feet through the rubber, blinding white light lining both sides of the makeshift stadium. As the fireworks continue to crackle around them, James is first on his way, screaming at Charlotte to follow.

Doug and Cass are next, arms flailing either side, trying to work up some momentum.

"Steph!" Bryan screams, glancing behind and catching the eyes of the flesh eater. "Run!"

She's frozen to the spot, the sounds and brightness overloading her circuitry. She can hear the things behind growling, can hear her husband screaming for her to run, but it's as though she's forgotten how. She shuffles forward a couple of steps, seeing the others out in front on either side, already getting themselves tangled up in the rope net. Willing herself on, she takes another strained step and another.

"Fuck!" Spinning himself around, Bryan begins dashing back towards the starting line, left arm outstretched. He clasps at his wife's wrist and gives it a yank, almost toppling her off balance. She finds her feet and stumble forward, momentum working in her favour. And just like that, she's off, arms pumping, bingo wings flapping, legs pummelling the rubber. She glances either side. To her left, James is already straddling the bar, Charlotte slapping away his offer of assistance, and to her left, Doug and Cass are still only halfway up, caught in the net like a couple of overcooked lobsters, faces brighter than the orange goblin's.

Deep-seated muscle memory kicking in, Steph begins making good ground, her and Bryan at level pace and spurring each other on. "Step and pull," Bryan rasps as they approach the net. "Step and—fuuuuuuuuuuuck!"

The pain is sudden and explosive, surging up his right side. He staggers forward best he can, face held in a grimace, teeth buried into his lower lip until he slumps to the ground. He clamps a hand around his right calf. "No! No! No!" There was nothing but a niggle the day before yesterday; he was sure it would sort itself out. His good leg, too; overcompensating because of arthritis in his left. "Fuck!"

Steph takes in the opportunity to suck in mouthfuls of air, affording a glance behind, relieved to see the flesh eaters still caged. She wonders for how long. "Can you walk?"

"I think so." Every step now painful, Bryan winces as he approaches the obstacle, grateful for the short reprieve as he lets the netting take his weight. "I should have listened to you, Steph. I'm sorry."

"No time for that. Let's do this." She lets out a groan as she heaves herself up the first two lengths of rope. "Are you coming or what?"

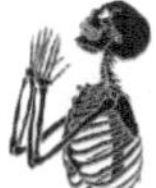

"Start the full sweep now." Tristan instructs from the starting line, finger on his earpiece, partly to drown out the growls from behind. "Home in on their faces. I want to see every jowl movement, every bead of sweat spilling down their crusty old skin, the fear in their eyes when we announce the release of the flesh eaters. I want the figures through the roof!" *I want the bonus. I want a passport. I want a promotion. I want it all.*

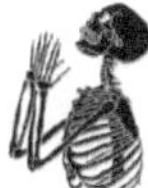

Malcolm brings the drone in on the current leaders, James and Charlotte. Only one sucker would take his bet this week, one of the nameless in costumes, and only then prepared to bet a twenty. Still, it's an easy win—firm favourites all the way and showing why as they approach the wall, the others not even close to finishing the first obstacle. He's about to sweep the drone across to second placers, Doug and Cass, but he notices a quarrel beginning to unfold between the leaders and nudges the lens closer towards them.

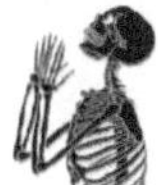

"If I go first, I can drag you over from the other side," James says, doubling over and catching some breath.

"That's not going to work, you fool. Give me a leg up, and then you can get yourself over. All that cardio, and wrestling metal doors, it shouldn't be too difficult."

"Fuck's sake. We haven't got the time for this, Charlie. Just do as I tell you!"

The slap is instinctive, catching him a good one on his right cheek. "And where has that ever got me, James?"

His mouth falls open, and he lets out a little shiver. There's an adrenaline rush of frustration and anger, and it takes all reserves not to return the strike. "It's a good job the cameras are on me."

"Oh, such a big man. But you're all hot air when it comes down to it, aren't you? Little baby James and his tantrums."

His eye and arm twitch simultaneously. "Can we do this when we get to the finish line?"

"Crouch, peasant, I'm going first."

Reluctant, James lowers himself to the ground until he's on all fours, just where he thinks she's always wanted him. He grits his teeth even harder, sure some of them might crunch under pressure. He even offers the drone a snarl as it floats away towards Doug and Cass in lane two.

"Get your leg over, Cass. You can do this," Doug cries from the other side of the netting, ignoring the drone that stops just inches from his scalp. He glances over to lane three to see Bryan and Steph catching up. "Do it, Cass. Commit."

"I'm knackered, Doug. I can't feel my effin legs!"

"You won't have any legs if they set those bloody things loose. Count down from three, okay?"

"The fucking thing won't stop moving!"

"Grab the knots and keep your body close to the rope." It's only the second time he's ever heard the F-word leave her lips, the first at the starting line. "Three."

"My arms are burning."

"Two. Come on, Cass, where's that optimistic little bundle of joy?"

"At home, sipping on a cup of tea, admiring her roses."

"One."

"Fuck you!" She gives it everything, letting out a high-pitched war cry that transitions to a wail as she flops to the other side, embedding herself in the netting like a trapped fly.

"You've done it! You're over, Cass. Now relax your body." Doug tries to keep his voice calm but knows they've spent too much time on this one. "Well done. Well done." In the distance, he eyes the flesh eater, its nose poking through the cage and sniffing at the air, hands clasped around the bars. "Okay, now slowly start stepping down. I've got you. I've always got you." He glances to lane three to see Steph already over, Bryan nearing the top, any advantage now all but clawed back. "That's it, Cass. That's it!" From peripheral vision, Doug notices the drone leaving them, and his mind fills with thoughts of just how bizarre the entire situation is—viewers back home filling their faces with popcorn, laughing and mocking the frailty on display, no heed paid to their own mortality.

Bryan lets out another stifled scream as the drone floats past his right thigh. He eyes Steph through the netting, her features angular and urgent.

"We're catching up, Bry. Come on!" Steph yells.

Calf feeling like it's on fire every time pressure is applied, Bryan relies on his arms to do the bulk of the work, but they're beginning to sing, too, already aching from yesterday's full upper body workout. As blood-curdling growls continue to fill his ears, he tries to recall every zombie movie he owns but realises it's not a good distraction at all.

"Come on, Bry. That's it."

The top part should be easy, just a case of supporting with his left leg and throwing the right one over. *Inhale. Exhale. Inhale. Exhale.* And—he's over. Accompanying pain prompts a high-pitched yelp and a vacuous feeling in his stomach for what lies ahead.

"Give me your hand, Bry."

"I'm fine. I'm fine."

The fire ignites as he tries to find his footing, but he knows every second counts. Progress is slow, but he makes it onto the rubber just before Cass falls into Doug's arms in lane two. Steph offers her hand, but he soldiers on, hobbling towards the wall, knowing there's a whole world of pain waiting. A glance behind confirms the flesh eaters are yet to be released, but they look more frenzied than ever, rocking the cages from side to side.

"Give me a shove," Steph yells. Hands gripping the top, she readies herself. The wall seems so much higher now, insurmountable without a rope and proper climbing shoes. "Bryan!"

"I'm coming!"

With his wife's buttocks spilling over his hands, Bryan thrusts with everything he has, letting out a wild scream towards the drone as it sweeps around his head like an annoying bug. He follows with a maniacal laugh, imagining someone innocently switching over to the stream, thinking they'd stumbled upon amateur old-folk porn.

"Why—are—you—" Letting out a pre-emptive rush of air, Steph makes the drop, pain rattling through her legs, but the rubber taking the brunt of the impact away. "Laughing?"

"I was just thinking—" He jumps, clasping his hands around the top of the wall. *All those push-ups, side-planks. Time for return on investment.* Muscles crunch as he grimaces and scrambles against the wood, hauling himself up and throwing his legs towards the top. Hooking an ankle over the wall, he leverages his heel, using his arms to bring himself up. *I did it. I only bloody did it!* He takes a moment to rest atop the obstacle, preparing himself for the inevitable, painful drop. "Holy shit!"

"What is it, Bry? And will you get down from there, for the love of God."

He sees James and Charlotte wading through something resembling treacle or tar, up to their chins in blackness. They look exhausted but still have the energy for squabbling, Charlotte swatting at James's offered hand. Behind them, there's a two-metre-long wall with a small tunnel boring through and ahead, and what caused his stomach to almost fall out is a pit of what resembles large broken bits of honeycomb, wisps of smoke swirling above. Hot coals laid out in a ten-metre stretch of unfathomable pain.

"Bry!"

"I'm coming." He turns his glance to see Cass straddling the wall, face frozen in terror, looking towards the ground as though it was a ten-thousand-foot drop.

"What were you laughing at before, Bry?" Steph asks.

"I've already forgotten." *Timing.* "Let's go."

"And what did you see up there?"

"Just Doug and Cass closing in."

"What's this?"

"It's a fucking tunnel, Steph!" His body trembles with relentless pain, ranging from ten to off the charts each time his right foot finds the rubber. "I'm so sorry. Sorry, pet."

Steph crouches, inspecting the warren that looks nowhere near large enough to even squeeze into, never mind wriggle out of. "I hate small spaces, Bry."

"If truth be told, I hate your beef cobbler, but I still eat it every Sunday."

"You're in so much trouble if we make it out alive." Lowering her body to the ground, Steph takes a deep breath and submerges herself into relative darkness. From behind, Bryan watches her squirming through the burrow like a sluggish boa that over-divulged at feeding time. On his front, grateful for the weight to be off his leg, he readies himself to follow. "Good work, darling. Try to use—"

The explosion reverberates through Bryan's spine, the tunnel ahead framing his wife's body with flashes of brilliant white. Over the sound of the accompanying blaring siren, he hears the crackle of fireworks and the electronic fanfare. "Oh, shit." The eruption pales insignificantly to the excited roars of the predatory flesh eaters he knows are now free.

"Bryan?"

"Hurry, Steph." He digs his elbows into the rubber matting. "Don't think, just move."

And she does, buttocks swinging side to side as much as the tight space allows, Doug's comment about her cobbler still taking space in her head. And coming from him, the only person she knows who makes soup so thick the spoon stands upright. She drags herself through, muscles screaming, relief kicking in as her hand falls in the soft light cast on the rubber. With a final groan and haul, she pulls her shoulders from the tunnel. *I'll give him beef cobbler!*

Full-volume madness falls across her ears once again as she eyes the two pits ahead, the first, a pool of uninviting darkness, the second, a steaming pile of glowing skin-singeing agony.

"Keep going, Steph." Bryan pushes at her ankles, encouraging her to get the fuck the move on. "Don't think, just move!"

At last, Steph scrambles to her feet and staggers towards the first pit, swatting at the drone only just out of reach. Warm thickness swallows her ankles as she plunges herself into the darkness, prompting a vague recollection of a weekend jaunt to the seaside—running into the sea against the breeze, seaweed wrapping around her legs, the sun disappearing behind a cloud, turning the blue sea to grey. Bryan laughed so hard as she squealed and fought against the slimy tendrils to return to shore.

It's up to her waist, getting deeper all the time and harder to walk through. So damned thick. To her left, she sees Cass and Doug, both out of the tunnel, lumbering their way towards the first pit. Cass looks up towards her, their eyes locking for just a second, but the exchange lucid enough.

Steph glances behind to see Bryan's lined face as he hobbles into the blackness. Just over his right shoulder, she catches sight of the flesh eater's head. But it's gone just as fast. *Over the wall and on its way to tear us limb from limb.*

"Go!" Bryan screams, his face so white it's almost translucent.

Joints screaming, Steph forces herself on, half walking, half swimming through the murk, warmth spilling over the neck of her sweater. A growl comes from behind, louder, even more primal, the thing starved of food just for the occasion.

Up to his knees, Bryan squeals as he fights against the viscosity, watching Steph sink into the blackness until only her scalp is visible. As another snarl erupts from behind, he throws his arms forward, desperate to put as much distance between him and the flesh eater as possible. Another lunge, but this time he overcommits, losing balance and sinking into the murk. For a brief slice of time, the world is quiet and dark, and he wonders if this is what it's like to be dead.

He breaks the surface, sucking at the air, squinting into the bright lights. Wiping the warmth from his eyes and giving his head a shake, he stretches towards Steph's offered hand, who is out from the deepest part, eyes wide, gasping for air, skin oozing with watery blackness. His fingers only inches from hers, he takes another laboured step forward, but just like that, he's back in the black, holding onto a scream and scrambling for the surface, his right leg on fire, his left knee locked. Quiet, desolate warmth surrounds him once more. He feels Steph's hand brush across his head, but in his panic, he flails it away.

All that fucking training, Bryan!

With an agonising thrust, he manages to break the surface, but this time, to an ear-piercing scream and his wife's pale face, a crumpled portrait of fear. "Steph!" But before he can even reach for her, something plunges him back into darkness, his mouth filling with heat, his chest already feeling like it may burst.

Not like this. Not like this.

What feels like a foot presses into his spine, pushing his head to the bottom of the pit. He tries to fight against it, but his arms are leaden, his lungs screaming for air. *The needle would have been so much easier.* As the pressure on his spine is released, he takes the opportunity and begins to scramble, the pain in his legs secondary to the burning in his chest. He breaks the surface once more, sucking in as much oxygen as he can. Cries fill his ears but change to dampened gurgles. "Steph!" The flesh eater straddles her, one hand across his wife's mouth, the other wrapped around her throat, blood pooling next to her on the rubber.

Desperate, he tries to heave himself through the thickness. As he notes the fear in his dying wife's eyes, all Bryan can think is one thing: *I should have done more leg work.* The flesh eater snaps its head towards him, lips curving into what looks like a smile. It lashes out with its right arm, sending Bryan tumbling back into the void.

"Stay on them," Tristan cries, excited. "Get it all. Make sure you get close enough; I want the spray across the lens. People love it. Are the other drones in position for the finish?... Good. Get the relief on their faces as they cross the line. We'll do a quick 'how does it feel', then snap back to lane three immediately! Got it?... Good, this is what people want to see!"

Tristan dances on the spot, watching James and Charlotte cross the finishing line. As the metal boundary shoots up from the floor, the pursuing flesh eater runs into its own reflection. It puts its hands to its throat, letting out a pained howl, sinking to its knees as electricity courses through its collar.

What a final it will be if Doug and Cass make it across the line, Tristan thinks. A change-up this week, but he knows the fans are going to lap it up. He finds himself rooting for them, fists clenched in anticipation as they scream their way across the hot coals, the raging leather skin in tow. *And—made it!* "Yes!" He does another little spin and punches his tiny fist in the air. "This is going to be phe—nom—e—nal."

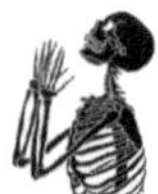

Malcolm sits back in his chair, chucking a handful of chocolate raisins down his throat, thinking them not a patch on the peanuts. He was in a rush this morning and picked up the wrong packet, swearing down he'll never make the same mistake again. *What a show, though.* He watches the screen, affording a smile as blood catches the bottom corner of the lens. *Bingo.*

Desensitised? For sure, he is. Worried how fast this became his norm? A little. But this is the lay of the land now, he figures, and if they weren't doing it, someone else would be. He sends the drone in further, making sure it picks up the sound of teeth on bone.

"Roger that... Okay, we'll switch in four, three, two, one." He presses the button and shovels more of the raisins down, watching Tristan do his stuff.

"Hurdy gurdy, what a race!" Tristan sings. "Congratulations, Doug and Cass; that was a close one. I bet you could almost smell its breath. How do you feel?"

"My fucking feet!" Cass is pink, choking on mouthfuls of air. She looks frantic, on the verge of screaming or crying. "Where are the others? James and Charlotte. And Bryan and Steph—they were ahead of us? Where are they?"

Tristan bows his head in a gesture, but the sparkle in his eyes is still there. "James and Charlotte declined to talk," he says, "and Bryan and Steph, I'm afraid, were DNFs. But you're in the final, guys!"

"DNF?" Cass looks to her husband, eyes wide, face creased in confusion. "Doug?"

Malcolm watches as Doug leans in towards his wife, whispering in her ear. She shakes her head, refusing to believe or attempting to throw the information right back out again. Either way, Tristan's ready to move on and get back to his original question. "You're in the final, guys." He repeats, teeth on show again. "One step closer to the money and passport. You must be pumped?"

Cass lets out a scream, the information hitting home. Aided perhaps by a tinge of goblin fury, Malcolm thinks. She crumples to the ground, palms slapping against the floor, tears splashing onto the brilliant white tiles of the hair and make-up slash picnic room. The frenzy continues, a series of incomprehensible words spilling from her trembling lips.

Doug rests a hand on her shoulder. "Cass."

"Get off me!" she screams.

"Any words for our viewers before we head into the final round?" Tristan persists. "What are your plans if you win the money?"

Doug offers a scowl and turns his back on Tristan, arms reaching for his wife as he crouches next to her. "Go away, shit stain."

Tristan smiles for the camera. "Well, let's give our finalists a bit of time to get ready, shall we? I can tell you now, viewers, we have an absolute doozy lined up. Brand new and coming your way soon."

Shit stain. Short and to the point, Malcolm thinks. As he kicks off the latest ReGenevate ad in the background, he catches up on some of the comments.

Oh shit, that was tense! What happened to Bryan? He was all over it for a while.

Little baby James—priceless! Crouch peasant!

I want to know why Bryan was laughing. Was it something to do the little sex show he and Steph performed? I guess we'll never find out.

Can't wait to see what the final is! 'Something different,' Trist said. Great episode so far, though!

James and Charlotte all the way. I'd love to see Cass make it, though. Kind of hoping we get at least some winners this week!

Final Preparations

Cass is still inconsolable, hysterical, a bubbling mess of jiggly damp flesh. Regardless of what happens from this point on, Doug knows she will never be the same. The positive current of electricity that was his wife is no longer, and he blames himself for that, thinking he should have done everything he could to keep her from this horrific savagery. "They had a daughter," she says. "It should have been us. It should have been us!"

It's a no-win situation. Death, or living another few decades trying to come to terms with what they've been through. Doug likens the whole thing to watching an old war movie. The viewer, the outsider, can establish some emotional attachment to the characters, them, and their plight. Still, the trauma is something only those who have experienced war could ever truly understand. And now those two worlds have collided for him and Cass, and things will never be the same again.

"I just want the injection," Cass cries. "I just want to go."

He wraps his arms around her, relieved she's no longer fighting his affection. "It's going to be okay, love." But his words of comfort bring only self-hatred. "I promise." He looks to the other side of the room to see James and Charlotte engaged in dampened bickering. Charlotte glances over her shoulder and offers a smile, but he doesn't have the energy or inclination to return it.

"Charlotte, what the hell are you doing?" James mutters.

"This is horrible." She feels a tear running down her right cheek. "What have we become?"

"Stop showing weakness," James says. "We're nearly home and dry."

Charlotte looks her husband in the eye. She can still see the man she fell in love with, but also the demon standing by his right shoulder whispering in his ear. Somewhere along the way, ambition gave way to greed, and greed gave way to something dark and hateful—the true form of which stands before her now. He almost converted her, too, but she knows his loyalty is to the demon, not her. "I used to love you," she says.

He curls his fingers into his palms and narrows his eyes. "I used to care."

"Is it a good time?" Tristan asks, poking his thick-skinned orange head around the door. "Oh, well, I'm coming, ready or not." He enters the room, two of his goons following close behind. Doug thinks one of them might be Silas, but he can't be sure and doesn't really care.

"This is it then, folks." Tristan rubs his little elf hands together. "The big one! Even our viewers don't know what's coming next." As if sensing the tension in the air, he shuffles back a couple of steps into the shadows of the big men. "Ears open as it's time for the brief, people."

Cass lets out another whimper. "Just give me the goddamned injection."

"Oh dear," Tristan says. "Did she forget her Xanax?"

"She'll be fine," Doug replies. "Just say what you've got to say and piss off, will you?"

In response, Tristan offers a smile and a bow. "Bring the boxes in, please."

CHOOSE YOUR WEAPON

Four wooden boxes are rolled in on a huge trolley, each of the group asked to select a number between one and four. Charlotte kicks them off after Cass refuses to choose. She opts for two, which turns out to be a pair of kitchen scissors. Doug is next, ending up with a pizza cutter. James gets the pan, and Cass gets the rolling pin.

You'd forgive anyone happening on the channel into thinking it a homage to past cooking shows. Alas, the viewers watching from the beginning know better.

"Roger, that," Tristan says, eyes on the ground. "I'm just taking them through it now... Of course... Is the arena ready? All in place?... Phenomenal." He removes his finger from his ear and lifts his head. "We're on in ten. Now, listen up, folks."

The subsequent brief is short, explosive, and had it been given to the group on arrival, their reactions might be exponentially worse. But as the goblin's squeaky words fall on their ears, a numbness prevails. Shock perhaps, disbelief maybe, or even an element of relief their ordeal is coming to an end, one way or another.

"Whatever happens, it's been a hoot, ladies and gents. You've got a lot of fans out there." And just like that, with the harrowing guidelines provided for what will be a fight to the death between the teams, "last couple or last person standing," he heads towards the door with a skip in his step, security in tow. "We'll be back for you shortly."

The room falls silent under a cloud of death, the group dressed in their brilliant white ReGenevate sweaters and shorts, complete with a built-in heart rate monitor for the pleasure of the viewers. They exchange nervous glances, feet tapping incessantly, heads shaking, mouths opening and closing.

"I'm sorry, Cass," Doug whispers.

She reaches for his hand, and he begins to cry.

Charlotte clasps her fingers to stop them from shaking, wondering how the hell she's going to get through the next few minutes. She watches Doug and Cass, suddenly wishing she had someone to hold her hand. She opens her mouth to say something to them.

"It's nothing personal," James says, getting to his feet. "It's just survival. Whatever happens in there, I wanted you to know that."

Squirming in her chair, Charlotte wills her husband to sit down.

"But rest assured, we'll show no mercy. And we expect none in return." James clamps his hands behind his back and begins pacing up and down, much to Charlotte's further discomfort. "If by some miracle, and I think we all know it would have to be just that, you two start getting the better of us, we expect you to finish it quickly. We will duplicate such sentiment. We have ten minutes in there before they release those things, and then we all die." He opens his mouth to say something else but instead retakes his seat, exchanging a scowl with Charlotte. "I'll show you who the big man is," he mutters.

Doug chooses not to respond. Throughout the prick's speech, he felt Cass's hand tightening around his, and could hear a low growl emerging from her throat. He thinks, under the circumstances, it might have been the best possible pep talk they could have received. He knows they're the underdogs, but for sure, they're going to go out fighting.

Iᴛ's Tɪɪɪɪɪɪɪɪɪᴍᴇ!

The arena is a thirty-foot area surrounded by caged flesh eaters, arms poking through the bars and jaws snapping towards the approaching contestants. Cass, the last in the group, steps into the circle, fingers gripped hard around the rolling pin handle. Shortly after, the final cage is slipped into place, providing the group with a cacophonous wave of roars in full surround stereo.

Tristan works his magic from beyond, introducing the viewers to the newest game, *Too Many Cooks in the Kitchen*. A fanfare erupts to flashing lights from above, and the timer floating above their heads begins ticking down from thirty, each flicker of a number accompanied by an ominous beep which Doug feels to his core. A drone hovers above, ready to capture the carnage.

Doug and Cass on one side, Charlotte and James on the other, the couples eye each other, agenda set in the waiting room, emotions stifled as much as possible. Fingers clench and unclench around their weapons. Breathing is heavy. Nervous feet shuffle on the rubber.

As the timer flicks down, James performs a lunge and shifts his hips from side to side. He breathes in deep, lets out a dramatic exhale, and brings the pan's base into his left palm, creating a soft thud. Eyeing his performance, unimpressed, Charlotte wraps her right hand around the scissors' handle and runs the fingers of her left hand across the blade. She turns her attention to Cass, who taps the wooden rolling pin against her thigh and shifts from one foot to the next. To Cass's left, Doug rolls the pizza cutter down his cheek; he's not sure why, perhaps a subconscious and foolish demonstration of bravado or a way to stop the surrealness of the situation from getting the better of him. As a kid, he used to pinch himself in the dentist's chair on the approach of the drill.

Twelve seconds left on the timer.

"I'll make it quick," James says.

"I'll make it last," Doug replies, now rolling the cutter across his palm.

Ten seconds.

Charlotte's fingers clench around the scissor handle until they ache. "I'm sorry, Cass."

"Save your apologies for Heaven, petal," Cass replies. "You never know your luck."

Seven seconds.

Six.

Five.

James lets out a roar, bringing the pan against his chest.

Cass raises the rolling pin above her right shoulder, ignoring the swaying bingo wings. Less time baking and more time walking would have helped, but it's too late now.

Two.

One.

The horn is deafening, and the accompanying fanfare meant to set hearts racing is nerve-shredding. Flesh eaters roar in accompaniment, their thrashing more urgent and violet than ever. And the timer, having restarted at ten minutes, is already down to 9:52.

They begin to shuffle clockwise, Doug and Cass rubbing shoulders, Charlotte and James, more than two feet apart. Ominous beeps of the countdown sounding above their head, the sinister stand-off continues, eyes darting from each other to the enslaved beasts rattling the cages against each other, lips pulled over teeth, battle-worn skin flapping against limbs.

Movement stops, tension continuing to build as knobbly fingers sing from white-knuckling their weapons. The timer continues its ominous countdown.

Beep.

Beep.

Beep.

James looks like he's about to go, pawing at the ground with his right ReGenevate sneaker. It's palpable, strained, a bottled frenzy of violence, cork ever so slowly heading towards its release. Cass offers a strange grunt. Doug's unsure if it was intentional, but he lets out a similar warning. James inches the pan further behind his head. Charlotte swings the scissors at the air in front.

9:32

The group can feel it, the atmosphere approaching an inevitable crescendo.

Doug readies himself, his unwavering stare fixed on James.

James lets out a roar, tapping the pan once against his chest, once against the side head, and then raising it back above his shoulder.

It's coming. It's coming.

Another nervous grunt from Cass. Another swing with the scissors from Charlotte.

9:02

Oh, it's coming.

8:59

The roar, the beeps, the fanfare, the lights, the sweat uncomfortably dripping down their back. An unbearable, claustrophobic melting pot of emotion.

8:46

James lifts his foot from the ground, grips the pan somehow even tighter, narrows his eyes, furrows his brow, exhales—and takes a step to his right—the dance beginning again, only this time anti-clockwise.

8:32

Still coming.

8:24

Sweat running down his back, James tells himself it will be this time. His stomach flutters, the clamminess of his palms making it feel like the pan's handle is slipping from his grip. He knows his mask is slipping, too. Charlotte was right—he's all hot air, her scathing summary hitting home further as a stream of gas escapes between his sweaty butt cheeks. As he takes another step to the right, starting yet another countdown from ten, a more disturbing sound emerges from his ass, lending thoughts a bad situation has just taken a turn for the worse. *Oh shit.*

As the timer clicks below eight minutes, Cass reminds herself to breathe. She knows someone needs to make a move; otherwise, they're all on the menu, and she's damn sure she'd rather die at human hands. Another nervous grunt escapes her lips, once again duplicated by her husband. She flicks him a glance, but he's otherwise engaged in a stare-down with James, teeth bared, left eye twitching, slicing at his right leg with the pizza cutter. She can't recall the last time they had pizza. Hawaiian with extra pineapple was—*is*—her favourite, sometimes with mushrooms. *Focus, Cass.* The rolling pin feels heavier in her grip, and without even lifting it, her arm aches. She sets her sights back on Charlotte, offering another nervous grunt, once again copied by her husband. It's like a match to her flame this time, though. A disproportionate annoyance to something so slight, as if years of ignoring the bad habits, putting her smile on, and glossing over cracks in their marriage, finally comes to a head. She's off, charging towards Charlotte, rolling pin raised.

Now or never, Doug thinks, but knowing there isn't really a choice. He takes a deep breath and makes his run towards James, who steps back, eyes wide, mouth agape.

Cass is the first to get a swing off, but the end of the pin only glances off a left breast as the tall lady recoils, missing the clutches of a flesh eater by inches. Letting out a yelp of pain but grateful for her expensive dual airbags, Charlotte straightens and brings the scissors down, but just in time, Cass snaps back the rolling pin, blocking the attack. Weapons redundant, their tussle begins, a battle of height versus bulk.

James and Doug are in a wrestling match of their own, the pan never making it down, James's arm pinned in the air by Doug's left hand. Spittle sprays across each other's faces as Doug tries to force the cutting wheel towards James's chest, but the floppy-haired bugger is strong and keeps it at bay, extending Doug's arms away. As they inch backwards and forwards, Doug catches the scent of something foul.

"Fuck you, Doug!"

"Fuck you, baby James!"

But the look on James's face is beginning to change, eyes narrowing, and snarl growing. Doug knows his window is closing, shock giving way to adrenaline, the man before him getting stronger still, as though just realising what his muscles are for.

Out of his depth, Doug knows he's the weaker man, and by some margin. As the pizza cutter starts coming back on him, heading straight for his throat, Doug tilts his head, grits his teeth, and braces for pain. Veins explode with an audible *pop* as his arm crunches inwards. He knows he needs a game-changer. A change of tack. *And what the hell is that fucking smell?*

6:32

Her shoes squeaking against the rubber, Cass is winning the battle, inching Charlotte ever-closer to the grotesque grey hands reaching out from the cages. Sweat drips from her chin and rolls down her back. She lets out a growl, managing another half-step forward. And another. Noting the fear in her competitor's eyes, but also the defined muscles running up and down her arms, Cass digs in deep, knowing if it comes down to stamina, she doesn't stand a chance; her training diet the last few days made up of pumpkin pie, tiramisu, and gallons of tea. Another half step. A full step. The grey hands behind swipe past Charlotte's taut neck by a whisker. *Now or never,* Cass decides. And with a throaty scream, she lunges forward with everything she has. "RARRRRRRRR."

But she didn't anticipate the side-step and release.

Before Cass knows it, she's stumbling towards the arms of a flesh eater. She tries to stop herself, but her balance is lost, the thing already clutching at her shoulders. It lets out a growl and moves its hands to her neck, bringing her headfirst into the metal bars. The thud is soft, but the pain is off the charts. She screams. The rolling pin drops to the floor. Warmth trickles down her eyelid. She screams again. Hot, rancid air rushes across her skin as the thing brings its face towards her and smiles. A dry tongue works down the right side of her face. She tries to push away, but its smile grows wider. With a roar, it brings her head into the bars once more.

5:12

"Let fucking go!" Doug can see his wife, one of those things with its arms around her neck, her continued cries filling him with desperation. He releases James's pan arm and lets the pizza cutter drop to the floor. "Cass!" He tries snapping his left wrist away, but James's fingers remain locked in place. "Get off me, you fuck!"

"I'm sorry," Charlotte cries, stabbing the scissors into the side of his defenceless wife. "I'm so very sorry."

Doug continues fighting, the sound of Cass's blood-curdling screams ringing in his ears. "GET OFF ME!" But he's weak, exhausted. The battle is lost. Helpless, he watches Charlotte pull back the scissors and plunge them again into his wife's flesh. "Stop! Please! Leave her—"

White light swallows everything, the ringing in his ears drowning out his wife's screams. He can feel the heat of the evening sun, see the shimmer on the glass, the tiny bubbles floating to the surface. *Promise me we'll come back to this place again, Doug. Promise me.*

As the fog begins to clear, he raises his right hand, pain reverberating down his arm as the pan strikes bone. Another piercing scream fills him with hopelessness. And another. *Plan B.* Grimacing, ready for agony, Doug turns and brings his reconstructed knee full force into James's manhood. The contact feels soft, heavy, and ineffective. But as James lets out a pained exhale, brown watery liquid running down both his legs, Doug allows himself to believe.

"You rotter," James says as if Doug has just broken one of the rules of their newly established fight club. "Foul play."

Half expecting his competitor to shout for the referee, Doug takes the opportunity and brings his knee up again, causing James to retch towards the ground. Another for good luck. And another. And another. And another. "How do you feel about that, you floppy-haired fuckwit?"

3:32

Doug rushes towards Cass just as Charlotte steps back, doubling over, sobbing, and mumbling apologies. It doesn't register at first, the sight of the scissors emerging from his wife's neck, one of those things pulling her in towards the cage, its teeth clamped around her nose. "Cass!" He tries wrestling her free, but the thing has no intention of releasing its catch. "Get off her, you filthy fucking beast!"

"I'm so sorry," Charlotte mumbles again from behind.

"You left the scissors in there, you stupid bitch," James yells from the ground.

To the sound of watery gurgles and the roar of the caged savage, Doug pulls at his wife's waist, but he knows there's no coming back from this. Tears run down his cheeks as the scent of his dying wife fills him with instant loneliness. The creature yanks at her, prompting Doug to grab the scissors from her neck. Offering a war cry, he plunges them into the beast's right eye. It squeals and releases its clutch, and together, Doug and his wife sink to the floor in an ever-growing pool of blood.

"Grab the rolling pin," James squeals. "Do it!"

2:42

"We're on the balcony in Rimini, love," Doug whispers. With arms hooked under Cass's elbows, he thrusts his feet against the ground to create distance from the cage. "Low evening sun, the sound of waves gently clapping the shore. Will you dance with me?" As he threads his fingers through hers, he can see the sun going down in her eyes, too, the sparkle of the blue fading to the bleakness of an off-season ocean. "I told you we'd come back."

Her heart thumping in her chest, Charlotte stands over Doug

and Cass, her tears creating ripples in the puddle of red. She raises the rolling pin again.

"Do it, Charlie," James yells. "Do it!"

Doug lifts his head and smiles at her. He mouths something and offers an imperceptible nod.

With a wail, Charlotte brings the weapon down full force onto Doug's head. She strikes again. And again. And again. With the taste of blood at the back of her throat, she lets out a maniacal scream, shifting her stare to the still-entwined hands as she continues delivering blows. An incredulous wave of jealousy sweeps over her as she finally drops the rolling pin and steps back, gasping for breath, violent trembles rippling through her body.

1:58

James drags himself from the ground, his stomach feeling like it's been turned inside out. He surveys the scene: the savages in their cages, the blood on the floor, his wife standing over Doug and Cass as she inspects the blood splatter on her skin. He takes a few pained steps towards her, eyeing the forever flicking display hanging above their heads.

1:37.

Thoughts already filling with new cars, holidays, tailored suits, and visiting friends to flaunt his reacquired wealth, he wraps an arm around his wife's waist and brings in her close, nestling into her hair. It's the closest she's let him get for as long as he can remember.

"We're done. Let us out," Charlotte says. She aims her voice towards the timer, confused as to why they're still surrounded by caged filth. "I said, let us out!" She stifles a sob and caresses her husband's elbow. "I want what they had, James."

James puts his lips to his wife's ear, feeling their pulses beating against each other. *Last couple or last person standing.* "I want it all."

There's no scream as the pizza wheel slices into her neck—shock perhaps, or numbness for deeds done. Only as James starts rolling the cutter along her flesh do instincts kick in, and she begins clawing at his arm, thrashing her legs out in desperation. Pulling her in closer still, James continues working the sharpness across, veins in his arms popping and his once-perfect white teeth a watery canvas of yellow and red. Charlotte lets out a garbled cry, but James can already feel the life oozing from her. He lets out a growl as he tightens his muscles and offers the time a glance. "I'll toast you tonight with the finest champagne, dear."

1:02.

Charlotte releases a series of rasps, her sneakers squeaking against the rubber. Until they don't, and her head lollops to the side. Feeling no pulse, James kisses his dead wife on the back of the neck and lets her crumple to the ground.

0:41

"Come on! Let me out!"

But the roars of the flesh eaters continue, and the timer keeps on ticking.

"Let me the fuck out! It's done!"

0:35

"Hey! Can anyone hear me?"

And ever so faint from below, James hears gentle wheezing.

"You've got to be fucking kidding me."

Cass snaps her eyes open.

James reaches down for the rolling pin. "Lovely day."

Roll Credits

Malcolm brings the drone in over James's right shoulder. "Thank you, Frank... Yeah, we sure did smash last week's figures... Oh, thank you... It's a pleasure working for such a great boss... Thanks for the opportunity... Yes, see you for drinks later... Thanks again, Frank... Bye, Frank."

"Can I suck that for you, Frank?" Fiona says, mimicking Malcolm's pathetic voice. "Please, Frank. It would be such a pleasure, Frank."

"What the hell are you doing here?"

"Come to say goodbye. I'm done." She grimaces, trying not to watch the carnage on screen. "Sent in my resignation."

Malcolm shrugs. "You'll be back."

"I can't remember the last time I slept. I can't do it anymore. We're glorifying everything that's wrong with humanity. Look at that prick on screen. Just look at him!"

Without shifting his attention from screen one, Malcolm continues picking at the meat between his teeth. "Oh, he's a prick, for sure." To the sound of fireworks and music, he watches James raise the blood-stained rolling pin towards the approaching shower of golden confetti, a victorious smile splitting his face in two, shit still dribbling down his legs. "Worst of the worst, and that's saying something."

"How can you do it, Malcolm? How can you live with your-self?"

Swilling the too-liquidy milkshake around his gums, he shrugs. "It's just what we do." As the cages are pulled back, he studies the screen, fingers at the keyboard, ready to sweep the drone towards the orange goblin. "We adapt."

She lets out a sigh and makes her way out. "I guess I'll see you then."

"Yeah. Look after yourself, and—"

"Jasmine!"

As the door behind him slams shut, Malcolm relaxes back in his chair, replaying his conversation with Frank, the bloody CEO of the company! As if they were old friends, Frank had confided so much. All hush-hush, of course, for his ears only—talk of Jake getting too soft and having to let him go. How sad it made him, what with all their history, and knowing Jake's salary was the only thing keeping his wife alive. "It's probably for the best, though," Frank had said. "He'll thank me one day. It will set him free."

Malcolm slides further down the chair and lifts his feet to the desk. A big old smile begins creeping across his face, even challenging the one James wears on screen as the goblin approaches, announcing him as the sole winner.

Over drinks tonight, I want to talk about offering you the position, Malcolm.

"We adapt."

As his mind fills with thoughts of surgery, fine restaurants, nice suits, and a different woman each week, he turns his attention to the comments.

That's it! I'm done with this shitshow, and I'm not just talking about James's legs! No more! How can people watch this? It's so sad and pathetic. JK. See you next week, folks!

James is a fucker and a half! I need his phone number.

Poor Doug and Cass. I was rooting for them so much.

Baby James, marry me, please! I have loo roll and stuff for nappy rash.

What a fighter Cass was! I don't think I can ever get over this. Not until next week's show anyway.

I can't take any more of this world; it's too cold. I love you, Mum, Dad. My brother, Jack. I'm so sorry. See you on the other side x

Fuck yeah! I can't wait to see how they're going to top that next week.

THE END

MY NAME IS BRIAN

At some point between the early years and adulthood, there's a tendency for people's passion, imagination, and hunger for the unknown to fade into oblivion, never to be seen again.

Pass me the motherfucking knife!

You can see it behind their eyes. It flatlines, along with dreams and aspirations. And starved of such awe and wonder, there's a danger of shrinking into acceptance, nodding in the right places, and settling into a resentful acceptance that this is all there is. Until, without answers, it's time to leave this place.

Come on, piggy. Oink! Oink! Oink!

It was back in the summer of 1986 when Brian first came into our lives, and that momentous day and subsequent events have kept my inner child alive through all the arduous trials life has thrown at me. It was a big year for news: Chernobyl; Halley's Comet, the explosion of the Space Shuttle *Challenger* that killed all seven astronauts, not forgetting Hands Across America. Hell, even the cows went mad that year. But, nestled between all that are a multitude of theories about what happened to those school kids in the middle of summer. You only have to search for it on the web for pages and pages of uneducated guesses and conspiracy theories. In the end, though, it went down as an unsolved case. It still is today.

My name is Tom Harper, and it's time to tell my story. Some might even call it a confession, but I'll let you be the judge.

They all had a piece of me at the time—my parents, the police, starchy councillors whose glasses never seemed to fit, not to mention a host of new-age therapists incapable of growing a full beard. None could coax a rational explanation or anything close to an accurate account of what happened. "Trauma" was the word they all kicked around, explaining that my mind shut down for self-preservation.

I'm gonna make you squeal again, piggy!

I think part of me might have felt somewhat responsible. Perhaps I could have prevented the carnage and done something before things got out of hand. At the time, though, I was lost in my private universe, carried above the threshold of reality on currents of grief and implausibility.

Squee! Squee! Squee!

It's time. The truth is well overdue.

Near the half-empty whisky bottle is a framed photograph of Eddie and me. We're at the air museum, chests puffed out, standing next to each other against the cockpit of a Spitfire. The picture has faded, but the memory hasn't.

I raise my glass. "To you, Eddie."

Fingers shaking as they hover over the keyboard, Prince's "Purple Rain" spinning on the turntable, my skin crawls with nostalgic dread.

"Come on, Tom, get a grip."

It's not just that the old feelings are beginning to return or that this is the first time I will have relived the experience, far from it, but now I have the challenge of making you, the reader, believe me while accepting any judgement that follows.

One more mouthful of scotch.

Ah, the burn.

Last one.

I've hardly touched a drop over the last few years, but today I'm making an exception. You'll understand why soon enough.

Okay, no more procrastinating. Let's do this.

Inhale.

Freshly cut grass, a nearby barbecue, and a multitude of other scents carry through my open study window. A dog barks in the distance. I hear children's laughter floating across on the warm breeze—

Exhale.

The scraping of chairs, echoey footsteps down the corridor, the hush as Mrs. Dunworth entered the room to introduce the new boy as "Ryan".

The First Days

"It's…Br… Br… Brian," the new boy said to Mrs. Dunworth, the words toppling over each other in a stammer. "My name is Brian." But no correction or further acknowledgement was made as she pursed her lips and pointed a bony finger at the seat beside mine. "Don't dilly dally, child."

After nervously scanning the room, the poor kid began to waddle towards me, pants half-mast, long black hair matted to his pasty white face. He reminded me of one of those ugly pug dogs, or "puglies", as my best friend, Eddie, used to call them. Infectious snickers made their way around while Daniel Slater started humming the theme tune to *The Addams Family*.

"Okay, come on, class," Mrs. Dunworth said without an ounce of commitment. "Let's try to make Ryan feel as welcome as possible, please."

"My name is Brian," the boy muttered again.

We knew nothing about the kid, only that *Brian* was in for one hell of a time.

"Fucking hell, is that an earthquake?" Richard said, holding onto the edges of his desk. Sleeves rolled up, ferociously chewing gum, and sporting a military-style crewcut that you knew had been in the family through the generations, Richard was the class knucklehead, a proper old-school bully. If you happened to be a boy with hair longer than half an inch—which was almost the entire class back then, bar Richard's side-kick Shane—you were automatically a "fairy." And may Heaven help you if you ever admitted to collecting anything other than detentions. "Your new boyfriend's a bit of a porker, Tom, isn't he?"

"Good one, Rich." I followed with a smirk because that's what you did when the school bully cracked a joke; you offered a grin, hoping it was the end of the interaction. On the days Richard came to school sporting bruises on his face, you knew never to look him in the eye.

"Show me the cookies," Richard said, his attention back on Brian, puffing his cheeks out and mimicking the boy's sway. "Where are the coooooookies?"

Mrs. Dunworth tapped her hand on the table. "Open your textbooks, please." But it was a lost cause, Richard needing less than an excuse to unsettle the class. "Cooooooookies."

More ripples of laughter made their way around the room, but acknowledgement wasn't enough to remove the look of menace that had manifested in Richard's eyes. It was no secret that he harboured a general abomination for most, but it's safe to say Brian went straight to the top of the list that day. Something about the kid, beyond the blubber, just rubbed Richard up the wrong way. "Space Shuttle *Chunker* is about to dock in T-minus five seconds," he said, covering his mouth with his hand.

"That's quite enough, Richard," Mrs. Dunworth said, looking close to tears before class had even started.

"T-minus four seconds."

Horrible to admit, but I think we all felt some relief that Richard had found his new fixation, a new obsession to channel his resentment towards. Since his last little project, Eric Chaplin, moved school a few weeks ago, we'd been getting more than our fair share.

"T-minus three seconds."

Poor little Eric Chaplin. A polaroid of the boy licking a white dog turd made it onto the school noticeboard for all to see. And I doubt it was curiosity that forced him into it.

"T-minus two—"

Stealing the end of Richard's sentence, the burp that emerged from Brian's shiny lips sounded more like a volcanic eruption than the simple passing of wind. It started as a low rumble, ending in a series of small explosions that had Brian all but doubled over. Even Mrs. Dunworth looked taken aback, her face a picture of confusion and disgust.

"B... B... Better out than in," Brian said, unfolding. He placed a belated hand on his lips and formed a smile.

"No, it fucking isn't," Richard retorted. "What the hell did you eat for breakfast, new kid? Poached skunk with a side serving of dog shit?"

Shane pinched his nose and collapsed across his table. "That smell...it's nuclear."

Avoiding eye contact, I slid my chair to the left by a good two feet, *preparing for landing.* Part of me wanted to reach out to the boy and tell him we've all been on the receiving end, but peer pressure has much to answer for. Besides, it was all I could do not to throw up.

"Class, please!"

Prompting the wood to creak, the new kid flopped in the chair with a sharp exhale. I recall the putrid waft of his breath and the subsequent cocktail of deodorant and sweat that followed on a draught of warm air. It was even more intense than the night Eddie had a few of us over to his house for an all-night Sega session. Six of us shoe-horned into the room the size of a closet, eating pizza, farting, burping, our T-shirts sticking to our skin.

The kid turned to me, a giant smile still splitting his face in two. "My name is Brian."

"My name is lard-ass," Shane muttered.

I turned away, Brian's rancid breath finding my cheek. Still, I could feel his sunken eyes on mine. From peripheral vision, I noted the large puffy areolas visible through the front of a damp, white polyester shirt straining under the pressure of his belly and giant breasts.

"Nice stack, new kid," Shane said, prompting more snickers. "I think you've just given Tom a hard-on."

"My name is Brian," he said, turning towards Shane. "B-r-i-a-n."

"L-a-r-d-a-s-s," Shane responded.

Not wanting to feel outdone, Richard drummed on the table. "He's got bigger tits than you, Sarah. Not that that's saying much."

At that point, I wanted to step in and be Sarah's knight in shining armour. I didn't, of course. Besides, Sarah was more than capable of looking after herself.

"Why are you looking at the new boy's tits anyway, Rich?" she replied. "Something you want to tell us?"

Although his stomach made up for it, the new kid never spoke a word for the next sixty minutes. And through all the relentless abuse and mocking, he kept hold of that goddamn smile. Even when Mrs. Dunworth let out a high-pitched, alien-like squeal of frustration at the class, that cheesy grin never faltered. Detention for all of us followed. All but Brian, of course.

Things would only get tougher as the days passed. We all knew it. Don't get me wrong, I felt sorry for the kid, but I've been on the receiving end many times, and I wasn't prepared to cross that border back into the land of persecution. "Am I a pussy?" I remember asking my Magic 8 Ball. "As I see it, yes," was its apathetic verdict.

As term got into full swing, we were all proven right. As I saw it, there were two problems. The first was that Brian was smart, so much smarter than the rest of the class, me included. Quiet at first, but whenever the teachers forced a response, he was all over it like a rash, unable to get the words out fast enough.

"Well done, Brian."

Always with his head in the books, even on lunch breaks, he was insatiable. There was no way I could compete.

"Excellent! Perhaps you should be teaching the class, Brian."

And although his chronic bouts of wind brought considerable disruption to the class, it was as if his intellect and otherwise well-rounded behaviour earned him a free pass from the teachers. Even I was beginning to feel some resentment towards the kid, and when he started sticking his hand up in the air to every question, that feeling only grew stronger.

"I think we have a genius on our hands, class."

The second and more serious problem was that despite Richard's fixation on the kid, he was getting nothing in return for his efforts. It had started as just the usual verbal abuse, nothing ground-breaking: Bitch tits, lard-ass, jelly belly, lunch bucket, and so on. Still, no matter how much Richard got in his face, Brian continued smiling, not the slightest hint of tears. This resistance to crack only made Richard more committed to the cause.

And then came the episode in the canteen.

Yoghurt-Covered Blubber

Eddie was explaining, in explicit detail, about the VHS cassettes he'd found at the back of his dad's wardrobe. He'd gone looking for his birthday presents, but instead, all his "Christmases had come at once." To me, it felt like there was something very wrong about sharing that stuff with a parent, but Eddie was on cloud nine, boasting about his seven-times-a-day habit. "Red raw it was by the time I'd finished, Tommy."

To be fair, I was still jerking off to the underwear section of my mother's catalogue, so I guess I had no right to judge. Across from us, Veronica and Sarah chose instead to discuss the previous night's episode of *Top of the Pops*, twisting their faces at us during lags in their conversation.

On the other side of the hall, with his banquet spread across the table, Brian was once again sitting on his own, alternating his attention between the packet of food in front of him and the open book.

"Anyway, I don't even think they were singing live," Veronica said. "You could see her lips—"

SCREEEEEEEEEEE!

We all looked across, watching Richard and Shane drag their chairs—deliberate, slow, torturous—towards Brian's table. Eddie gave me a sharp prod as if my attention might have been elsewhere.

As if. "Are you seeing this?" he said.

"Uh-huh."

I swear down that kid just carried on eating and reading, oblivious to the raucous noise and the impending sense of trouble etched on the other kids' faces. After offering a series of half-muted burps, Brian shoved in another cookie, licked his fingers, and turned the page. It wasn't easy to make out from so far away, but it looked like the kid was still smiling.

"Things are going to get real now," Sarah whispered. "Should we do something?"

"Like what?" Veronica replied, nursing her mountain of hair. "Boys will be boys, especially those two."

"Easy, Vee, I'm nothing like them," Eddie contested.

Veronica sighed. "Not exactly doing much to stop it, though, are you?"

"Hey, I'm a lover, not a fighter," he replied. "Ask Tom's mum."

My punch glanced off his skinny arm. "Go easy, Ed."

"That's what she said."

Sarah shushed us. "Here we go."

We watched, attentive and holding our breath, as Richard and Shane spun their chairs around and slumped into them on either side of the kid. Their faces twisted into scowls, only inches from his. I swear to God that Brian still gave them nothing. Instead, he crumpled the empty packet and slid each chubby finger into his mouth for degreasing. The tension was palpable, heading towards a crescendo where something had to give.

"Credit due," Eddie said. "Fat boy has lasted longer than most."

There was no doubt that was the case, but I prayed for him to break before things got out of hand. "They all crack in the end."

The sit-off continued for some time, Brian refusing to lift his gaze, his fingers working across the table like giant arachnid legs. Richard and Shane moved their chairs even closer until they were within kissing distance.

"I'm bored now," Veronica muttered. "Boys suck, that's all there is to it. Now, what the hell was I saying before? Oh yeah, anyway,

Bobby's taking me to the Drive-In at the weekend, but I doubt we'll see much of the movie if you know what I mean. *Big Trouble in—*"

"Oh shit." Sarah leaned across the table, offering Veronica a sharp elbow. "No way. There's just no way." Mesmerised, we watched Richard peel the lid off Brian's yoghurt carton in slow motion.

Eddie snorted. "Richie's having yoghurt-covered blubber for lunch."

We didn't laugh, though. Things were getting darker, and we knew it was just the beginning.

"Is he really going to do it?" Sarah said. "Is he? Do you think he—"

Mouths open, we watched as the pale, chunky substance slid down Brian's hairline to the bridge of his pudgy nose. I felt sure the kid was going to break. Instead, he raised his stare from the textbook, gave Rich and Shane a confused but cursory glance, and, as God as my witness, moved his gaze back to his book and carried on eating his packet of salt and vinegar chips as though he hadn't a care in the fucking world.

"Filthy fucking pig!" Richard yelled in frustration. The clattering of cutlery ended, and the few remaining heads that weren't already transfixed turned towards the drama. "Filthy fucking bastard pig!"

Silence aside from the kid's chewing.

"Hey, dump truck! Giganto!" Richard cried. "Fat-ass, do you hear me underneath all that fucking blubber?"

"Tactics, I reckon," I said to the group.

Veronica burst her bubble and carried on chewing. "What on earth are you talking about, Tom?"

"The kid's probably used to all this. Likely been bullied his entire life and had it drummed into him to ignore them."

"It ain't working," Eddie said.

"No, it isn't."

At this point, Richard's head looked fit to explode, a shade of red akin to that of a beetroot. You could see he didn't know what to do with himself, excess adrenaline causing his body to twitch, his eyes almost popping from his head. Even from the other side of the canteen, I could see the vein in his neck.

Eddie offered me another sharp prod. "He's going to smack the poor bastard."

And if Mrs. Jenkins hadn't walked into the canteen at that moment, I do not doubt that that would have been the case. Richard didn't immediately step away—as if the pull was too strong—but after what seemed like an eternity and with an imperceptible slump of his shoulders, he kicked the chair and turned, rewarding onlookers with a snarl. "What the fuck are you fairies looking at?"

"Oink. Oink. Oink," Shane uttered before following his leader. "Oink. Oink. Fucking oink."

The hum of conversation once again commenced, as did the clink of cutlery. And to detailed descriptions of Bobby Taylor's biceps and how comfy the backseat of his car was, we carried on eating our lunch. "He's got a soft side, too, you know. When he went to the bathroom, I looked through his record collection; found a Lionel Richie album amongst all the Metallica and Megadeth. He said it was his sister's, but his face turned bright pink. And last week, when we went to..."

Through the incessant barrage, I kept an eye on Brian, watching him digging his hand into packet after packet until he'd worked through everything on the table. Just when I thought the show was over, he began to finger the yoghurt from his face into his mouth, and finally—I kid you not—he licked that table clean of crumbs. On the way out, he offered us a nod, followed by a squeaky fart that sent us all into hysterics until the invisible gas cloud sent us packing.

We all knew the canteen was just the beginning of next level bullying, and as predicted, the escapades became worse each time. Tacks on the chair, stink bombs in his locker, steel rulers against the back of his legs, and more food play. Through it all, Brian remained close to stoic, the familiar smile planted across his face. Goodness knows how many detentions Richard received in his pursuit to break the kid, but all he had to show for his efforts over the weeks were multiple black eyes and bruises upon bruises.

Once after class, Richard moved into an even higher gear by relieving himself in Brian's locker, drenching the *Teen Wolf* poster that once belonged to the white dog poo licker. I guess it was his way of asserting dominance, letting Brian know that this was his school, that things would be done his way, and God help anyone who stood in his way.

"That's what you get," Shane said. "Owoooo."

Once again, efforts went unrewarded—no tears, scampering feet, or cries for help from one of the teachers. That said, it was the first time Brian gave me anything other than a preoccupied glance, a sort of bemused interest etched across his chubby face as he offered a shrug. I turned away, shoving my books towards the back of my shelf, seeking relief in the ocean-blue eyes of Heather Locklear and her cheeky and comforting smile.

"Why the fuck are you always smiling, fat boy?" I heard Richard say from behind my locker door. "Come on, what's on your mind, you big sack of lard?"

"My name is Brian."

"Shanks!" I heard Shane say.

And to the booming voice of our headmaster, Mr. Shanks, enquiring if everything was "tickety-boo," Richard withdrew, topping up his rage for another day.

"That kid's going to get the beating of his life unless he caves," Eddie said. "Never seen Rich so worked up before."

Eddie was right. I was scared, not just for Brian but for all of us. Richard was getting more volatile every day, the look in his eyes manifesting into something beyond hate. You could feel it in the air, that same sensation before the weather turned bad, and this was heading towards the storm of the fucking century.

All the relentless anxiety wasn't good for me. I broke out in spots, couldn't focus on my work, and couldn't sleep. I just wanted the holidays to come so I could hang out at the arcade with Eddie. I had so many plans. The latest Schwarzenegger film was showing, and I wanted to finish the Stephen King book I was reading. *Thinner*, that was it. I always remember thinking Brian could do with a few of those strawberry pies. Yeah, it's safe to say I longed for easier times when my mind was full of video games and thoughts of Sarah.

Sarah.

Sarah...

My first true love, if you can count something that never materialised into anything other than an innocent brush on the arm. Much more confident than I was; it was like she'd already lived a life. Often, I watched in awe her ability to see the good in everything, how she tried to spin a positive on the direst of situations. I remember one of our conversations from class, Brian, of course, being the topic of the moment. "He'll probably grow up to be super handsome," she said. "You see it all the time, once—what is it? Test—Testee—"

"Testosterone."

"That's it. You watch, ten years from now, I bet Brian will be driving a Porsche with a Michelle Pfeiffer look-a-like in the passenger seat."

Eddie smirked. "More likely a Fiat Panda with a bucket of chicken on the seat."

"If he makes it that far," I said. "We've all seen how Rich has been looking at the kid of late. Makes my skin crawl."

"He's just pushing limits." Veronica sighed and fingered a curl. "He'd never do anything serious."

"I'm not so sure."

"Well, what are you going to about it anyway, Tom?" Eddie said. "You going to stop him using those big muscles of yours?"

"Shut up, Eddie."

"It's alright, gang," Eddie said, raising his hands and offering a cheesy grin. "Arnold's little brother, Tommy Sweats-his-knickers, is on the job."

My cheeks burned. I'd often fantasised about taking Richard down in one of the wrestling moves from the TV, launching from one of the desks and wrapping my arm around his neck. The class would applaud as the school bully begged for mercy from the floor, doing his best to writhe free from an inescapable chokehold.

Sarah would be clapping the loudest of them all, even duplicating that same wolf whistle she did when Michael J. Fox first walked on screen.

"I'm sure Tom could kick Rich's ass if he wanted to," she said, following with a wink. "But I imagine him to be more of a lover than a fighter, just like you, Eddie. How many girlfriends is it now, Ed?"

My friend turned red.

Outside of those rare dreams when deep sleep found its way through, I knew I'd never have the courage to ask her out. I still remember one such scene, walking with her hand in hand through an endless field of gold. Upon seeing a small clearing, I pulled a blue-and-white chequered blanket from my backpack and laid it out, gesturing for my love to sit. By the time I was done, almost every square inch of that blanket was covered with the best snacks and drinks pocket money could buy. I reached for her hand and asked if she'd be my girlfriend. Sarah lifted her gaze towards me and smiled, eyes glinting in the sun. "I thought you'd never ask." Then, to a rustling sound behind, we turned, only to see Brian on all fours galloping towards us, chins and belly swinging, saliva spraying from his jowls. We ran hand in hand, only turning once to see Brian gorging himself on our picnic.

THE DAY BEFORE

Whichever way I look at it, there's no denying my part to play in the events that unfolded. Our part, I guess. We should have done something, but to reiterate and dress down the verdict the Magic 8 Ball provided, I was a pussy. And hindsight is a bitch, pure and simple, something that one day takes a bite at your ass, gets a taste for it, and then doesn't stop until it has consumed you whole. Hell, if there were a DeLorean parked outside, I'd be screeching down the street and out of here quicker than you could say, "Great Scott!"

The day before the carnage, we had double P.E. in the afternoon. The showers were terrifying for us kids—naked, and at our most vulnerable. There were no luxuries like separate cubicles in those days; it was open range, and everyone was fair game. Shane was the one that rallied us all out. "Right. Everyone out, or I'll fuck you up."

No, it wasn't anything along the lines of Shawshank or anything like that, but they did take two wet towels into the shower area and lash poor Brian until there wasn't a single white patch left on his body. And that was no mean feat. Proper determination. Proper hatred. "Squeal, piggy! Squeal!" But still, Brian gave them nothing, silent to the end.

When Richard emerged from the changing area, face bright red, and breathing as though he'd just run a marathon, the look of defeat on his face was plain for all to see, as were the fresh bruises that lined his body. "What the fuck are you hard-ons staring at?" he shouted, prompting us to divert our glances and carry on dressing in our little paranoia-filled worlds.

That should have been the end of it, torment dealt out. I prayed for that to be the case, but the words that emerged from Richard's lips came with such venom that the skin around my skull contracted. "I'm gonna fuck him up," he said.

We all heard him, our stares following him to his changing bag, silent as a grave, watching him bring out the six-inch blade and return to the shower area. I'll never forget the look on my friend Eddie's face. White as a ghost, he shrugged, but I saw raw fear in his eyes.

Nobody said anything. No heroes rushed into battle. Even Shane just stood there, mouth hanging open as Richard marched past him.

"He won't do it, Tom, will he?" Eddie said.

As if seeking confirmation that normal service would soon resume, heads snapped towards me, Shane's too. Offering a half-assed shake of my head, I shrugged, no longer sure what Richard was capable of anymore. The place fell into silence for what felt like an eternity, a simmering pot of tension. Naked, or close to it, we held our breath and exchanged nervous glances, for once concerned about something beyond our tiny, shrivelled peckers.

The shriek took us all by surprise.

I can't find the words to describe the cry, but it sure wasn't like a movie scream—this one was piercing, the sheer volume making my ears ring and giving me an instant headache. I felt it, too, inside of me, rattling deep in my core, so much so that I had to reach out to the bench to steady myself.

"Fuck," Eddie muttered. "Fuck."

My first thought was that Richard had finally lost it and killed the poor bastard. I imagined him emerging from the shower, watery blood running down his arms and legs, even visible between the cracks of his yellow teeth as he twisted his face into a manic grin.

"Gutted the fucking pig, I did."

"Fuck," Eddie said again.

Not a single boy in that changing room looked to be carrying anything but anguish, their faces all taut and pale.

When Richard came back out, his hands were over both ears. "Wow, that bitch can scream," he said. "Jesus Christ!" He ran his eyes across the room and laughed. "Relax, I didn't even touch the sack of shit. Hearing him squeal was enough for today."

"Is it finished now, Richard?" Eddie asked with venom. "Are you fucking finished now?"

As another eerie silence fell across the room, a shudder rattled down my spine at my friend's new-found bravado. I swear I could hear the vein in Richard's temple ticking like a time bomb. People froze, still half or fully naked, paranoia on hold again and fully aware a line had been crossed. It felt like my heart skipped a beat when Richard rushed towards Eddie, knife still in hand, those godawful discoloured teeth clenched together.

Helpless, I watched, wincing at the sound of Eddie's skinny frame slamming into the lockers. My friend gave a high-pitched cry but still had anger in his eyes.

"I'm sorry, fuckwit," Richard said. "Perhaps it was because I had my hands over my ears at the time, but for a split second, I could have sworn you asked if I had finished." He let the blade rest against Eddie's pale right cheek. "Is that what you asked me?" Spittle sprayed across Eddie's face as his eyes found mine. "Is it? IS IT?"

At this stage, I'm beginning to feel your judgement, but I was a pussy, remember. And Richard's eyes carried a wildness, reminding me of the predators on the nature shows my dad sometimes watched on the TV.

"N-No," Eddie stammered, his flash of bravery a distant memory.

"Thought so," Richard said. "It's finished when I say it's finished, dumb shit!"

"Sure, Richie. You're the boss."

Only when Richard slid the knife back into the bag, did I feel close to human again.

"If any of you say anything about this, I will cut you all. Do you understand?"

We nodded in unison, thinking him more than capable. There was no way out, or at least, that's what we thought back then.

"Pussies."

Shortly after, Brian emerged from the showers, redder than a cherry snow cone, stark-white towel wrapped around his midriff. Not even bothering to collect his gear, he ran straight for the door, pasty butt cheeks slapping together.

"Run, sloth, run," Richard yelled.

The new gear of unpredictability had us all on edge, and we knew Richard had no intention of letting this go. "Listen up, fuckers," he said, singling out myself and Eddie as punishment for my friend's earlier outburst. "Tomorrow, we meet straight after the bell, just inside the gates to the field. There's a hole in the fence bordering the old cemetery that I've seen fat boy struggling through. Be there or be dead."

"Why?" Eddie the idiot said. He swallowed hard. "I mean, just so we—"

Richard laughed and put a hand on Eddie's shoulder. "Relax, Edster. I just want to make sure this little piggy runs all the way home and never comes back. Can't stand looking at the bloater anymore. He makes me sick, and don't tell me you don't feel the same way."

Eddie grimaced as Richard pinched at his shoulder. "I guess the kid could do with a salad every now and again," my friend muttered, aiming his stare towards the ground.

"Exactly. And Tommy-boy, I've seen the way you look at the kid. Can't tell me your life wouldn't be better without that steaming pile of white dog poo sat next to you every day?"

Eddie let out a yelp as Richard's fingers dug into his flesh.

"Yeah," I said, just wanting the ordeal to end. "I guess."

Richard relinquished his grip. "That's what I thought. Now, you know better than to let me down, so I'll see you two numpties tomorrow. Oh, and make sure your two little girlfriends come with you. If they ask why, tell them it's because Eddie asked the same." He gave us both light taps on the cheek before nodding towards Shane. "Sleep well, fairies."

And just like that, the ordeal was over, or at least on hold for a while.

"What are we going to do?" Eddie said.

"Couldn't keep your mouth shut, could you?"

"Fuck!" He launched a series of punches into his locker in a renewed burst of machoism. "Fuck! Fuck! Fuck!"

"We haven't exactly got much of a choice. We turn up. Rich does his angry dance. We leave."

"You saw him today, though." Eddie sighed as he packed his towel away and nursed his hand. "It just doesn't feel right."

"You mean like eating salad?"

"Funny. Real funny. Do you think we should tell someone?"

I shot him a look.

"Yeah, okay," he muttered. "Bad idea."

"His bark is worse than his bite."

"I fucking hope so, Tommy. I fucking hope so."

As did I.

Donkey Kong

After zipping up our bags, we collected our BMXs and cycled to the amusement arcades. Legs going like the clappers, we never uttered a word on the ten-minute ride. Even when we got there, dripping with sweat, we pooled our clammy coins together in silence before claiming our machine: *Donkey Kong*.

"You first, Eds," I said, breaking the tension. "Make it count."

I watched him feed his coin in, fingers sweaty and twitchy. His body language wasn't right; he was like a different kid. The Def Leppard T-shirt he wore—the one I always teased him about as he never actually liked them—looked far too big. Also, the smattering of light hair above his lip looked silly rather than cool. He looked younger, smaller, so damned fragile all of a sudden.

Richard Clark had a lot to answer for.

Richard. Fucking. Clark.

Even when Stacey Barlow walked in, sporting a bubble the size of her head and tight fluorescent green leggings, we only offered her a cursory glance. We both had plenty already stored in the wank bank, for sure, but just to put things into context and to emphasise our distraction, she was the best-looking girl in school. A Madonna fan, which resulted in most of the school following suit; what you might call an influencer in modern terms. According to Veronica, though, she was dating a twenty-year-old grease monkey who'd already done time. None of that really bothered me; it was Sarah that I had a secret crush on. Only Eddie and my mum knew that. Perhaps Sarah, too.

"What the hell are we going to do, Tom?" he mumbled, moving the joystick in sloven, half-hearted attempts.

"Don't know, Eddie. I hate the guy, wish he was dead."

"Brian?"

"Richard, dummy."

"Hate them both. Wish they'd both just die."

"Eddie!"

"Yeah, I know, but this truly sucks. Why doesn't the school do something about it? Why don't they kick Richard out or tell Brian he's too fat for class."

"Easy, kiddo. Richard's the baddie here."

"I know. I know. Christ, I feel so fucking pathetic when he's around! So damned weak. I've got a real bad feeling about tomorrow; the kid's a fucking psycho."

I had nothing for my friend. My eyes were on the screen, but my mind was elsewhere. In the background, I recall *The Final Countdown* playing over the sound of the machines, the full irony of the song yet to hit.

"Your turn," Eddie muttered, giving the stick an aggressive yank to the right. "Might as well have been playing with my fucking eyes closed."

We were both off form, thoughts racing with the events of that afternoon and what might occur the next day near where dead people lay. We couldn't get near our high scores, but it didn't stop us from pushing more coins in, anything to try and take our minds off things, even for a second.

"I tried talking to him once," Eddie said. "Brian, I mean. Sat next to him on the bench near the basketball courts."

As I watched another life disappear from the top row, I recall a few of my own painful attempts to do the same. "What did you talk about?"

"The weather."

"The weather? How old are you? Forty?"

"I only happened to mention it looked like it was going to piss down, and the next minute, he launched into a run-down of all the different clouds and what they meant. Five minutes in, I told him I needed a shit, then fucked off. I tried, Tommy, I really did, but he's just so—"

"Different."

"Odd."

"Fuck!"

We stared at the machine long after its mocking tune had finished. And even though all the money was gone, we lingered, seeking comfort from the relentless bleeps and bloops and the violent revving of engines. It felt safe, a sanctuary of stale sweat and acrid farts, just like that time in Eddie's bedroom.

I'm not sure what time it was when we finally left, but I chose to walk home, wheeling the bike next to me instead of riding it, because home meant dinner, dinner meant TV, TV meant bed, and bed meant tomorrow.

"Are you okay, love?" Mum asked as I walked in the front door. "You look like you've seen a ghost."

I recall the lump at the back of my throat and the swell behind my eyes. "Fine, just tired."

The cheeseburger and fries Mum made to cheer me up went untouched. And on the verge of breaking as my parents fired more questions of concern, I told them I felt sick and rushed up to my room. There, I spent the rest of the night staring at my *Karate Kid* poster, this time imagining taking Richard down with a vicious leg sweep and finishing him off with a sharp strike to his nose. Rapturous applause erupted, the entire class on their feet. "That's my best buddy," Eddie shouted. And to enthusiastic chants of my name, the class lifted me high into the air and carried me to where Sarah was waiting with a medal and a kiss.

I did it for you, Sarah.

My hero.

But I knew there'd be no *Karate Kid*. And as I ran my eyes over the rest of my posters, I also knew there'd be no turning green or spinning webs. No laser vision, or perfectly aimed Batarang would save the day. It was just me, a scrawny kid, and his even scrawnier sidekick, Eddie.

"Pussy. Pussy. Pussy. Nothing but a fucking pussy, Tommy-boy."

Usually, I would read a while before sleep, but not that night; things had me knotted inside. I couldn't think about anything else. Hour after hour went by as I contemplated how to get out of it. We didn't have a Mr. Miyagi down on our street, nobody to teach me to wax on, wax off, catch a fly with chopsticks, or, more importantly, how to kick a bully's ass. And If I didn't turn up for school, I knew I'd be back on Richard's radar, ready to collect the shit that travelled down.

D-Day

The last day of term should have been fun, anticipation for the long summer holidays and all the adventures to be had. But the tone was ominous, guilt and dread drawn across our tired faces. Even the teachers picked up on the morose undertone. "Are you going to miss me that much?" Mr. Turnbull joked.

When the final school bell rang, I wanted so much to run home and bury myself under my duvet. I'm sure I wasn't the only one, but like sheep, we flocked to the designated meeting spot—me, Eddie, Veronica, and Sarah—the lucky ones selected for the evening's events.

Veronica was far from happy about it. "What the fuck are we doing on the last day of term, hanging around with those fuckwits?"

"I told you, Vee," Eddie said. "I'll get you two specials and the vanilla shake."

"Extra fries, too?"

"Jesus. Alright."

"I don't like it, Tom," Sarah said. "It doesn't feel right."

"I know." I felt about two feet tall. "But he's gonna kick the shit out of me and Ed if we don't turn up."

"Hate the fucking creep. Wish someone would teach him a lesson."

"You and me both, Sarah." *Pussy, Tommy. Nothing but a fucking pussy.*

When we arrived, Richard and Shane were sitting at the edge of the clearing near the tall grass, tugging on cigarettes and spitting balls of mucus into the straw-like grass. "Fat boy shouldn't be too long. I've watched him walk the field a few times," Richard said before blowing an impressive smoke ring and heading towards the decrepit barn. "Make yourself at home."

Trying to get my bearings as I followed, I wondered where the field provided a shortcut to. There were houses on the other side, but that would be at least a four-kilometre walk. And the grass was so long in patches—I mean four-foot high—hardly a comfortable stroll.

I cleared my throat, not wanting to sound as weak as I felt. "What are we doing here?"

He snapped his head around, face twisted into a manic sneer. "*We* are not going to do anything, Tommy-boy. You've just volunteered yourself." With that, he plucked the knife from the back of his pants and thrust it into my palm. "Pig. P-i-g. That's what you're going to write across fat boy's chest. And if you don't, I'll write it across hers instead." Without turning towards her, he raised a finger towards Sarah. "And then Eddie's. Then Veronica's."

My skin prickled. The knot in my stomach made itself known again. "Come on, Rich, you've had a laugh. It's time to—"

"Give me the fucking knife back," he said. "Shane, bring her to me."

"No, wait! Rich, please."

"Give me the fuckin' knife back now, you pussy." Teeth gritted together, he took a step forward and rested his forehead against mine. "Give. Me. The. Knife."

"He's bluffing, Tom," Veronica said. "Just hot air."

"I'll fucking show you who's bluffing, Vee," he said, tobacco-flavoured spittle spraying into my mouth. "Give it, shit-stick."

I remember wanting to stab him, to sink the blade into the side of his neck. It was a perfect opportunity that I still think about today. I'd watch as he gurgled and choked on his blood, his face registering disbelief and new-found respect. Instead, I looked towards Sarah, her eyes wide as she frantically tried to wrestle from Shane's hold, the boy who would cut his own head off if Rich gave instructions to do so.

"Okay, okay."

"That's my boy," he said, giving me another sharp slap across the cheek. "And make sure you go deep enough to—"

"He's coming!" Shane whispered.

There were six of us nestled behind the grass, and I was sure as hell Brian would see or hear us. I remember praying for it to be the case, that he would veer off and find a different way home. But he kept coming, in his own world, munching on a Snickers bar as though he'd not eaten for a week. When he was close, Richard stepped out to greet him. "Fat boy, you left without saying goodbye. Didn't your mama teach you any manners before you ate her?"

Silence, aside from the chuckle from Rich's sidekick.

It makes me feel dirty just thinking about it, but at that moment, I despised Brian for having us endure such an ordeal. How twisted is that? Even as Richard approached him, the kid just stood there, forcing the remainder of the melting chocolate into his mouth.

Cry, fucker, cry, I remember thinking.

Shane crept out from the other side of the barn, dropping to all fours a couple of feet behind Brian. And then, with that same manic smile plastered across his face, Richard lunged forward, thrusting his hands into Brian's chest and offering a sharp grunt.

That kid did not move an inch.

Not a fucking inch.

Richard's face turned red, a combination of embarrassment and rage. "Pass me the knife, Tom."

I recall studying the dull blade still sitting in the palm of my hand. I also remember wanting to throw it into the long grass and get it as far away as possible.

"Pass me the motherfucking knife!"

That look on his face—twisted into the meanest thing I'd ever seen. Hating myself, knowing something terrible would happen, I started walking, sheepish, eager to rid myself of the knife's ever-increasing heaviness.

I'll never forget what happened next.

It was halfway to Richard that I noticed Brian's eyes grow wide as he caught sight of the weapon. It was as though a switch had been flicked, a subsequent scream filling the area so loud it made the trees shake and the ground tremble.

Breaking point.

"What the fuck?" Veronica muttered. "What the fuck? What the fuck? What the fuck?"

Brian backed up, stumbling over Shane and landing on the dry summer ground with a thud, an audible rush of air gushing from him.

"Come here, piggy," Richard said. And even though his victim had finally—*finally*—shown something more than bemused interest, Richard appeared manic as he snatched the knife from me. "I'm gonna make you squeal again, piggy," he said, the kid's eyes still gaping wide and not leaving the blade.

"Stop," Sarah shouted, but Richard was already on the kid. "Stop, Rich!"

As quiet as a mouse, I watched it unfold, an almost out-of-body experience I've relived countless times. Brian's terrified, wide eyes darted between us, but we just stood and watched as Richard waved the knife in front of his face.

"Richard, that's enough," Eddie cried. "He's done. Congratulations."

"Shut the fuck up," Richard replied. "Come on, piggy. Oink! Oink! Oink! Squeal for me again, piggy. Come on. Come on!"

Even Shane looked as white as a sheet, realisation dawning that his leader was losing any control he might have had. It was the look in Rich's eyes, beyond hate and obsession, the same relentless and unmotivated fixation that I guessed his father might have had on him.

"Squee! Squee! Squee!" Richard sang. "Let me hear the piggy sing."

When Brian parted his lips, I remember thinking he was about to blubber and plead for mercy—give Richard a reason to end the chaos. But what came out bore no resemblance to the English language, instead emerging as a series of sharp piercing cries that fast escalated towards a deafening crescendo. The ground shook again, causing me to thrust my arms to my side to keep my balance.

"What the fuck," I heard Eddie say.

I looked down to see a crack forming in the ground. "Oh, shit." It began to extend through the dried grass, creating a chasm of oblivion between us. "Crack," is all I managed to say. "Crack!"

Then it ceased.

A warning, not a plea; I know that now. I guess we all got our notice.

"We need to leave," Sarah said. "Leave the kid alone, Richard."

But red mist still fogged Richard's mind. He was gone, lost in his campaign of loathing as he leaned towards the kid, knife gripped tight in his right hand. "You think you're so smart, don't you, piggy?" He adjusted his grip, pointing the blade towards Brian. "But school's over now. Time for an education in real life."

The kid squealed again, forcing my hands over my ears, the subsequent tremor sending me to the ground. The others, too. Even Richard lost his balance, the knife sinking into the yellow grass only a few inches from Brian's right ear. Cursing under his breath, Richard pushed himself up until the blade was again only a few inches from its target.

"Was that you, fatty? Did you break wind?" Unprepared to drop his vendetta, he grabbed Brian's shirt, ripped it open, and rested the blade on the doughy white flesh. "Whoa, look at all that blubber! I think I'm going to need a bigger knife."

As Sarah helped me to my feet, a large tremor almost took our legs away again. Veronica screamed, the ground continuing a rattle that rode up our bones.

What followed from Brian, I can only describe as a cartoonish gaseous fart.

FRAAAAAAP!

It filled the area with immediate pungency, causing Sarah and I to dry retch towards the ground as we held hands for support.

"Richard!" Sarah pleaded.

Undeterred, he put the blade to the poor boy's skin. "Now, piggy, this might hurt a—"

Brian opened his mouth, letting out an almighty burp, a subsequent spray of green bile hitting Richard square on, covering his face and hair with thick, gloopy vomit.

"Fuck," Shane whispered.

"My name is Brian," the kid said.

Sarah broke the silence with a nervous giggle, her eyes projecting disbelief and immeasurable fear.

"I can't see!" Richard yelled, beginning to dance. "I can't fucking see!"

Shit was getting serious, and I wanted to go home. Veronica screamed again. Eddie looked towards me, but I had nothing. Opening and closing his mouth as though catching flies, Shane began swaying left and right as though about to pass out.

"Help me," Richard sang, rubbing at his eyes with a frantic circular motion but failing to displace any of the green substance. "It's burning! Please help! Someone—"

Brian burped again, another powerful jet of liquid spraying from his mouth straight into Richard's, cutting the bully's manic pleas short. Hands around his throat and head still covered with green spew, Richard let out a series of horrific muffled choking sounds. I wanted to run, dragging Sarah with me, but even then, Richard had a hold over me. "Where did you fuck off to, shit-stick?" I imagined him saying the next time he saw me. "Now it's your turn."

"What the fuck?" Veronica called out. "What the fuck-ity fuck fuck fuck?"

"Somebody do something," Shane said, finding his voice.

But we all just stood there, observing Richard writhing around, performing a series of tribal-like manoeuvres as he clawed at the unmovable green stuff on his face. Blind, he stepped forward, catching his foot in the crack and sinking to his knees. He wavered for a while before toppling headfirst onto the yellowing ground, the muffled chokes becoming few and far between and his kicks growing weaker by the second. Hands still clasped around his neck, he looked so small, like a child. I recall feeling no gratification, only dread.

And then he stopped moving.

Shane was first to run for it, leaving his fallen comrade behind. Letting go of my hand, Sarah also retreated. "Tom, let's go," she muttered, but my legs wouldn't move. "Tom, come on!" Veronica screamed again, stepping over the crack, leaving me and Eddie to stare at each other, Rich's lifeless body between us.

"Tom!" I heard Sarah cry again.

When Brian began pushing himself from the ground, Eddie broke his stare and made his run. "Eddie, wait for me," I cried, but he made no effort to turn. Brian offered another almighty eruption on the way up, the ground shaking more vigorously than ever, only momentum keeping my friends from falling. I watched the crack widen, finally finding the courage to move before it could swallow my right foot.

Anger.

That's what I sensed. He was done with the warnings, the poker face well and truly gone.

"My name is Brian," he said, turning to my fleeing colleagues. Another deafening burp—loud enough to wake the nearby dead— left his lips. What followed was the wildest tremor yet, sending my friends and me immediately to the ground. From the sharp grass, I could only watch as the subsequent jet of green liquid sprayed with impossible accuracy across what must have been forty feet. Starting with Shane, it covered each of them, bringing them to a sticky halt, some catching the end of my sneakers en route and setting like concrete.

"My name is Brian."

"Help!" Sarah cried. "I can't move! I can't move!"

Even from there, I could see the fear in their eyes as they snapped their heads around, only to see Brian starting his approach.

"Tom!" Eddie shrieked, a plea that still haunts my dreams. "Tom, what do we do?"

I managed to stand but was helpless, unable to move or make a sound other than a whimper as Brian edged towards them, only their heads and necks unhindered. And then, two steps in, something started to happen, something that if I hadn't already witnessed previous events, I might have put down to my eyes playing tricks.

Brian's head started to split.

I kid you not; that noggin cracked like a fucking egg.

"Oh fuck," I said. "Oh fuck."

The huge, jagged crevice continued working its way down the entire length of his torso just like the chasm that worked through the grass.

They all crack in the end.

Holding my breath, I watched both sides of his body peeling away like banana skin. Beyond him, I could hear the screams and cries of my friends, but from the other side of the chasm, they sounded so distant.

"My name is Brian."

A strange and garbled cry left my lips as the sack of flesh fell to the floor with a soft thud.

I can't imagine what my friends saw, but even the back of what stood before me was enough to send my heart pounding and my stomach fluttering to the brink of vomiting. With glistening yet scaly skin, the creature appeared almost amphibious-like, its pulsating black veins and green pearlescent skin like something from one of those B-movies I used to watch with my dad.

"Ed-Eddie," I managed to stammer.

My friend looked towards me, his face pale and his eyes wide. He tried again to pull himself away, launching into a childish blubber I'd not seen for years. To his right, Veronica let out a series of rasps, and further along, Sarah was beyond manic, offering a series of incoherent cries. Sometimes, I see her face in my dreams, teary and confused, nostrils unnaturally flared.

"I should get back for dinner," Shane muttered from the floor. "I'll be grounded again."

Sensing Brian was far from done, we went into panic mode, desperate to pull ourselves free, all rational thought and composure out of the window. We cried, screamed, and pleaded, but not once did we apologise or try to reason with the creature that had imprisoned us.

"My name is Brian." And with that, its colours faded until we could no longer see it. "B-r-i-a-n."

"For fuck's sake," Eddie said, his voice breaking all over again. "Where is it, Tom? Where the fuck is it?"

"I don't know, Eddie. I don't know."

On that brightest of summer evenings, we were as good as blind.

Shane let out a high-pitched wail. "Have to get back for dinner."

"Please, Brian," Sarah uttered. "Please don't hurt us."

My heart was in my throat. I never really knew what that expression meant until that day, but I feared for my life, my entire body pulsating with raw terror. I swallowed hard, not a drop of saliva in my mouth.

We waited.

"Shh," I said, lifting a shaky finger to my lips.

And waited.

I remember hearing the distant bark of a dog, thinking it sounded from the other world, the one before Brian shredded his skin. There was a thought for my parents, wondering what mundane things they were getting up to at that precise moment and wanting more than anything to hug them. I had no idea how much time had passed, but it felt like an eternity. The hot summer breeze wafting my hair was barely audible over my erratic breathing. But when the warm gust dropped, I held air in, frightened I'd miss something.

Silence.

"Has he gone?" Veronica uttered after an eternity. "I think he's gone."

It was torturous, the waiting. It still gives me the shivers today just thinking about it. Such a heightened level of trepidation would put the fear of God into the most hardened of people, not to mention a bunch of wet-behind-the-ear adolescents.

I cleared my throat. "I think—"

Sarah's blood-curdling cry still haunts my dreams today, as does the memory of the jagged hole in her belly through which I could see sharp blades of grass rustling in the breeze. Darkness spilled down her Levi's, and to the sound of cries from the others, I watched the light go out behind her eyes.

"Sarah!" I began to cry then, a helpless sob for my make-believe girlfriend, who was dead but still upright, held in place by Brian's vomit. "Sarah!"

We screamed and yelled for help until our voices faded to hoarse rasps. But the only other people in the area were already dead, Brian's squeals ultimately unable to wake them.

"I want to go home now," Eddie cried. "*Family Ties* is on."

Veronica was in the worst state. "We're all going to die," she muttered, her lips trembling. "I love you, Mum, Dad." It became too much for her when the flesh-tearing, bone-crunching sounds commenced. She closed her eyes, spewing a series of unrecognisable words that further fuelled my fear. At this point, I was already gone, bubbles popping from my nose, vision blurry from tears, and warmth leaking down my right leg.

We're all going to die.

Still, I couldn't take my eyes off the carnage. There was little of Sarah left, just her head and a shiny bit of gristle. I remember thinking the head must be its least favourite, or the part it savoured most. And then it spat out her torn clothes and chewed sneakers onto the grass.

"Fuck! Fuck! Fuuuuuuck!" Eddie cried to the sound of more bone chewing. "I want to go home. I want to go home." His eyes found mine as he continued trying to pull his leg from the solidified gunk. "I love you, Tom Harper," he muttered. "I love you."

Sorry, I just need a minute...

Damn, those words still eat away at me.

Sorry.

Inhale. Exhale.

Okay.

With all his bravado gone, Shane looked like a ghost. His watery eyes caught mine as he continued his struggles against the green stuff. I saw fear and regret. Without his commander, he was just one of us. Perhaps less.

I happened to turn towards Veronica just as her left leg disappeared. It all felt quite surreal until the delayed spray of blood tainted the dry yellow grass beneath. She didn't fall, still locked in place like a limbless statue. There was no scream either, her silence scaring me more than the missing limb. Only when she looked down did a muted cry leave her lips. "My leg," she said. "Has anyone seen my leg?"

She lifted her gaze towards me just as a chunk of her midriff disappeared, more horrific chewing and crunching following. With a soft thud, her torso squelched to the floor into a lumpy and bloody puddle. She let out a series of watery rasps as she clawed at the grass, dragging herself a couple of feet before her eyes changed like Sarah's, unplugged from the mains and never to be switched on again. Then her head disappeared.

Eddie began to pray. I knew his parents used to drag him to Sunday mass, but before that day, he never gave any indication he bought into it all. I felt an odd jealousy—at least he had something, a distraction. All I could do was listen to the sound of Veronica's skull being crushed and my laboured breathing that had started to sound a lot like Brian's.

The chewing stopped.

"—undeserving of your grace and presence—"

It was just the three of us left.

"—ask you to forgive me—"

I watched Eddie's arm disappear from the elbow and as magnificent red tarnished the only exposed white bit of his Nikes. He looked down, his prayers turning into nonsensical garbles.

"Eddie!" I screamed. "Look at me. LOOK AT ME!"

He looked up, a knowing in his eyes that his time on Earth was coming to a premature end.

"I love you, Eddie MacGuire," I said.

His head was ripped clean off. It didn't seem real, cartoon-like, similar to one of the video games we'd played at the arcade, except there was nowhere to insert a coin to continue, and the stuff emerging from his neck seemed legit. "Eddie!" I screamed towards his headless body. "EDDIE!"

Halfway through the creature's latest meal, there was a sharp and loud thunderous sound that I can only assume was gas, the subsequent stench making my eyes water. "My name is Brian," he—*it*—said between chews. "B-r-i-a-n."

In seconds, what remained of my best friend was gone, and I was still on the menu.

"I'm sorry, Tom. I'm so sorry."

I turned towards Shane's voice to see his face, a puffy and watery mess. "I'm sorry," he repeated, beginning to bawl. "I'm so so—" His bowels were ripped open, entrails falling to the floor in a gooey purplish heap. Unlike Veronica, his scream was loud and blood-curdling, a prelude to what was in store and a chilling farewell from someone who knew they were about to die. In seconds, his screams ended, leaving a horrific and just as unbearable silence.

Unplugged. Dead.

Images of my parents and sister flashed through my head, all of us at the breakfast table that morning. Business as usual, apart from the dread that had lodged in my stomach from what the day might bring. I recall *Sledgehammer* was crackling through the radio, and Dad was complaining someone had put the empty orange juice carton back in the fridge. My sister was painting her nails, and Mum danced around the kitchen making pancakes I had refused with a smile, thinking I'd be unable to keep them down. The thought I'd never see them again was like—well, it was like having my insides ripped open.

I prayed then. To any fucker that might have been listening, I prayed for the first time in my life.

One by one, Shane's limbs disappeared in a frenzy of flesh and blood until he, too, was nothing more than a glistening pool of darkness.

It was me next. I was dessert.

Accompanied by another tremor, a rush of putrid wind swept over me. As the chewing and crunching sounds drew closer, I remember squeezing my eyes shut so tight that I thought they might pop. It swallowed then, bringing the inevitable even closer.

"I'm sorry, Brian," is all I could think to say. "I'm sorry I didn't try to stop him."

Standing there in that clearing, as the thing finished grinding what was left of Shane, I still held on to a glimmer of hope that I would make it out alive. It was inconceivable that my life would be cut so short. I wasn't such a bad person, just a weak one.

Silence.

I prayed some more.

With tears running down my cheeks, I started arranging my Nintendo games in alphabetical order. I got as far as *Ghosts 'n Goblins* before the pain came, incredible agony that spread through my entire body like wildfire. It felt like someone was pouring boiling water onto my nerve endings, the scream leaving my lips otherworldly and devoid of hope. Some part of me was missing; that's all I knew.

"I'M SORRY, BRIAN! I'M SORRY!"

With thoughts of Mum's apple pies running through my head and with my eyes still screwed shut, I began to whistle the theme tune from *The A-Team*, bracing myself for a painful departure from this world. No joke, I whistled the hell out of that fucking tune as though my life depended on it, all the time able to smell *its* breath and hear its rasp.

I didn't want to die. I wasn't ready to die.

But all hope was gone.

And then nothing short of a fucking miracle happened.

Tyres screeched, and car doors slammed, leaving a picture in my mind of Hannibal puffing on a cigar while giving the signal to move in. A series of gunshots crackled around me, my instincts causing me to jolt, the spatter on my foot beginning to yield.

Slowly, I opened my eyes. Metallic silver it was, I remember that much. But it was fading, disappearing before me until only an empty clearing remained. I recall voices screaming from behind. I turned my head to see two men running towards me, both dressed in grey suits, black ties fluttering, their guns unholstered.

"You okay, kid?" one of them yelled.

"No." The last thing I recall is looking down to see the puddle of darkness collecting on the grass next to me.

THE LAB

"What do you remember?" a deep voice floated from above.

"Everything." I tried to push myself up, squinting into the bright lights. "Where am I? What's happening?"

"Relax, kid. You passed out. Tell me what you remember."

"My friends."

"Gone, kid. And I'm truly sorry about that, but we need to crack on."

I already knew it, but I'd half hoped the entire ordeal might have been a dream. *Gone, kid.* The smell of fresh summer air had been replaced by disinfectant, and the sound of the breeze by a series of monotonous beeps. My eyes began to adjust, offering a view of bright-white sheets, and as I looked even further down, I saw my arm bandaged up to the elbow, flashbacks of the carnage running through my mind. *I love you, Tom Harper.*

"I ain't got all day, kid." One of the grey-suited men that had rushed towards me was leaning against the far wall, arms folded, cigarette dangling from the corner of his mouth. "Sooner we get this done, the sooner we can get you home."

"Who are you?" I asked.

"You don't need to know."

"My hand. It hurts so bad."

"We'll give you something another shot of something soon."

"I want to see my mum and dad."

The man grabbed a metal chair and dragged it towards me. "In time, Tom."

"How do you know my name?"

"We know a lot." He spun the chair around and slumped into it, blowing a cloud of smoke towards me. "We need to chat, man to man."

"My friends are dead." It still didn't seem real even when the words left my lips.

"And I said I'm sorry for that. But we need to get on talking."

"About what?"

"The birds and the bees. Come on, Tom, what do you think?"

I shrugged. "Everything."

The guy nodded.

And with thoughts of returning home, I talked, words coming out so fast they almost rolled into one. "His name was Brian." *B-r-i-a-n.* "Quiet. Really quiet. Sweaty. Fat. Really smart, too. And then he turned into a lizard and sprayed Richie with a green gloop. He—he—"

"Slow down, Tom. Take it easy."

"He kept burping and farting. It made my eyes water. And when he saw the knife, he went—"

"Knife?"

"Yeah, Rich was going to cut him a little. P-i-g. Pig." I swallowed hard, trying to catch my breath. "I'm sorry, I'm sorry. I should have stopped him. If I had, Eddie might still be here. It's my fault. It's all my fault."

"Calm, Tom. Calm."

"Am I under arrest? Am I going to jail? Can I have some more drugs now, please?"

"Nobody's under arrest, Tom." He leaned in closer. "Breathe and tell me the rest."

I was sure I would pass out again, the room starting to spin. With my good hand, I grabbed a handful of the sheets and focused on the guy's nose hair. "There was this alien noise that made the ground split. I think he was angry or scared. Then he threw up."

"Threw up?"

"Yeah, it was super gross—this gloopy green stuff that turned into cement. We couldn't move. And then—then he started eating us one by one like a...buffet." I broke off then, tears filling my eyes, images of the carnage I'd witnessed—the blood, the screams from my friends, the looks of pure fear drawn on their faces—things I'd take to the grave.

"When you're ready, kid."

"I had to fucking stand there while he ate my friends—chewed them all up and burped out their clothes. Then it felt like someone set my hand on fire. And the next thing I remember after that was feeling dizzy and hearing gunshots. I opened my eyes and saw the metallic ship in the field, a trail of bright green on the ground. Was that its blood?"

The guy nodded.

"Did you kill it?"

"I don't think so. Lucky shot, but not that lucky."

"How did you know—about Brian?"

"Our equipment has picked up those sorts of tremors before, but we've always been too late."

I nodded. "Then it just vanished. And I turned to see you and the other guy rushing towards me. And then I looked down and saw my—"

"I think I have all I need."

"Told you. I remember everything."

The guy sighed. "And that's going to be a problem."

"What—what do you mean?"

"None of this happened."

"Yes, it did."

"No, it didn't.

"But it did."

The man let out another sigh and leaned in closer still. "Tom, listen to me and listen well. You saw nothing. You know nothing. Okay?"

"But—but—"

"Say after me, Tom. I saw nothing. I know nothing."

I couldn't believe my ears. Everything I'd been through, and this prick in a suit was asking me to forget it all. It was fucked up, like something from a movie. I shook my head, wincing as pain shot up my arm. For Eddie, Sarah, and Veronica, the truth needed to come out.

"Do you want those drugs or not?"

"I saw everything. Everything."

The man sighed again, leaning all the way in and putting his lips to my ear. "I really didn't want to take this route, kiddo, but you're forcing my hand." The hot breath on my neck made nerve endings prickle. "Let me put this another way. One word of this gets out, and we'll come for your parents and your sister." He leaned back in his chair, aiming a smoke ring towards the ceiling lights.

"I don't understand."

"You're a smart kid. Figure it out."

"That thing killed Eddie. And Sarah. And—"

"After that, your grandparents and anyone else close to you. We'll save you until last, Tom. That way, you can live through the devastation you've created." He inhaled the cigarette, then flicked a flurry of ash towards the grey floor. "Brian's gone, at least for now, but we're here, Tom, and we're the ones you should be afraid of now."

I remember feeling so much rage and confusion but, most of all, a desperate need to get home to my family. "How do I explain the hand? What about my friends?"

"You passed out. You can't remember anything after arriving at the field. Leave the rest to us, we're good at making things disappear."

"It's not fair."

"Life isn't."

"Shit. Shit. Shit. I don't know anymore."

"This isn't optional, Tom. Twenty-three Arlington Road, forty-seven Cloverfield Lane, twenty-nine Mulholland Drive. Do you want me to go on?"

"No." Exhausted and broken, I would have agreed to almost anything if pushed, the guy's message received loud and clear. "Please take me home now." Desperation had won, together with an overwhelming desire to feel part of the ordinary world again, the one full of mundanity, rules, and people who cared for me. "I swear, okay. I swear."

"We will know, Tom. We will know."

"I swear, okay!"

Someone resembling a doctor entered the room, administering an injection that helped numb the pain and made me feel light-headed. They put me into a wheelchair and escorted me into a long corridor lined with glass-walled rooms. Everywhere I looked, there were people with white suits, rushing from one room to the next to an orchestra of high-pitched beeps. And even though sedated at the time, I recall the contents of the very last room, the fat human shell that was once Brian laid out across a silver table and the crowd of people gathering around, prodding with their silver instruments.

My name is Brian.

Through the glass doors of the main entrance, I spied the black car waiting for me, complete with tinted windows. Tears filled my eyes at the thought of soon seeing my parents, but I clenched my fists, determined not to give 'grey suit' the satisfaction. Along the way, he swiped a non-descript card at several locations until we finally arrived at the main foyer, two burly security guards armed to the kilt offering a nod on the way past.

Fresh air had never tasted so good as when those doors opened, and I recall taking an extra-large gulp of the stuff before "grey suit" helped me into the back seat. "Remember what I told you, kid," he said. "We are for real."

I'm not sure how long I was in the back of that car until I was dropped at the real hospital, not an armed guard or fat suit in sight. The nurses were so kind, rushing to assist, attentive, and listening as I fumbled through what the driver had told me to say.

We will know, Tom. We will know.

My time at that hospital would become a blur, but I remember my parents being beside themselves when they saw me. Even my sister had a little cry. Strange to say, but it was the smell of my mum's perfume that set me off into a childish wail, and even my father's habitual, annoying rustle of my hair had me close to going another round.

We'll come for your parents and your sister first.

And that's pretty much where the story ends, the juicy stuff anyway. The funny thing is, I'm not even sure anyone will bother running this. I've lost count of how many alien stories I've read in the newspapers over the years. But I have to hope, not just for the sake of my fallen friends but also because it's been a painfully bloody slow process typing this story with one hand.

All said and done, through all the trials and tribulations life has offered, events of that day have helped me maintain an unwavering state of childhood wonder, one I'll take to my not-so-far-away grave. On the warm evenings when I lean against the doorway, surveying the sky and saying a prayer for my lost friends, I might claim to understand the science behind the twinkling stars, even follow the mathematics behind the two-million-year-old light that makes it down to us. However, my mind still races with all the possible life forms that could be out there, all the magic behind the black veil. It's humbling, for sure.

Well, that's it, readers. That's all I've got.

A hell of a ride, eh?

Oh, one last thing. Just be sure to keep a look out for smart kids with a sweet tooth.

THE END

THE NAUGHTY CORNER

The Fowlers

The pain comes fast and intense, Helen's lungs on fire. She tilts her head back, squints into the light and tries to blink the stinging soil away. Fighting the urge to scream, she tries raising her arms above the surface, a need for some part of her to stretch beyond earthy oblivion.

But her limbs fail her.

Hope fades that this might be just another lesson, another peak in a never-ending nightmare of sustained fear. From the neck down, she's unable to move, ever-growing pressure compressing her bones, her life reduced to a claustrophobic world of darkness and pain.

I'm sorry, Jake. I'm so sorry.

The leaf above is so alive, green, and lush, the stark light behind it highlighting intricate venation. Something so beautiful and innocent, she considers, yet the very soil that nurtured its life is taking hers away.

I don't deserve this!

Death's coming, she knows it. Everything she was, no more, as if she was herself but a speck of dust in the wind.

Eyes screwed shut, minimal light making it through her eyelids, she wills herself to pass out while instinctively forcing air into her lungs. Only a teaser makes it through this time, bringing some solace that it will surely be over soon.

We are good people!

Earth sprinkles across her face. And another load. She retches only for more to replace it. Eyes fixed on that damned leaf, her neck stretching back as far as it can go, the soil finds its way into her ears, her nostrils, her eyes, grainy bitterness laying at the back of her throat.

This is it.

Unable to hold onto her scream any longer, not even a whimper emerges.

Images flash through her mind, a relentless barrage of happier moments decompressing from memory, likely for the last time. Her husband, Jason, and her son, Jake—shared lives soon to be nothing more significant than roadkill. In total darkness, she holds onto her last breath for as long as possible, knowing they are both on either side of her, inches away, struggling or already dead. She wishes she could hold their hands one final time.

The pain is extraordinary for a while.

Veronica Davenport

Sitting behind the desk of number forty-three Melody Drive, Veronica waits patiently, studying her street below through the gently wafting curtains and pink glow of fairy lights decorating the outside of her window.

Her skin prickles with the knowledge they'll be here soon.

She strokes the glistening pouch hanging from the edge of the mirror and begins practising her smiles. There aren't many variations, one for the insiders and another for outsiders, but the reflected grin she reserves for the in-betweeners.

It's nearing the end of a long and hot summer, and the breeze sneaking through the ajar window already carries notes of autumn, her least favourite season. The trees lining Melody Drive will soon change colour and shed their leaves, creating an awful, ugly mess on roads and pavements. No, she doesn't like it one bit. The scale model behind her, the one that Daddy built, is how the street would look year-round if she had her way. Daddy and Mummy can fix most things, but nature is an unruly beast.

She takes some time to marvel at her beauty in the ornate mirror. The warm pink light accentuates the softness of her skin and gives a shimmer to her eyes. Her teeth are a brilliant white, and straight, and her auburn hair falls across her shoulders in perfect waves. At church, she's always sure to thank God for being created so flawlessly. And she's seen how boys look at her—the way Mummy told her they would once they realised what their thingies were for. As Mummy instructed, she ties her hair back in a tight bun and applies a layer of red lipstick.

An engine.

Reaching over her desk to draw the curtain back halfway, she eases to her feet. She holds her breath in excited anticipation, listening to the approaching hum, eyes fixed on the large gates at the end of Melody Drive.

It's definitely them, she thinks. *No reason for anyone else to be around here at this time of day.*

She swallows hard.

It's the perfect spot to keep an eye on the neighbourhood, to catch up on all the goings-on, the slightest of noises exploding through the usual quiet always a prompt for her to take her position.

The white van rolls towards the gates, and as an arm extends from the driver's window to enter the appropriate code, Veronica tucks herself a little further behind the curtain. She's not a fan of the music arriving with the new residents, but Mummy tells her it always takes a little while for people to adapt to their new surroundings. She thinks she can even hear them singing.

Hairs bristle across Veronica's neck as the van enters through the opening gates, followed by the removal truck. She watches both vehicles crawl towards the driveway of number twenty-four. Change is necessary sometimes; she knows that, but it's not something she relishes. She likes quiet, consistency, stability, and order. It's just how she was raised.

Veronica continues watching from her window, keen to lay eyes on her new neighbours. She'll begin applying the rest of her make-up soon, not that she needs it, but Mummy says it shows effort.

Number 24, Melody Drive

They're all at it, screaming incoherent lyrics to *Bohemian Rhapsody* and not caring one iota. It's a song Charlie hates, but he can't help himself if it's playing on the stereo. His dad, Frank, is well off-key, but they expect it, and it's more funny than irritating. His mum Sheila is much more serious with it, veins in her neck popping, fists clenched as she belts out the words.

"Dad, you sing like you always need the bathroom."

"I generally do these days, son."

Caught in the moment, Charlie knows sadness will return when he stares at the ceiling of a brand new room, one without a crack running across the middle. For now, though, he'll take excitement over melancholy. He had to blink away tears even before they'd reached the end of their old street, a case of not knowing what he had until it was in the rear-view mirror. The house, the park he spent hours in, his best friend waving them off at the end of the driveway. "You'll make new friends, son," his dad had said. "Even better ones."

Melancholy aside, the journey had been quite fun, the battery percentage on his iPad hanging on for dear life. Helped by gorging on endless snacks, four hours went by in no time.

"It's perfect," Sheila says.

Frank switches off the engine and rests his hands on the steering wheel. "It's pretty close." The truth is, the place is better than he remembers, like something from the technicolour TV shows he watched as a kid. Paintwork as white as advert teeth and a contrasting, colourful garden at odds for such a dry season. So quiet, too. He never dreamt he would end up living in a gated community, such a thing reserved for the rich, not teachers or wannabe writers like him. "Not sure I'll ever get used to plugging a code in just so I can get into my street, though."

"First things first, I'll put the kettle on," Sheila says. "And then you and Charlie can start bringing the rest of the stuff in from the van while I go Mary Poppins on this place. Ask the men if they want a cup of tea, will you?"

As pre-autumn evening air rushes into the van, Charlie's teeth begin to sing. He scoops up what's left of the candy, pushes himself up from the centre seat, and steps out onto the mosaic brick to take in his new home. "Not bad," he says. "Nice one, Mum."

"Hey, punk, we're a team," his dad says, stepping out from the driver's side.

"Yeah, but Mum's the one with the good job. No offence."

"Offence taken, you little shit," Frank says, giving chase.

And for the first time in a while, the blanket of silence across Melody Drive is disturbed by laughter and the sound of thumping feet across manicured lawns and perfectly spaced-out flowerbeds.

"Okay, children, that's enough." Sheila notices the curtains twitching, thinking herself far too exhausted to entertain the thought of jibber-jabber. "Frank!"

But they don't relent; they chase and guffaw, running around the removal truck, weaving in and out of the men as they begin their stoic unloading. Usually getting a kick out of seeing them like this, Sheila winces at every noise, every cackle, every playful scream accentuated by surrounding silence. It makes the show appear forced, even though she knows it isn't. "Frank, we've just got here," she says, firm. "Please don't show us up."

"Yeah, Dad!"

Offering a salute, Frank makes his way to her. "Sorry, love." He wraps an arm around her waist and leads her to the door. "This is your moment. Best lawyer in the county."

Sheila smiles. *Yes. Yes, it is.* Years of having to stomach the ego-stroking between her male counterparts, the constant attempts to undermine, and all the backhand comments, but it's her that got promoted to head office, and this is her reward. She feels an overwhelming sense of accomplishment and pride as she slides the key into the door. "I made it, Dad," she whispers.

"Holy shit!" Charlie says as the door opens.

Frank offers him a playful slap across the back of the head. "Language boy." He follows Sheila across the threshold. "Fuck-a-duck!"

It's as spacious as they recall, with ample room for their furniture, and a perfect excuse to buy more, Sheila thinks. She's already planned where everything will go, almost to scale on the back of a coffee-stained work notepad. "Oh, yes, this will do just fine."

"Excuse me," the short man says from the doorway, giant hands wrapped around the bottom of a louvre cabinet. "Where's this going, love?"

Charlie notes the guy's back-to-front baseball cap, thinking him too old for that malarkey. The tiniest amount of skin visible through all the tattoos on the man's massive arms provides further alienation.

"Just against the far wall next to the bottom of the staircase, please," his mum answers.

The second man through the door is much taller and skinnier, with no sign of tattoos. Bottled glasses give Charlie the impression of intelligence and that the man looks more like a professor than a removalist. It's a strange match, little and large, but one that appears to work well, the first bit of furniture already in place.

As soon as the men are on their way, the Harpers begin exploring their new home, dodging boxes, claiming each new area as their own, a base for future memories. It's spotless; no evidence anyone was ever here before them. The place smells brand new, too. Untainted. At least that is before Sheila fills the air with a sickly pink sugar wax melt.

"Oh, no. Brace yourself, Charlie," Frank says. "I know that face."

Crinkling her forehead further, finger resting on her chin, Sheila begins snapping her head this way and that. "It's hard to say until you're in," she says. "Just a few changes, boys."

Frank sighs. "Bloody knew it."

She gives out her orders, instructing Frank and Charlie to reallocate the already once-positioned furniture, an action Frank knows will be repeated several times over the coming days. Regardless, they oblige, knowing resistance is futile.

"That one goes upstairs, please. And be careful, there's glass in it."

"Yes, boss. Charlie, you okay on your end?"

Charlie nods, putting on a brave face. "It's not even heavy." The staircase is wider than their old house, making it appear less steep, but only three steps up, his arms are already singing. "Have you talked to Mum about where the PlayStation is going?"

"Working on it. You can't rush these things. Timing is everything with your mother."

"You mean you're too chicken?"

"Yeah. I'll get to it, though."

"Can't wait to kick your ass on the big screen."

"I miss the days when you didn't know your arse from your elbow."

They take it slow, Frank bringing up the rear, bearing the brunt, and Charlie in front, determined to ask for a break. By the time they reach the top of the stairs, he's on the verge of conceding, his arms numb.

"Just here for this one, bud," his dad says.

Relieved, Charlie lets his end down, noting how the cabinet appears smaller in the expansive hallway. "Do you think you'll miss—"

"Hellooooo," a voice sings from somewhere below.

"Hide," Frank says, eyes wide with panic as he drops behind the banister.

Charlie also sinks to the floor, a smile breaking across his face. Together, they huddle, taking refuge from the uninvited shrillness already disturbing their energy and undoing all the claiming they've been doing.

"We brought piiiiieeeeeee, neighbours." The intrusive voice continues. "And apple and ginger tea."

From the safety of the second floor, Charlie observes the intruder. Sporting bright red lipstick and large hoop earrings, the tall lady leads the way with her nose in the air and an almost too-upright posture. It looks to Charlie like she's clinging onto a fart, keeping her nose out of the way just in case. Already wearing a smile, the lady holds a pie in front of her.

"I'm sure that front door was closed," his father whispers.

Charlie continues studying the lady, thinking she looks like an actress, even prettier than the ladies he sometimes spends time with behind the locked bathroom door. The thought makes him shudder and long for lights out.

Holy shiiiiiit.

Following behind is the prettiest girl Charlie recalls ever laying eyes on. She's a carbon copy of the mother, only smaller, even carrying herself the same way. She has an I'm-too-good-for-life look across her face, and a small paper bag pinched between two fingers. "That girl looks mean," Charlie says. *I think I'm in love.*

"Answer me honestly, Charlie. Is that man better looking than me?"

Charlie studies the man bringing up the rear. "Yes."

"Whoa, cowboy. Do you want to take a minute to think about it?"

"If it makes you feel better, Dad."

As though on their way to somewhere formal, the uninvited guests are all dressed up in straight-angled clothes. Their hair, too, so damned tidy—the dad with a short, straight cut, and both mother and daughter's pinned back in a bun, lending them a look of severity, much like his old-school nurse from back home. Bar the jowls, moustache, and tattoo on the wrist.

His dad elbows him, eyes wide, standard goofy smile on display. "They brought pie, Charlie." Frank puts his hands together in a prayer-like pose and closes his eyes. "God, please let it be cherry. Amen."

Charlie shrugs, unimpressed, Grandma's blueberry pie ruining things for him. One grey hair, most likely from her head, but it had a curl to it that put him off pastry for life.

As the girl's glance falls across different areas of the house, Charlie thinks their eyes meet for the shortest—but longest, timeless, magical—time. She wrinkles her nose and carries on with the inspection. There's a little golden pouch hanging from her waist, one Charlie's quite taken by. Figuring there must be something important in there for her to carry it around, he's filled with a sudden and inexplicable urge to know what's inside.

"Hi. Hello there." His mum enters from the other side, wiping her hands on her jeans and wearing the smile reserved for strangers. "Hello," she says again. "Sorry about the mess."

Charlie studies his mum, hair all over the place, her shirt untucked, and a layer of dust decorating her left leg. She looks awkward and flustered as though caught doing something she shouldn't have been. It's not a sight he cares for. He also wonders why his parents are so willing to apologise to complete strangers but never to each other.

"No need to apologise." Still wearing the smile, the woman steps forward and presents the pie. "The wine is from us, but the pie is from the lady at number twenty-three. Oh, and this tea is from the gentleman at number seventeen. It's apple and ginger, your favourite, I believe."

"That's so very kind—"

"It's Patricia," the woman says. "This is my husband, Nick, and my daughter, Veronica. Veronica has some liquorice straps for Charlie."

"That's a lovely name, Veronica," his mum says, bending her legs and arching her body towards the girl.

"Thank you, Mrs. Harper."

"Call me Sheila, please."

Still watching from the landing, Charlie and his dad exchange a look. "Did Mum just bow?" Charlie whispers.

"Either that or she let one rip," his father mumbles back. "Silent killer."

"We're the Davenports from number forty-three," they hear the lady say, turning their attention back on her just in time to see her sniff at the air. "Hope you don't mind us dropping by?"

"Not at all," his mum says, flustered and rosy-cheeked as she collects the pie. "Let me just put this in the kitchen. Would you like a drink?"

Patricia marches after her. "Yes, let's all have a cup of that tea you're so fond of. And shall we slice off a bit of that pie?"

"Frank! Charlie!" Sheila hollers in a tone they know all too well. "Visitors!"

Frank and Charlie offer each other a defeated glance and crawl along the landing until they're behind proper cover. "Fuck's sake," Frank says, pushing himself from the floor. He brushes himself down, raises an arm towards the ceiling, and buries his nose in his armpit. "Do I smell?"

"If you have to ask, Dad," Charlie says, also feeling a strange sense of unworthiness, as if they're about to meet royalty. "As if their shit doesn't smell" is one of his mum's favourite sayings. But she bowed for fuck's sake.

They descend the stairs, gripping the banister for comfort, an unconscious effort to offset the inevitable awkwardness of superficiality. It was theirs; they claimed it, put the flag down, and now it feels like no man's land again. They'll have to start all over once the Davenports have gone.

"Nick, is it?" his dad asks, knowing full well it is and offering a hand.

The man with the tidy hair takes it and gives it a firm shake. "Nice to meet you, Frank. Welcome to your new home."

"I'm Veronica," the girl volunteers, offering her hand and a perfect-toothed smile. "Very pleased to meet you."

Regretting not changing his shirt, Frank takes her small hand in his. "And this is my son, Charlie. Charlie, say hello."

"Hi," Charlie mutters, hands in pockets, eyes fixed on the pattern of the oak floor. He knows there's more coming, though, his throat already dry. One hell of an ordeal for a bit of red liquorice, he thinks.

"Now, how old are you, Charlie?" the well-groomed man called Nick asks.

Shit fuck. "Thirteen. Nearly fourteen."

"It's his birthday next Sunday," Frank adds.

Nick smiles. "Veronica's thirteen, too."

"Oh, which school does she go to?"

"Veronica's home-schooled, Frank," Nick replies. "Patricia likes to know where she is and what she's doing. Not that we don't trust her." He lowers his voice. "It's the others, you see."

Frank nods and gives a thin-lipped smile. "Riiiiight."

"My favourite subject is maths," Veronica says. "I'm already up to complex algebra."

"Charlie likes to write, don't you, Charlie? Just like his dad."

Charlie nods, avoiding eye contact with the prissy girl who just shook hands and does complex algebra. *And what's with the sickly smile.*

"Pie's ready," his mum hollers.

They walk through to the kitchen in an awkward herd. "The real estate agent said you were a teacher, Frank," Nick says. "Have you anything lined up?"

"I'm taking some time off right now. Trying to finish writing my book."

The response prompts no further comment, hanging in the air like a bad fart.

Six bowls await on the kitchen table, along with the heavy silver spoons reserved for Christmas or special occasions. All smiles and glances, they take their seats, Charlie nipping at his thigh to distract from the unbearable discomfort.

"And what about you, Nick," Frank says. "What do you do for a crust?"

"Nick's an architect," Patricia answers. "He designed most of the houses down the street, including this one."

"Wow, that's pretty cool," Frank replies. And he is impressed. No two houses look the same, curves seamlessly blending with natural surroundings, and for their size, that's no mean feat. He recalls writing about a street like this in one of his stories. He hopes it ends better than it did for those residents.

"Daddy built me a scale model of the street," Veronica says. "It's huge. You'll have to come up and look at it sometime, Charlie."

Charlie winces as his fingers dig too deep. *Daddy!* It's like she's from a different time. And this conversation is beyond boring. He sighs under his breath, knowing it won't get any better. As someone kicks him under the table, he lifts his gaze, his mum's eyes waiting for him. "Kay" is the best he can muster.

Patricia spoons a small portion of cream atop her pie, her little finger at a right angle to the others. "You're a lawyer, Sheila, the real estate agent tells me."

As his mum begins to respond, Charlie's eyes draw to Patricia's fingers, adorned with the longest nails he's ever laid eyes on. He studies them, mesmerised almost, wondering how on earth the lady wipes her bottom, and ponders if she might have someone or something that does it for her. They seem the sort.

"—thus the move to the city. Exciting but terrifying."

"Well, if there's anything we can do, anything at all, please sing out." Patricia runs her eyes around the table. And again. "It's a lovely street, so peaceful and orderly. I'm sure you will all be very well received."

Sheila smiles and nods, acknowledging Frank's wide-eyed glance.

"So, what's this book about, Frank?" Nick asks.

Sensing his mother's internal groan, Charlie begins to zone out. He sees his dad's lips moving but pays little attention to the words, knowing he could almost recite them verbatim. He studies the others around the table—their nods, glazed eyes, and the offered grunts that only conjure pity for his father.

As the monologue *finally* ends and the two families continue eating their pie in relative silence, interspersed with infrequent bursts of mundane and awkward conversation, Charlie wishes for the floor to open up. But it doesn't. Instead, he continues pinching at his thigh and squirming in his seat as the Davenports and his mum sip on posh tea from cups Charlie didn't even realise they had. It's unbearable, suffocating, like when he had to go to church for Grandad's funeral, old people he never knew raking their crusty fingers through his hair or their puckered lips attacking from all directions. He eyes his mother, who shows no signs of letting, but his dad looks more than a little edgy.

"Amazing pie," Frank comments. And it is one of the best cherry pies he's tasted, melt-in-the-mouth pastry and full of flavour. "Truly amazing." Frank figures he'd be enjoying it much more without their presence, though, the whole experience sapping his now already low energy reserves. As he catches his son's eye, he offers him a wink and a nudge under the table.

Dad has a plan, Charlie thinks. *I love you, Dad.*

"Certainly enough to give us a second wind," Frank says, hoping the hint lands. "Fuel to finish the job."

"Oh, dear. Look at us taking your time up when you have so much to do." Patricia stands and begins collecting the dishes. "Veronica, did you have a little something to show the Harpers before we go?"

The pie was good, the conversation all but done, and now he will find out what's in the golden pouch, not to mention the stack of red liquorice waiting on the counter. As his mum often tells him, things are never as bad as they first appear—just like the first day at a new school. He hopes. A wave of controlled calm, of order, washes over him as the girl prises the package from the small bag. She places it on the table and begins to unfurl the embroidered cloth.

Hands clasped together, Charlie leans in, letting out an involuntary shudder. *Pegs.* Not just ordinary pegs, though. It's them, the Harpers, as plain as day—his mum's green dress and his dad's pale blue sweater with the beige pants that Charlie hates. Leaning further, he studies the peg version of himself, complete with tiny blue shorts and his favourite white T-shirt.

This is fucked.

Charlie eyes his mum, who in turn eyes Frank before they all turn their attention back to their peg selves, laid out on the kitchen table.

"She makes them herself, cuts and stitches all the fabric," Patricia says. "Isn't she adorable? She saw you the day you came to look at the house, and when she found out you'd got it, she was so excited."

"They're really...wonderful," Sheila says. "How very talented of you, Veronica."

"Thank you."

Veronica hands them out, Charlie offering a grunt as he takes the miniature version of himself. They're actually pretty good, well detailed. He notices the black dot on the right cheek of the makeshift face and runs a finger over his mole. *A bit too good.*

"What does it say on the handkerchief?" Frank asks, arching his neck for a better look.

"The handkerchief is for you to keep," Veronica says. "I made that, too. Can I use your bathroom, please?"

"Of course," Sheila replies, beginning to question her parenting skills. "Upstairs, first on the right."

As Frank starts running his eyes over the far-too-neat writing on the cloth, his face crumples and he offers a half laugh, half sneer. "What's this?" He picks a line from halfway down. "No loud music?"

"That applies to entering the street, too," Veronica says, nearing the staircase.

With her opinion of the girl going up in flames, Sheila joins Frank in inspecting the fabric. An awkward silence ensues, one more palpably volatile than the previous ones, full of glances and high energy. Tension continues notching up as Frank huffs and shakes his head with ever-growing intensity, running his finger down the fabric. "This is some bullshit."

Nick leans in, offering a cough. "Just something to bear in mind, Frank. It's a great street, we just want to keep it that way. A few simple initiatives like this help set us up for a truly harmonious living."

"Rules?"

"We prefer to call them guidelines, Frank," Nick replies.

"Any homeowner would usually have to sign an agreement for such regulations." With her eyebrows knitted together, Sheila leans forward in full lawyer mode. Not that it took years at law school to know such legislation was never scribbled onto a piece of cloth. "Our estate agent, Rebecca, never mentioned anything."

"Oh no, no," Patricia retorts, offering a detestable snicker. "Sorry, Harpers, we're misleading you a little. As Nick said, these are more of a guide to help us all enjoy our time on Melody Drive. It's more of a friendship pact, really, one that all the residents are on board with. We just want to keep the place...decent."

"Residents must mow their lawns between three and four on Sunday afternoons only?" Frank lifts his head, studying the Davenports, looking for signs this may be an elaborate joke played on the new people.

"There's nothing more annoying, I think you'll agree, than the sound of a lawnmower when you are trying to read the newspaper and enjoy your orange juice and croissants." Nick asserts. "This way, it all gets done in one go. It makes perfect sense when you think about it."

Unable to recall the last time he ate a croissant or sipped on orange juice, Frank continues studying the fabric, every now and then breaking the heavy silence with a snicker. "Residents are to attend Sunday service without fail."

"To thank our good Lord for keeping us safe and gracing us the fortune of living in such a harmonious environment." Patricia follows this up with a smile and a gentle nod. "We'll give you a pass this Sunday, what with the house being upside down, but we will expect you after that."

Charlie turns, searching for Veronica. She's been gone a while, and he's keen for the Davenports to leave now. He can almost feel the fire in his father's eyes.

"And what's this bit about a curfew?" Frank asks, his face now set in a permanent state of crinkliness.

"The gates close at seven, and streets are to be clear by nine," Veronica chirps, finally emerging onto the landing. "It helps make people feel safe. We don't want people loitering outside in the deep hours."

Charlie screws up his face, wondering who the hell talks like that. *In the deep hours.*

Drumming his fingers loud on the table, Frank continues reading the lines of notes, his grunts becoming more frequent and pronounced. Sheila picks up on his agitated state and makes her move. "Well, it's been a pleasure," she says, offering a smile and launching into a speed walk towards the front door. "Thank you for the pie and tea."

"They're not unreasonable requests," Patricia comments, leading her family through the corridor behind Sheila. "Just have another looksie at the rules tonight, and I'm sure when the dust settles, so to speak, you'll agree."

"Guidelines, you mean?" Sheila says.

"Beg your pardon? Look, it really doesn't need to be such a big deal. Everyone else is on board, and I'm just as confident you will fit in just fine. For the greater good."

"Chilly out there now," Sheila says, holding the door open, grateful for the embrace of fresh air. Fit in fine. Well received. It's terminology that sends a shudder down her spine.

"Oh, I need those back," Veronica says as she approaches the door. "The peg people. They live in my bedroom with the rest."

"Crazier than a soup sandwich" is one of Charlie's mum's sayings, but it fits like stuffing in a turkey. Something about the girl having a version of his family in her bedroom makes Charlie's skin crawl as he grabs them from the kitchen table and heads back towards the starchiness.

Nick's first out. "Knock if there is anything we can do, won't you?"

"As long as it's before nine, eh?" Frank shouts after him.

Through the narrowing gap in the door, Charlie watches the weird girl putting the peg-Harpers back into her golden pouch. It swings around her waist as she skips across the road, the effect inducing a strange nausea. "Thank god for that," Shelia says as the door clicks shut behind the Davenports. She doesn't know whether to laugh or cry.

"It says our grass must not be over an inch long," Frank mutters. "What the hell have you got us into, Sheila?"

They break into a series of giggles, which escalates to full-blown, eyes-streaming laughter; exhaustion, disbelief, and nerves all playing a part. Over mugs of hot chocolate, they study the embroidered fabric, mocking the rest of the rules and praying the other residents aren't half as creepy as the Davenports.

"No cats or dogs." Charlie reads out.

"Does it say anything about crocodiles?" his dad comments. "Sheila, any of this legal?"

"Of course not." She settles back into the chair, wiping away a tear. "I don't think we should read too much into it. It's obviously a nice neighbourhood, and they just want to keep it that way. And as Patricia indicated, albeit with the silver spoon wedged up her arse, they're just a guide."

"For the greater good," Frank says.

Charlie and his mum smile. "For the greater good."

"And who made her queen of the bloody street anyway?"

"I guess they were just trying to nip things in the bud early," Sheila replies. "Set their expectations. And you can't deny that we've had problems with neighbours before."

"What does this mean?" Charlie comments, running his finger about three-quarters the way down. "No unauthorised guests. Residents are allowed a bubble of five people only."

"It means," Frank says, "that we are in an episode of the bloody twilight zone." He picks up where Charlie left off. "Any guests must be booked in advance and leave the premises, that is, the street, by seven p.m."

Sheila sighs. "I'll have a chat with Rebecca in the morning. I'm surprised she failed to mention any of this malarkey before."

"At the risk of losing a sale?"

"Perhaps she didn't know."

Frank offers a sharp laugh. "Yeah right."

"I know, I know, but I really thought we hit it off. And with all those questions she kept asking, she seemed genuinely on our side." And she did; the tied-back hair and initial hard face that Frank likened to a bulldog chewing a wasp gave way to such warmth and interest.

"If it's any consolation, she had me fooled, too. Could talk the hind legs off a donkey, that one."

Charlie looks at his dad with a look beyond confusion across his face.

"A hell of an anti-climax, eh?" Sheila sighs again, placing a hand across her forehead.

Charlie smiles, taking his opportunity to be an ass. "Things are never as bad as they first appear."

"Shut up, Charlie."

"It's a load of old bollocks," Frank replies. "There's no way I'm setting foot in a bloody church. I think my skin would fall off."

"Me too," Charlie says. "They give me a funny feeling inside."

"Okay, boys. I think we've had enough talk of the Davenports tonight." Sheila drops her shoulders and offers a long exhale. "Let's give them the benefit of the doubt, okay? Positive intentions and all that."

"Bloody nutters," Frank mutters. "All church folk are the same."

Hoping it serves as punctuation to move on, Sheila claps her hands together. "New car on Monday," she says. "Shame it wasn't ready for the weekend, but I'm giddy."

"Show off." Frank winks. "I bet it doesn't have a tape deck like the van, though."

"Bloody hope not," Charlie says.

The Harpers turn in just before nine, with no chance of breaking curfew. There's still much to do, but the visit from the Davenports has left them exhausted and with a bitter taste.

"Did I tell you about my new story idea, son?" Frank perches on the end of Charlie's naked mattress.

"Can it wait until tomorrow, Dad? I'm pooped."

"I guess. You know it's three strikes, and I'm out with Mum, though. You're my only outlet."

"Tomorrow, Dad. Please."

"Fine, fine. Sleep well, bud."

"Night, Charlie," his mum shouts from along the corridor. "Love you!"

"Night, Mum," Charlie yells. "Love you, too."

The lump in Charlie's throat has returned. *In the deep hours.* He takes in the expanse of stars, the night sky much clearer than back home, but it only worsens things. Everything is different, even the room's smell and the height of the ceiling. He flips to his right side, and more for comfort than warmth, pulls the bundle of blankets across, appreciating the familiar scent of the fabric conditioner. It's the first proper chance of missing home. A single tear had rolled down his best friend Max's dirty cheek as they said their goodbyes, a promise pledged to stay in touch, one Charlie knows they'll keep for perhaps a few weeks. They were inseparable, sharing everything, even birthday parties. He bites down on another strap of liquorice but doesn't chew.

So damn quiet.

He closes his eyes, but the silence becomes off-putting, deafening, blood beginning to pump loud in his ears.

Good liquorice, though.

Tomorrow, they'll set up the PlayStation, hopefully on the big screen. *No hum of traffic.* There's a new move he knows his dad will never see coming. *No voices from the street.* They'll probably get takeaway tomorrow. *No meow of a cat or bark of a dog.* He pushes himself up and slides open the window. *Not a sound.* As he settles back into the mattress, staring at the smooth ceiling, his stomach begins to churn, knowing further down the street, a young girl has a peg version of his family in her room. It takes quite some time before he falls into a restless sleep.

Cherry Heaven

Charlie's mum is already downstairs, nibbling on a slice of toast. "Morning, love," she says. She looks pale, and darkness underlines her eyes. "How did you sleep?"

"Did Dad talk to you about the PlayStation?"

"Morning, Mum," she mutters. "And I slept like shit, thanks for asking. But to answer your more important question, yes, and I'm still thinking about it. Maybe if you help him out today, and I mean *really* help, I'll consider it. As long as it doesn't interfere with my shows."

"Thanks. Where is he anyway?"

"Just gone to get some stuff from the van. Do you want some tea and toast?" She's trying her best to be chipper, but her head feels fuzzy, and there's a dull ache behind her eyes.

"Nah, I'm good."

"No, thank you!"

"You're welcome."

"I'm popping into my new office today to get things ready, pretty it up with a few plants and whatnot. I'll pick up some juice and stuff on the way back. Hopefully, you'll have both worked up an appetite by then."

Frank arrives at the back door with his toolbox in one hand, a pie wrapped in a red ribbon in the other, and an envelope wedged in his mouth. He gestures for help with frantic nods of his head.

"Got any liquorice?" Charlie says through the glass. "You can't come in without any liquorice."

As his father's eyes widen, Charlie opens the door, noting the dark circles under them, no doubt from last night's events that also added to his own restless sleep.

"Thanks, Charlie," his father says after letting the envelope drop to the counter.

"Welcome."

The smell floats across, filling the place with mouth-watering wholesomeness and making Charlie's belly rumble. He must admit he's tempted, the seductive colour of the fruit in the centre drawing his stare. *Granny's hair. Granny's hair.* But the smell fills him with yearning. *Dry and curly. Dry and curly.* And that pastry, a perfect gold, like a warm beach.

Frank slides the toolbox onto the table and grabs a knife from the counter. "Cherry again," he says, inspecting the blade bathed in magnificent red. "It's still piping hot. They must have just left it." He makes a strange whimper and takes his first generous bite.

It's too much for Charlie, the urge overwhelming. He doesn't bother with the knife and scoops a handful.

"Charlie!" his mum scolds.

But he's already lost in cherry heaven. It tastes even better than it looks, pastry melting in his mouth, giving way to exquisite warmth that explodes with flavour. It's been an age since he's had good pie, but this, he considers, could be the best he's ever had. "What's that?" he asks his dad, glancing at the envelope as he shoves in another handful.

Sheila's already there, prising it open. "Welcome to the neighbourhood, from number twenty-three."

"Well, there you go," Frank says. "This might just turn out okay, after all."

"Or it could be some attempt at bribery," she replies. "Another nicety to help us fall in line. Christ, it's like something from a bloody novel."

"That reminds me, Sheila, did I tell you about my new story idea?"

"I'm going to shower and then pop into work for an hour or so to get things sorted," she says, ignoring her husband. "Don't each too much pie, boys."

"How much is too much?" Charlie asks, scooping another handful of warmth.

Frank shrugs, carving another generous slice onto a plate. The lyrics of *Bohemian Rhapsody* bouncing around in his head, he familiarises himself with their new home again, at last wandering into the lounge and easing himself into the bay window seat that offers a panoramic view of the street.

"What time is the internet being switched on, Dad?" Charlie follows, dragging a sleeve across his mouth.

"Tomorrow, I think."

"Tomorrow? That's not a frigging time! What am I supposed to do in the meantime?"

"Hell, I don't know, Charlie. Read a book, maybe. Make some peg people."

"That's not even close to being funny." Charlie folds his arms in silent protest. "I'm going to have to play offline, for Christ's sake."

"Oh, poor Charlie. So hard done to. Half an hour, though, and I want you back down here. You're not getting away scot-free."

"Tomorrow, for fuck's sake," Charlie mumbles as he stomps up the stairs. "And ask Mum again about the big TV, will you?"

What Lovely Petunias

Frank chases the remaining crumbs around the plate with his fingers, after a while landing a decent catch and shoving it in. He looks down at his ever-growing belly, part and parcel of the extra writing time, trying to convince himself he doesn't need another slice. Just as he's about to admit defeat and refill his plate, something—someone—catches his eye.

"Shit on a stick."

He offers a quick, paranoid glance behind, half expecting the image to be gone as he turns back to the second-floor window of the house opposite. But she's still there. Unable to tear his eyes away, he takes in her naked form, skin prickling with excitement but also a tinge of danger that she'll turn her head and catch him ogling, a risk he's somehow prepared to take.

"Holy cow."

Usually, he takes pride in turning his head the other way when attractive women pass him on the street, feeling a slight sense of victory, but his eyes are on her like a tractor beam.

Perfection.

He considers what that means. Different for everyone, he supposes.

But she is *his* perfection.

He knows he should turn away, but it's as if there's an invisible devil on his shoulder, holding his head in place. Everything outside the window becomes blurry, out of focus, drifting into insignificance, while she remains as clear as a sunny day. With a stirring in his pants and butterflies in his stomach, he crosses his legs, wincing at the discomfort.

Oh shit! Oh shit!

Impossible to deny; he knows she sees him now. Their eyes are on each other. What is she doing? He considers his next move—pretend to clean the windows, or offer a neighbourly wave, perhaps? Too late for any of that, he decides. Instead, he watches as she runs her right hand across her chest in slow motion, stopping to caress one of her delicious, pert breasts. The other hand moves out of sight, disappearing behind the window baskets, but Frank knows where it's going. The woman opens her mouth and slides her tongue out, bringing it across her top lip.

"Frank."

He snaps his head around, his heart thundering.

"I've been talking to you for ages," Sheila says. "Did you not hear me?"

Placing his hands over the already shrinking pants tent, he says the first thing that comes into his head. "How long do you think our grass is?"

"What?"

Already, he's contemplating what he could say for damage control. "The grass. Is it an inch yet?" Heart pounding, he thinks he's done, caught out.

Sheila leans over him, craning her neck to get a good look up and down the street. "Those baskets are lovely across the road, aren't they?" she comments.

He grimaces, ready for the explosion.

"Are they petunias?" she says.

Heart now in his throat, *Bohemian Rhapsody* still thrumming in his ears; he turns, straining his neck and squinting his eyes for effect. The blind in the window is down. Nothing to see here. "Erm,

I think they might be actually." *Thank god. Oh, thank the bloody lord.* "Yes, petunias."

"Hey, that's number twenty-three," Sheila says, "the one that left the pie."

Frank's stomach drops, and his nuts begin to shrivel. He aches for another slice of pie.

"Alright, I'll be gone a few hours. It will be nice if you finish the house by the time I return."

"You mean it better be."

She nods and smiles. "And be a darling. When you get the chance, go across to number twenty-three and thank them for the welcome, will you?"

"But—but that's a together thing, Sheila. Can't we go later or tomorrow?"

She sighs. "Everything's always left to me to sort out."

"You know I'm not good with—"

"Just do this one thing, okay?" She gives him "the look", not the one of love. "It will make a good impression. Besides, you're the one shovelling it down."

He sighs, holding up his hands in defeat.

"Oh, and I just got off the phone with Rebecca, the estate agent. She said she knew about the guidelines but didn't consider them worth mentioning. It's getting quite common these days, especially within gated communities apparently—just a 'few golden rules to happiness', she called them."

"A few? That fabric's nearly two feet bloody long!"

Sheila shrugs. "I'm off. Now, get busy tidying or get busy—"

"Dying." Frank finishes. "Don't be too long."

A Lovely Gesture

Charlie sets to work helping his dad, trying to make the last few liquorice straps last as long as possible. They're miles better than the ones from home, but he can't imagine ever having the balls to ask the "royals" where they get them. By late morning and the last of them gone, the house resembles a home, and Frank and Charlie afford themselves a rest, perched at the back of the van, kicking their legs in the air.

"Does this place seem weird to you?" Charlie comments.

"It will feel like that for a while, Charlie. Everything's new, and it takes time to settle."

"What about the rules?

"We're good people. I guess the Davenports are just trying to make a point and get us to respect their authoritah!"

"You're too old to do *South Park*, Dad."

"Oy!"

The sound of the engine draws their attention to the road, and they watch in silence as a large black car pulls into the driveway next door. Frank offers an exaggerated nod as a youngish couple emerge, but they either ignore him or fail to see him, disappearing behind the back of the car, emerging seconds later with several shopping bags.

"Howdy neighbours," Frank says. The couple hurry down the

path, offering the slightest of nods on the way past, shopping bags clattering against their legs. "Maybe a little weird," Frank mumbles. "Hey, do me a favour, kiddo. Come over to number twenty-three with me to thank them for the pie."

"Nah."

"What do you mean 'nah?'"

"I mean, I've done my bit. Done what was asked." Charlie jumps down from the edge of the van and offers his father a smile. "Mum never said anything about talking to anyone, so no dice, Daddo."

"I'll pay you."

"You can't afford me; you're a writer. Anyway, I'm off to enjoy what's left of the school holidays."

Laughing, wondering when the kid got so smart, Frank turns his attention to number twenty-three. *Act as if nothing happened. Hell, tell her you were admiring her baskets if she asks.* He glances up and down the street and starts a slow walk over.

Baskets. Baskets. Baskets.

Frank arrives at the door, for a moment considering just lying and telling Sheila there was no answer when he knocked. He wonders if she'd buy it. *Everything's always left to me, Frank.* Approaching footsteps removes the burden of decision. The handle turns.

Frank swallows hard. "Nice baskets," he says as the door opens.

Close up, she's even more alluring, a movie star, all wrapped up in a silver sequined gown like an expensively wrapped present. *Shit. Shit. Shit.* There's not a drop of saliva in his mouth.

"Come in," the woman says, a wry smile creasing her eyes and the bridge of her nose.

Damn, she really is perfect. Perfection. "Oh, I don't want to disturb you, Miss. I just came over to say that Sheila and I really appreciated your lovely gesture. The pie is—was—so good."

"Really? What was so good about it, Frank? Tell me."

He opens his mouth, but unprepared for the question, his mind draws a blank. "It was—fruity."

"But was it fruity *enough*, Frank?" Her voice is sultry, making Frank feel like he's melting.

"Yes, very fruity," is all he can think to say. "Very fruity indeed."

"Well, come in then," she says, extending an arm. "I won't have you standing on my doorstep like this, the neighbours will gossip."

Her grip is warm, her essence that of a summer meadow. *A summer meadow? Fuck's sake, Frank, get a grip.* He can smell cherries, too. *What is wrong with you, man?* But he's at once exhausted and exhilarated, floating in a dreamy haze. He imagines them walking across a soft, green forest floor, sky-punching snow-topped mountains on either side, and the sound of a trickling stream nearby. She brings him in close, her warm flesh on his—

"I saw you looking, Frank."

"Huh?"

"I saw you. Don't deny it."

"Baskets."

"That's what they all say. Have you got room for a little more dessert?"

"Huh?"

The woman leads him upstairs without further small talk. "Don't pretend you don't want this."

Her voice. Her skin. Her smell.

"Petunias, aren't they?" he says, following her up, unable to recall the faces of his family. The sway of her bottom, the touch of her hand, all becoming too much for his circuitry. He catches sight of the bed through the ajar door, knowing he's already lost, his mind blanketed with her heavy-scented fog of far-off and forbidden places. She pushes the door and drags him through. Before he can speak, her lips are on his neck, her tongue exploring his flesh. His body shudders as the woman's nails run across his chest and begin working on the buttons of his shirt.

Frank offers a garbled rasp. "I don't even know your name."

"It's Florence. Now get on the bed, Frank."

And he does.

She's on him fast, their bodies melding into one, no giggling reticence, but exploring each other in ways Frank would describe as pornographic. Sheila often calls him prudish, never the one to take the lead, but he's in the driving seat here, self-deprecating paranoia out the window.

Move over, Frank Harper. Make room for Don Juan.

All thoughts of his family are long gone. He's surrounded by mountains, rolling on soft grass, doing things—depraved things—to the mysterious pie lady of number twenty-three. He feels harder than he can ever remember. Her body is magnificent—flawless, smooth, warm—and with a fragrance that drives him euphoric. He can't get enough.

"Yes, Frank! Fuck me, Frank. Any way you like, Frank."

And he fucks her with as much intensity as he can muster until sweat drips from his forehead and chin. She squirms beneath, offering delicious moans of pleasure that bring him to the verge much sooner than he'd like. She feels and smells like warm pie, and he's insatiable.

Hang in there, Frank, he tells himself, but he's so close. *What the—*

"Meow."

There's a fucking cat on the bed! "There's a cat on the bed."

"It's just Archie."

"But you're not allowed cats. It's in the rules."

"Times change, Frank."

"Huh?"

"Just fuck me, Frank!"

Brushing its rear end against Frank's thigh, the cat plants itself on a patch of duvet beside Florence's head. Frank gives it a hiss, and it hisses back. *Oh, Christ, I'm coming.* He digs his teeth into his lip to try and delay, but it's no good, his body erupting into a series of spasms as he continues eyeballing the moggy. *Oh shit. Shit on a stick.*

Beneath him, Florence moans and squeals with pleasure. "Oh, you little fucker, Frank!"

Sucking in the spicy air, shaking some of the sweat from the end of his nose, Frank drops next to her into the damp sheets, wild heart pounding.

Not once has he come close to doing anything like this before.

He would even be so bold as to say he hasn't even thought about it. But self-esteem evades as the haze lifts, the realisation kicking in of what has just happened. *I'm such a prick. What the fuck? What the fuck?* The now clear images of his wife and son flash in his head as the black cat saunters across the pillow, eyeing him with disapproval.

"You can let yourself out," she says. "See you again soon, Frank."

Swings and Things

Pacing up and down the carpet and carving multiple tracks, Frank intends to tell Sheila as soon as she gets home. He clasps his hands behinds his back, running off a thousand poor excuses in his head. Rip off the bandage. That's what they say, but he's doubtful if that also applies to fucking someone else.

Oh shit. Shit. Shit. Shit.

He imagines his life crumbling. Shaking his son's hand, a kiss if he'll let him. *See you on Saturday, son.* A tear falls down his cheek as he pictures himself picking up his cases, Sheila unable to look him in the eye, her face raw and red. He wonders where he'd go, alienated from all his friends by countless weeks locked in a room, writing his stupid fucking book. "What have I done?"

"Dad?"

"Charlie." Frank turns, hoping he manages to blink the tear away. He swallows hard. "You good, son?"

"Fine."

"I love you, Charlie. You know that. More than life itself."

"Yeah, alright, Dad. Calm down. I just came down for the last of the cheesy twists."

"Yeah, of course. Okay, son."

Frank watches the back of his son's head disappear into the kitchen, followed by the familiar creak of the snack cupboard door.

He considers it a noise he'll soon be pining for from the confines of some poxy bedsit. This is brand new territory. Terrifying. No secrets. It's what they agreed: everything out in the open as soon as they hooked up, nothing insurmountable.

Stupid fucking pie.

He snaps his head towards the window at the sound of the music.

Shit! Shit! Shit!

The room spins. He feels heavier, feet sinking into the carpet as though it was marshy ground. His fingers ache as he coils his fists even tighter, heart pounding as he watches and waits.

She had a cat. That's not allowed.

Frank shudders as he eyes the van into the driveway, music blaring.

"Is that Mum?" Charlie shouts from the kitchen. "Thank god. There's nothing to eat."

Feeling dizzy and lightheaded, Frank ducks behind the window, waiting for the music to stop and the creak of the van door. *Am I going to do it now? Make her a cup of tea and then tell her?* He takes another peek, but no movement. He can hardly breathe, as though something is wrapping around his chest. *Hey, love, how was your day? Good. Good. Hey, I made you a nice cuppa. But...I fucked one of the neighbours. Shit!*

"Charlie, why don't you go out to play?"

"Out to play? What does that even mean?" Charlie screws his face up. "And why are you hiding? Are we going to scare Mum? Cool!"

Frank hears his wife's voice. She's on the phone. Lord Christ and saviour, this is unbearable. "Go play, Charlie. There's a park down the road—swings and things."

"Swings and things? Have you had a stroke, Dad?"

"What about that young girl from down the road?"

"Peg girl?"

Frank takes his son's arms and pushes him towards the doorway. *Just go away, Charlie.* "It's creative. You like to write; it's just the same."

"No, it isn't." Marching back upstairs with his paltry half-bowl of powdery cheesy twists, Charlie lets out a dramatic sigh. "World's gone mad."

The music ceases. The car door opens.

Shit on a stick. Shit on a stick.

Frank takes a nosy to see his wife stepping out. *You've got to be fucking kidding.* "No, no, no." He blinks hard, but Florence is still there, breasts pressed against the upstairs windowpane of the house opposite, lips to the glass.

"Fuck off. Fuck off." He flicks his wrist towards her but turns it into a wave as Sheila catches him through the window. He watches his wife's forehead crinkle, eyeing him as though he's just absconded from the funny farm. She begins to turn, and once again, Frank's balls draw into his chest as he follows her stare.

Just baskets. Petunias.

As Frank breathes a sigh of relief, he sees an old man striding towards his wife, a frail arm in the air. He guesses the fucker is on his way to complain about the music his wife had blaring. Attempting to eavesdrop on the conversation, he moves towards the glass, eyes on the baskets across the road. There's a flashback to that room, the intoxicating smell, the softness of her flesh, the irresistible taste of her skin, and the warmth like freshly baked pie.

Fuck, Frank, get a grip!

As muted voices fade, Frank peeks out to see his wife and the old man crossing the street. Momentum all but gone, he watches them make their way up the path of a house to the right.

Was I really going to do it? Right here, right now. He begins to doubt it very much.

In the kitchen, waiting for the kettle to boil, he studies the photographs on the fridge—last year's holiday to Greece, considering it the last time it will just be the three of them, Charlie insisting on bringing a friend from now on. But realisation hits, that might not be the reason at all. He traces a finger across Sheila's smile, guilt gnawing at his insides.

It was all too easy, he thinks. Dream-like almost. "I'm so sorry, love. I'm truly, truly sorry."

The knock on the door snaps him from melancholy, and he crouches behind the couch, in no mood to entertain. An almost immediate thumping from above puts pay to his attempts at stealth. "I'll get it, Dad."

"Fuck's sake, Charlie." Frank straightens and clears his throat in preparation for dealing with another human outside of his unit.

"It's another pie," Charlie yells, emerging from the hallway.

"Who was at the door?"

"Nobody, just the pie."

"Just the pie?"

"Just the pie."

The smell prompts more images in his head and that familiar haziness. He's lost again. Back in that bedroom, the heat, the moistness, the hot breath against his neck. He feels the stirring in his pants. *Oh, Florence, yes.* There's a voice behind her bedroom door, but he can't make it out. *Yes! Yes! Yes!* She's pinning him down, licking him from head to toe. That voice, though. Her tongue flicks at one of his nipples, her fingers squeezing at the other. The door creaks. She wraps her mouth around his firmness, doing things with her tongue. Already, he's close. The door creaks again. It's Charlie. "Dad, I said, why do people keep giving us pie?"

Frank shakes his head, snapping himself from the dream-like state and back into the reality of the nightmare. "I don't know, son. Just being friendly, I guess." He takes the pie from Charlie and puts it on the counter—a work of art, flawless pastry surrounding a deep well of red fruit. Even with the knot in his stomach, he knows he won't be able to resist.

"Do you want a slice?"

Charlie shakes his head. "Nah, I'm on a diet."

"A diet?"

He smiles. "Not really. Mum promised me donuts. I'll get the stuff in from the car."

As Charlie disappears, on the hunt for his raspberry glaze, Frank grabs the still cherry-stained knife and slices through the pie. That smell. That crust. That vibrant, coloured fruit. *What's this?* He plunges his fingers through the cherry juice, pinching at the small, sealed plastic bag.

"Jeez, Dad, use a fork at least," the boy says as he comes through with two loaded carrier bags.

Frank forces a smile, scrunching the small bag into his pocket, cursing as cherry juice smudges across the fabric. "It's okay, Charlie, I'll unpack."

"I didn't offer." Charlie holds a donut in each hand, a big smile splitting his face in two. "Catch ya."

As soon as Charlie's through the doorway, Frank digs the plastic from his pocket, fishing out the note inside.

Frank, have a slice of cherry pie and then pop over for a slice of something else. You've got ten minutes, or it will be more than fruit that spills.

With no intention of jumping to her call, Frank sits on the stool, contemplating his next move and running a hand through his hair. *Fuck! Fuck! Fuck!* The thought of her getting there first, though—*spilling*—tightens the knot in his stomach. He winces as he uncurls his toes from the metal of the footrest. *I'm such a bastard! A fucker!* He sticks his hand into the pie and brings warmth to his lips. Just as amazing as he remembers. Shovelling in another mouthful, he begins to cry. Not a tear or two, but a full-blown sob that he stifles with a tea towel. Red juice hangs from his chin.

You fucking weak man!

He inhales so deep it hurts, counts to three, and lets the breath go. Again. Again. But there's still pressure, an invisible force against his chest, a heavy blanket of ever-increasing claustrophobia. Tossing the cherry and tear-stained towel into the sink, he jumps from the chair and heads for the front door. He sticks his head out, checking to see if the street is still empty and that there's no sign of his wife. Satisfied, he marches across the road to number twenty-three and gives the door a light tap, nervous anger building as he shivers on the doorstep.

Dressed in a lacy black number, Florence opens the door, her nose wrinkling in that same irresistible way. "Come in, Frank."

"I'm not staying," he says, stepping towards the warmth, that same intoxicating scent filling his nostrils.

More Than You Can Chew

"That was splendid, Frank, even better than this morning."

Frank rolls over, reaching for his briefs, the ones with the fountain pens on that Sheila bought him last Christmas. *I'm a bastard.* "I can't do this anymore, Florence."

"New rules," Florence says. "Each time I put a pie out, you have twenty minutes to come over. No more notes."

"Florence, I'm a married man. I have a child."

"Don't be late." She gives him that wry smile and blows him a kiss.

"Are you listening to me?"

The cat meows a reply as Florence turns over, bringing the blankets over her naked shoulders.

Frank fumbles at his belt, scanning the floor for the rest of his clothes. *God damn it! What's wrong with me?* As he threads an arm through his shirt sleeve, he peers through the window to the street below to see his wife making her way down the old man's path. "Oh fuck! This was the last time, Florence. The last time."

"Bye, Frank. Must rest now."

Almost stumbling down the stairs, Frank clatters into a picture of two old people on the wall. Assuming them to be Florence's parents, weathered and toothless, he straightens the frame and navigates the remaining steps. *Fuck. Fuck, Fuck.* He holds the door ajar and checks to ensure Sheila is out of sight. Satisfied, he makes his run across the road and down the side passage of the house.

Stealthily marching between the brickwork and the overgrown hedgerow, Frank considers what a big fucking mess he's got himself into, knowing the longer it goes on, the further past the point of no return he'll get. He grips the bricks at the end of the small passage and shimmies himself around, pushing himself flat against the back of the house. *Fucking idiot.* He sidesteps to the glass patio doors and arches his neck for a quick look inside. *Fucking arsehole!* She's in the kitchen, emptying the shopping that he didn't. He takes a deep breath, counts down from three, and slides the doors open. "Bit of a mess out there. Needs a damn good tidy and prune."

"Why wasn't this unpacked? It was just left here."

Franks lets out a dramatic sigh. "He hasn't just left it, has he? Why, the little bugger. I'll go and have a—"

"Just leave it," she says, deep lines carved across her forehead. "I'll do it like I do everything else around here."

Sensing her tone and body language, knowing words will be redundant, Frank offers them anyway. "Here, let me sort it, love."

"It's fine." His wife slams each item on the counter, sending a puff of white from the packet of flour.

"Please, love, let me help."

"I said it's fine!"

Frank recoils at his wife's tone, knowing this little scene is far from over. On eggshells, he treads, making his way across and resting a hand on her shoulder.

She flops onto the stool, burying her head into her hands. "Haven't had a migraine for as long as I can remember, but this one's a doozy."

Frank runs a towel under the cold tap, then presses it across his wife's forehead as she tilts her head back. "Just take it easy." He opens the Ibuprofen and pours her a glass of water.

"Thank you," she says. "I love you. I'm sorry."

"I love you, too," he says, planting a delicate kiss on her lips. "You taste like ginger."

"And you taste like cherries. Where's Charlie?"

"Upstairs. What did the old boy want?"

"Who?"

"The guy you were talking to."

She waves a hand, grimacing as she nurses her skull with the other. "Just some legal advice on something. Word gets around quick, I guess." She sighs and drops her shoulders. "Courtesy of Rebecca, no doubt."

"You don't look well."

"I need to lie down."

"I'll give you a hand."

"I'm fine." She tilts her head further back and swallows the tablets. "Honestly."

"Can I get you anything?"

"A time machine, maybe," she says, navigating the doorway. "Ever get the feeling you've taken on more than you can chew?"

Frank watches her disappear around the corner before angrily shovelling more pie into his mouth. *More than you can chew.*

"What's wrong with *her*?" Charlie says as he enters the kitchen. "She looks terrible."

"Shh. Migraine."

"What the hell have you done to that pie?"

Frank looks down into the dish, studying the carnage of what was once something so beautiful. "I fucked it, son. I fucked it good and proper."

"Jeez, a bit dramatic, Dad." Charlie grabs a spoon and begins chasing one of the cherries around the dish. "I'm bored. Do you want to do something?"

Absolutely not. "What did you have in mind?"

"I don't know. I'm just hoping the bloody internet kicks in today." Charlie gets his catch, but just as he's about to spoon it into his mouth, there's a knock on the door. They both snap their heads towards it, sinking into withdrawal mode.

"See who it is, Charlie."

"Why don't you?"

"Please, son. I'll make it up to you."

"I have to do everything around here." Charlie sighs as he eases to the floor. "Probably more pie for you, fat boy."

Once again, the sight of the back of his son's head, one he's taken for granted for so long, fills Frank with sadness. He bites his lip, feeling the ship sinking.

Dolls Are for Kids

"Veronica."

"I brought these for you, Charlie; I know you like them." The girl hands over a paper bag full of red liquorice straps.

"Thanks."

"Mummy said I should come over."

"My mummy—mum—said the same," Charlie utters. "Said I should go over to yours, I mean."

"Well, come on then."

She doesn't wait for any acknowledgement, she just walks across the road, humming a strange tune. Obedient, Charlie follows the girl, noting the familiar stiff posture and how the girl's nose tilts a little towards the sky. He mimics her but soon gets paranoid that someone might be watching.

"Are you settling in okay, Charlie?"

"I guess. I dunno." Nothing but the swirl of the sprinkler system as they walk across the road. No music. No TVs blaring, lawnmowers roaring, or hammers hammering. No people peopling. "It's just so quiet."

"We like it like this."

The breeze blows over him, bringing the scent of bubble gum and something else he can't quite put his finger on. "Doesn't it get boring?"

"Only boring people get bored, Charlie. Come on."

She leads him to the grandest-looking house down the street. "Whoa." Huge double doors await at the end of a long path, extravagant marble water features on either side, only outdone by the partially sunken concrete sculptures that look to Charlie like something from a science fiction movie. He follows her up the impressive steps, observing the thickness of the doors as they begin to move inwards.

"How the hell is—" He notices her finger pressed against a small panel. "Cool."

"Biometric. Daddy did it all. He's very clever."

Inside, the house is just as impressive. "State-of-the-art," Charlie's dad would say. Big home theatre with rows of seating, a giant chandelier spinning rainbow light across the room, and indoor water features leaking coloured water down mosaic walls. "Holy crap."

"No swearing in public, Charlie. That's number twenty-seven. Didn't you all read the fabric? You must."

"Crap? Is that a swear word? Crap?"

"Can you please refrain from using it, Charlie?" She turns, hands on her hips and lips pursed. "We'll put that down to experience, but from now on, I'll have to give you an official warning. Your mum's already on strike one."

"My mum? What for? What are you talking about?"

"Her punishment for the music. Next time it will be the naughty corner." Veronica offers an exaggerated tut as though she shouldn't have to explain. "Sheila was told, and as an adult, she should know better."

"My mum's a lawyer."

"My mum's a traveller and—"

"Where does she go?"

She sighs and leans in. "You probably know it is a gypsy, but she hates that word. Mum's and traveller and can break your back by standing on a crack." Veronica sticks her tongue out. "Come on. I want to show you something."

"Wait." Charlie inches forward, doing a double take to ensure his eyes aren't playing tricks. To the left of the enormous fireplace, framed by the thickest of timber mantles, there appears to be a young child facing the wall, dressed in corduroy pants and a chequered shirt. Like the removal guy, the baseball cap is turned the wrong way, a tuft of brown hair spilling from the closure at the back. He turns to Veronica with a "please explain" look written across his face.

"It's just art, Charlie. Daddy named it 'The Naughty Corner.'"

Thinking he might live to regret it, Charlie makes his way over to the sectioned corner of the room, the large gold plate above affirming it as The Naughty Corner in fancy embossed writing. "He's not real, is he?"

Veronica snickers. "No, that would be weird."

But as Charlie closes in, catching sight of the phone sticking out the boy's pocket, and even the tiny laced-up shoes, he thinks it's already a step beyond weird. As he leans in, he half expects the boy to turn around, a playful prank to trick the new kid. A little shudder runs down his spine. "He's got no—"

"Shh," Veronica says, bringing a finger to her lips. "Arnold gets upset if you say anything." And with a giggle, she's on her way. "Come on, follow me."

Without hesitation, Charlie begins backing away from the faceless wooden boy called Arnold, knowing there's every chance he'll have a visitor tonight once the lights go out. "I like the kind of art where the dogs play pool."

"Come."

Tracking her ascent up the magnificent spiral staircase, Charlie keeps glancing down towards the boy in the corner, just in case. "Wait up." Ahead of him, Veronica walks with purpose, not like a child. "Come on, will you?" she says, disappearing through an archway. Charlie follows without knowing what to expect, chomping on one of the red straps with a bit too much aggression.

"Holy cow," he says, spittle spraying ahead as he crosses the threshold to her room.

The bedroom is four times the size of his, large widescreen TV on the far wall and enormous bookcases lining the others. It's the giant table in the centre that grabs his attention, though, a huge sprawling model of the street taking up almost every square inch of its surface. The gardens, houses, cars, trees, so much intricacy, as if he's looking down on the street from the clouds.

"It's all perfectly to scale," Veronica says. "Took Daddy ages."

Charlie leans over, inspecting the top-floor window of the nearest house, running his eyes over the wooden replica furniture. He follows the stairs down to the living room, eyeing the four peg people scattered around the open plan kitchen and lounge. "Now, this is art."

"No, Charlie, this is security."

"I've heard of doll houses, but—"

"Dolls are for kids, Charlie!" Veronica snaps, her face puckered with rage.

"Pegs then. Whatever you want to call them." He moves on to the next house, inspecting the different layout, impressed. "Where are the people in this one? I mean, the peg people?"

"They're away at the moment, back Tuesday."

"Huh?"

"Did you not read the rules, Charlie? Residents must book vacation time at least three months in advance." She shakes her head and offers another sigh. "Your family must start respecting the rules. It's for your own good."

"So, you know where everyone is at all times?"

"We like to think so."

"That's creepy."

"Not at all. It means everyone is accounted for. Rules bring safety, an order to things."

"As I said. Creepy." He shifts from house to house, noting the uniqueness of each of the pegs. He sees beards, moustaches, and even tiny glasses. Padding has been shoved inside some miniature outfits, Charlie guessing to represent the meatier residents. So many questions fill his head as he tries to decide if this is weirder than the naughty kid downstairs with no face.

"Listen to this." Veronica smiles, flicking a switch on the wall that prompts a tinny voice from one of the nearby houses.

Charlie follows the sound, trailing a finger across the smooth road with the white-dotted marker running across its centre. Half-way down, the voice becomes a little clearer, and he narrows it down to the living room of number thirty-two. He presses his ear against a sidewall.

—rescuers tried to assist, but the woman died at the scene. Witnesses say they saw two youths—

Veronica flicks the switch and offers another smile. "Cool, isn't it?"

"Was that a TV?"

"Yes." She flicks another switch prompting the same tinny sound from the house next door.

—second incident in the area in the past few weeks—

"I don't understand."

"You really didn't read the rules, did you? Number forty-two states that residents must tune into both the lunchtime and evening news during the weekend and at least one during the working week. It ensures awareness of the dangers in the world, Charlie. How bad it is outside those gates. A reminder, if you like, of why community matters and how residents are better off because of it."

"You listen? To the houses? Their conversations, too? Our conversations?"

She nods. "Sometimes. Clever Daddy set it all up. As I said, this is no doll house, Charlie. This is a very adult toy."

A toy? "Do people know—that you listen?"

"Not at first. We ease them into it." She sighs as if bored of the conversation. "It's difficult for them to take on at first, but they all come around over time. It's for the greater good."

Charlie follows the street around to number twenty-four. He eyes his peg dad in the kitchen. "Where's my peg person? And Mum's?"

"Well, you're here in my house, silly, and your mum is upstairs with a headache for her misdemeanour."

"Mister what?"

She sighs. "The music she had blaring from the car."

In the small version of his parents' room, Charlie locates the peg in the green dress laid across the bed. He opens his mouth to say something, but words fail him.

"Your mum's headache will worsen, but it will be gone on Sunday, providing she behaves. If she does, I can take her out of the naughty corner, and Mummy can make her better."

"This is fucking nuts! And what are all the other switches for?"

"This is your last warning, Charlie. I'll give you the benefit of the doubt as you're just a kid."

"My parents won't like this one bit."

"I insist this will be our secret, Charlie. For now, anyway." She moves towards him, inching a half step at a time. "They'll find out eventually, but best let them settle in for now."

Those lips. Those eyes. That skin.

"Can we agree on that, Charlie? That it's for the greater good."

Charlie takes a step back, but there's nowhere else to go. He looks to the doorway, knowing he could make it if he wanted to, but the smell of her bubble gum and that other mysterious scent wafts towards him, wrapping him in a cloud of sweet rapture. Only a few feet between them, Charlie's left leg buckles. Something's happening, something weird.

Oh shit. Oh shit.

She's directly in front of him now, the model street behind almost a blur.

"I've never kissed a girl," he says. "Only my arm."

She smiles, reaches deep into his pocket, and brings out one of his raspberry straps. "Nobody likes this place at first, but people always come around. Because people are like sheep, Charlie, eventually just becoming part of the herd."

Charlie swallows hard but is unable to dislodge the lump.

"And we are good shepherds, Charlie. We keep them safe." She slides one end of the strap into his mouth and brings her face towards his.

Part of him wants to scream, but the other part—

"Can you smell it, Charlie?"

Bubble gum. And something sweet yet spicy. He presses the back of his head against the bookcase, blood pulsating in his ears.

"You can, can't you?" She wraps her lips around the other end of the strap and starts sliding her face towards his, stopping halfway and biting down. "I know what you do in that bathroom, Charlie. Naughty things."

"Huh?"

"Naughty, naughty things."

"No, no, I don't." The unchewed raspberry strap lodges in his throat, prompting a cough. "I haven't." He croaks, following up with a nervous cough. "I haven't."

She unzips his fly and lets out a giggle.

"What are—"

"It's okay, Charlie. It can be another little secret."

Charlie opens his mouth, but no words emerge. He studies her face, everything outside of it melting, spilling down the side of his vision like water down the walls. Her smell continues to wrap around him, a heavy blanket of mystery. Letting out another shudder, he feels his other leg giving way. "I don't think—"

"Shh," Veronica says.

"I think this might be inappropriate."

"Oh, Charlie, you're so—new."

He tries to distract himself, something he's learned to do in times of anxiety and stress. "It's my friend Max Flynn's birthday, the day before mine. Saturday. We were going to have a joint party until Mum got the new job. It was going to be cool."

"This is a community, Charlie. We look after each other. What happens inside these gates brings us closer together."

"He got an early birthday present yesterday. He sent me a picture of it."

"You'll be amazed at some of the things that go on, Charlie. Quite a shock to the system at first, but it's all for the greater good."

"I think he sent it to me just to make me jealous. New PC, top of the range, fully customised."

"For the greater good, Charlie."

"I must admit, I was quite envious when I first saw it." *But you didn't get this, Max, did you? You didn't fucking get this!* "The processing speed is out of this—"

Veronica smiles.

Words jumble in his head, beginning to run into each other. He opens his mouth again and leaves his jaw hanging. He tries to steal his glance away, but her green eyes, now offering unfathomable depth, draw him into a strange new carnival world of bubble gum hills and rollercoasters, *Bohemian Rhapsody* thumping from an invisible speaker system. He's climbing up the rickety track towards a pink-coloured sky, Veronica in the carriage next to him, blowing the biggest bubble he's ever seen. As the carriage creeps closer and closer towards the top, anticipation builds, his body tingling, his skin crawling. Up they go. Up. Up. Up. So close now. He feels dizzy and light-headed.

They're approaching the drop.

Three.

He bites his lip.

Two.

Inhales.

One.

They've reached the top.

Fireworks everywhere, lighting up the valley, flashes of brilliant white light filling his vision. Roman candles, fountains, spinners—you name it, no expense spared for this extravaganza. Charlie reaches for the safety rail, both legs buckling this time, his body crumpling into a ball of pleasure. At last, the rollercoaster levels out, brakes squealing, bringing them into a queue of faceless children waiting for their ride. Fireworks fizzle into dampness as the safety bar raises.

He's back, standing in Veronica's bedroom where the peg people live, his John Thomas now pointing south.

"Happy Birthday for Sunday, Charlie," Veronica says.

Whatever cloaked him begins to lift, and only the smell of bubble gum remains. Clarity returns, as does the familiar older-than-years starchiness of Veronica's face. He fumbles at his fly, grimacing at the wetness around the fabric. *Weird. Weird. All of it, just plain fucking weird.* "What did you mean before?" he says.

"What do you mean now?"

"You said your mum is a gypsy...er...traveller."

"Isn't that clear enough?"

"But—but they don't have flouncy hair, sharp nails, and smell like candy. And they don't live around here."

"You have a lot to learn, Charlie."

"You're nuts. Loco!"

"Charlie, Charlie, Charlie. Remember your family is on our watch list for now. It would be a real shame if your mum took a turn for the worse."

"I have to go."

"Bye, Charlie. Our little secret, remember." She wipes her hand down the front of her dress. "If you tell, I'll say it was all you. Boys are stronger than girls, so who will they believe?"

He grabs the banister and launches himself downstairs.

"'Bye, Charlie," Mr. and Mrs. Davenport shout from the kitchen. But he's already out the door, grateful for the breeze until it reminds him of his damp patch.

It can be another little secret.

Charlie marches across to his house, snapping his head left and right, feeling overwhelming relief as he wraps his fingers around their front door handle. He turns, the stillness of the street even more haunting and making his skin crawl. Veronica's still visible at her window, waving, smiling. What he wouldn't give to hear the sound of screaming kids. Hell, even the bloody roar of a lawnmower or two would be welcome. He opens the door, wishing more than anything else he was stepping into his old house.

Cosmic

"Charlie?"

Charlie freezes on the second step of the staircase. "Yup. Is mum still upstairs?"

"I'd leave her be, son." His dad's voice is morose from somewhere in the next room. "She's in bed with a cold compress."

"I'm sure she'll be okay." *I know she'll be okay.*

"How's Veronica?"

"Fine. I'm going upstairs for a shower."

"In the middle of the afternoon? Are you feeling alright, son?"

"Cosmic."

Afraid more questions will follow, and that somehow his father may bring his dirty little secret to light, Charlie takes the stairs two at a time, pausing at the top of the landing to peek through the ajar door. In the relative darkness, he can only just make out his mum's silhouette on the bed. "Love you, Mum," he whispers, and waits for a response that doesn't come.

Your family is on our watch list for now.

He tiptoes across to his room and grabs clean clothes from his cupboard and the towel from the bed, sighing as he closes the bathroom door behind him.

I've seen what you do in that bathroom, Charlie. Naughty things.

He ducks into the water and spends quite some time there,

reflecting on events.

Naughty, naughty things.

He shudders, adrenaline rushing through him—excitement, fear, shame, guilt, concern for his mother and the knowledge that things can never be right here.

I insist this will be our secret, Charlie.

I can take her out of the naughty corner, and Mummy can make her better.

But given the chance to ride that rollercoaster again, he knows he'll be unable to resist.

After a longer-than-usual shower, he begins towel-drying himself in front of the mirror, studying the child looking back, reality embedding itself.

If you tell, I'll say it was all you.

The room feels tiny, the walls closing in around him.

Boys are stronger than girls.

He grabs his pants, wrestling them over his still-damp legs, almost spilling over the side of the bath.

All you. All you. All you.

Snapping at his shirt, he slides his arms through and ducks his head under the hem. So damn hot. Halfway through the neck hole, his head gets stuck, and he begins to panic.

He reaches for the cold tap, tearing his glance away from the mirror and flicking water into his face. *Break your back by standing on a crack.* The starkness is jolting but does the job, plunging him back into an only slightly more bearable reality. He takes a few deep breaths, removes his head from the neck of the T-shirt, and retreats to the safety of his room, opting for an unworn button-up shirt. Then, he falls into bed and into a restless mid-afternoon sleep, where he dreams the strangest dream he's ever had.

Father and Son Time

Charlie plays a game, trying to dribble a pea around the brown food without touching it. He thought they were on for Chinese, and he's wearing his disappointment on his sleeve.

"You're quiet, son."

"So are you, Dad."

Frank nods.

"Dad."

"Son."

"Do you like it here?"

Frank lifts his stare from the gristle on his plate, considering the question with care. They've not even been here a full day yet, and somehow he's managed to destroy his marriage and ruin a six-week diet that saw him drop over thirty pounds. Add to that his wife being upstairs with what he would consider, if he was superstitious, to be a premonitory migraine, her first in almost a decade. He shrugs and lets out a sigh. "You?"

Charlie wants to tell. He wants to spill it all. It's like an aching inside, something heavy in his chest that he's sure would feel better out than in, like a fart.

Sometimes, we listen.

He studies his father's pale face, sunken eyes, and the new lines across his forehead, wondering where the joker has gone, the clown without the filter. With a shrug, he returns to chasing the pea around his plate, replaying Veronica's words in his head: "Boys are stronger than girls." But he doesn't feel strong at all. In fact, he feels as weak as piss.

They eat the rest of their dinner in silence, minds switching back and forth from the euphoria of recent experiences to memories of a more predictable time before Melody Drive. Each taking a generous helping of the cherry pie through to the lounge, they spend the evening watching comfort shows in front of the big TV.

"I'm going up, Dad."

"It's only eight."

"Yeah, I know. Just a bit tired." But even in a fresh bed, he doubts sleep will come. "Can I check on Mum?"

Frank shakes his head. "She's in a bad way. Frightened to death of being sick for her first day on Monday." He finds himself envying his son, not a care in the world, no burden to carry, no anxiety or stress, just floating from day to day in his little bubble of predictability.

"I'm sure she'll be fine tomorrow."

"Well, thanks, Doctor Harper."

"Night, Dad."

"Sweet dreams, Charlie."

As his son disappears through the archway, Frank returns to gazing at the imagery on the television, the words he knows before the characters orate them. Nothing unexpected, nothing out of the ordinary. He gets up once for more pie, finally calling it a night just before eleven, grabbing a blanket from the airing cupboard and curling up on the couch, figuring he might need to get used to sleeping alone.

Twice for god's sake. How the fuck did I let it happen twice?

He's going to tell her. He has to tell her. Will he tell her? He doesn't know anymore. As sure as shit, it will hit the fan at some point.

Twenty minutes to come over. No more notes.

Frank lies in the darkness for quite some time, wondering how the hell he's going to get out of this hole.

Just Another Day in Melody Drive

From his bedroom window, Charlie watches the cars begin to leave the street, the ball of his hand crunching at the sleep in the corner of his left eye. Silver and black, no other colours, just a convoy of blandness on their merry way to thank God for god knows what. But it feels like a small reprieve, as though some of the heaviness is leaving with them. He spots the Davenports' car, big and sleek, the hum of its engine reminding Charlie of a predatory cat. Imagining Veronica staring up at him from behind the tinted-black passenger window, wearing that smile, beautiful but sickly, he lets out a little shudder.

Boys are stronger than girls.

He picks his clothes from the floor, dresses, and checks his phone to find two messages from his best friend, Max. The first one reads: *Look at my setup, bro. Isn't she sexy?*

There's an attached picture of the corner of his friend's room, the glass desk basking in stunning purple lighting from the new gaming system. The effect should be warming, but it leaves Charlie feeling cold and longing for his old life. Beneath, the other text reads: *Looks even better for real. Wish you were here, Charlie.*

Charlie punches the keys. *I hate it here. It sucks!*

He deletes his text and throws the phone on his bed, hating his mum more than anything else in the world. She was all smiles and teeth when she relayed news about the job, trying to win him over, skipping the bit about ripping his life apart. He paces around the room, throwing a few kicks at the hem of the bed.

Everything feels different, the fleeting excitement of travelling somewhere new, all the singing and laughter, nothing but a distant memory. He clenches his fists and stifles a scream, letting the anger ride through him until there's only a residual nagging that nothing will ever be the same again.

"It's not fair. It's not fucking fair."

After composing himself, he tiptoes towards his parents' room and peeks through the door, the sight of the made bed providing a glimmer of hope. "Mum? Mum, are you up?" It's the scent coming from downstairs, though, that adds extra bounce to his step as he takes the steps two at a time. "Mum?" Something normal. Something routine. Something wholesome and kiddish, even.

Pancakes.

Following his nose, Charlie finds her in her dressing gown, towel around her head, shuffling a pan across the stove.

"You feeling better, Mum?"

She turns, colour back in her cheeks, but Charlie can tell something is off. "Much better." She offers not so much a smile but a forced flicker. There's an atmosphere, a post-storm cooling, but Charlie didn't hear any raised voices or doors slamming.

"You sure? No more headache?"

She shakes her head, offers another flicker, and returns to the pancakes.

Frank lifts his head from the newspaper to acknowledge his son's presence. "What are your plans, spud?"

"Well, even though we're not at church today, I started the day with a little prayer wishing for the internet to finally be switched on. Oh, and for world peace, of course."

"Do you fancy coming with me into town later?" His mum slides a plate stacked with misshapen, discoloured pancakes across the table. "I just need a few pieces for work, a couple of skirts and whatnot. There'll be something in it for you."

"Raspberry glaze?"

She nods and smiles. "Sure."

"Can you pass the syrup and anything else we've got that I can pour over this disaster, please?" Charlie offers his mum a wink to soften the blow.

Weighing up all the pros and cons, Charlie considers his mum's offer. On the one hand, he hates standing outside the changing rooms, trying to make it look like he's not staring into the cubicles even though he isn't. And on the other hand, he would be away from here for a while. But then there's the fact that he hates being out with his parents in public, not to mention the whiff of piss you get when walking past shop doorways. Crowds and noise bother him, too, but on this occasion, he thinks it could be a welcome relief from the overbearing quietness of the street.

A dilemma for sure.

"Well, don't fall over yourself with enthusiasm," his mum says, placing the syrup and Nutella on the table.

Charlie opens his mouth to speak, but Veronica pops into his head. She's standing opposite him, the length of a liquorice strap separating them, her green eyes burning into his. His stomach twists, his skin crawls, and his heart pounds. Fear? Yes. An ominous sense of dread? Yes. An overwhelming feeling of paranoia and guilt? Tick. But also an overwhelming urge to climb aboard that roller-coaster one more time.

"Charlie!"

"Huh?"

"Your mum's talking to you."

Charlie turns his stare to see his mum leaning against the table, eyes wide, a hand on her hip.

"Well, are you coming or what?" she says.

"I'll think I'll stick around, Mum. See if my prayers will be answered." He forks pancake into his mouth, grateful it tastes better than it looks. "Sorry."

"Suit yourself."

"Can you still bring me home a raspberry glaze?" He puts on

his little pout and flutters his eyelids.

She shakes her head and lets out a sigh.

"I can come if you want, love," Frank says, lowering the newspaper he was pretending to read.

"It's fine," she replies, not turning her stare from the table.

But Frank knows it isn't. Regardless, he nods and raises the paper once again, more than a little paranoid. "As long as you're sure."

"Yes."

"Are you seeing Veronica again today, champ?"

Charlie snaps his head towards his dad. "Why?" A globule of pancake fires from his mouth onto the tablecloth.

"Jeez. Just curious, son."

"I don't know. Maybe. No. Possibly." He scoops in another mouthful, eyes on the chewed blob beside the syrup.

Sheila takes a seat opposite Charlie. "What's she like?"

"In what way?" Sensing the inquisition, Charlie crams in more of the pancake.

Sheila smiles. "In a human way."

He chews maybe three times and swallows. "Erm, normal." *Normal? Far from it, Charlie. Far fucking from it!* He takes a deep breath and crams another mouthful in, hoping his mum will get the hint.

"And what's the house like inside?" she asks.

"Normal." *Faceless boy. Faceless boy. Faceless boy.* Halfway through the stack already but not taking the time to savour it, Charlie shoves more in, discarding the fork and opting for his fingers.

"Normal. Is that the word of the day, Charlie?" his mum says. "What did you do over there anyway?"

Charlie shrugs, no longer hungry but pushing more of the softness into his mouth. His mum's eyes won't let him be, though. "Normal stuff."

"Hang on there, cowboy." Frank lowers the paper and arches his eyebrows. "I'm sensing some tension here."

"Well, she is a very pretty girl," his mum says.

"Yes, a pretty little thing," his dad concurs.

It's all too much for Charlie. He stands, sending his chair sliding across the tiles. "No, she isn't! She's a fucking moose!"

"Charlie!" Sheila scolds, feeling an echo of the migraine.

"I'm going to my room." Charlie runs, blinking away the tears, swinging himself around the corner and up the stairs. The new bedroom, much larger than his previous one, offers little solace, and even as he pulls his blinds down on the eerie, quiet street below, and throws himself on the bed, thoughts soon turn to times gone, adding to the feeling of solitude.

All you. All you.

He cries some more, the walls closing in around him. Pressure builds on his chest until he's taking massive gulps of air.

My mum's a traveller and can break your back by standing on a crack.

"What should I do, Max? What should I do?" He prays for strength.

Boys are stronger than girls.

He prays for life to be simple again.

Our little secret, Charlie.

But still, when all is said and done, he still prays for one more visit to that magical world, and he hates himself for it.

Confession

Frank folds the paper and tosses it onto the kitchen counter. "I think the boy has a crush."

Sheila smiles and nods. "Be nice for him to have a friend, even if she's not at the school."

"I wonder if she has friendship rules, too. One must address me as Miss Davenport at all times." He thrusts his nose in the air. "And candy is only to be eaten on Fridays." The fake joviality burns inside.

Sheila turns to him, unsmiling. "Do you like it here, Frank?"

The question catches him off guard. "Charlie asked me the same thing earlier."

"And what did you say?"

"I shrugged." He leans forward, resting his clasped hands on the kitchen table. "Honestly, I don't know." Her voice. Her skin. Her smell. The ever-present knot twists again as he chews the confession over in his mind. *You fucker, Frank.* "On the surface, it seems fine, but—I don't know. There's something...off about the place."

"You mean apart from the Davenports and their embroidered rules?"

Frank nods. "Don't forget the peg people."

"I feel it, too, Frank."

Nursing his tepid coffee, Frank sighs and reaches for his wife's hand. She recoils at first but drops her shoulders and uncurls her fingers, allowing him to slide his hand into hers. It feels forced to Frank, something habitual now feeling alien. There's something different in her eyes, too, something off.

It's this place, he thinks, the oppressiveness, the isolation, the anti-climax of new beginnings. *The sheer fucking dirtiness of it all, you cheating little bastard.*

He wants nothing more than to return to a time before Sheila took that stupid job. How happy they were. No, not happy necessarily, but content, something he suddenly thinks is very fucking underrated.

I need to tell her.

With each additional day without his confession, he knows the stronger and more savage the fire will eventually burn. He wants something left to salvage, something worth living for. He shifts in his seat, squeezing her hand, swallowing hard and preparing himself for the long haul. "I love you, Sheila. You know that, yeah?"

His wife smiles and squeezes back. Frank senses her vulnerability, a side he imagines few others will ever get to see. They stay like that for a while, just discovering each other again. Frank thinks he might cry.

"Frank?"

He clears his throat and leans further forward.

This was the last time, Florence.

Their life together flashes in front of him—the good, the bad, the routine. He takes a deep breath, opens his mouth, closes it, and swallows dry.

"Frank, what is it?"

The words are on the tip of his tongue. This is the moment. "I...I was thinking maybe once you've settled in, we can look for somewhere else?" *You weak, weak man.* "Somewhere normal even."

"It's a nice thought," his wife replies. "But Rebecca got us such a great deal on this place. You saw what other houses were going for in the area."

"Do you think she stitched us up?"

"No, no way. She likes us, you can tell. Friendly as all hell."

"In that case, she might go all out helping us get our money back."

"We still probably wouldn't even break even, Frank."

"We'd manage."

Sheila sighs, gazing past him to the patio doors. "I don't know. And all that hassle again."

"We could move further out. We don't have to be so close to the city."

She shakes her head. "I just haven't got the headspace right now. My mind's full of work and—"

"I get it. I get it. It doesn't have to be now, it was just a thought." *New rules. Twenty minutes to come over.*

"Somewhere closer to the school even."

Bowing her head to hide the fresh tear, Sheila carries her hardly touched pancake to the bin and scrapes it in. "There's just too much to think about right now."

"I know, love. I'm sorry. I love you."

"I know."

Before he can utter another word, she's out the door and almost running up the stairs. He contemplates how fast things have started to rot after arriving on such a high. Paranoia works its icy claws around him again, and once more, he begins to wonder if she somehow already knows. The migraine, the change of mood, the unsubtle desire to not be alone with him.

But how could she? Florence perhaps? No. No way. Did someone see him?

But knowing his wife, her reaction would not be muted. The bitter taste of cowardice settles at the back of his throat as he remains seated at the kitchen table, listening to the songs of the birds and envying their freedom. *Fuck this place.* But on the eve of starting a new job, not just any old job, he considers how his confession would make things a trillion times worse. And that's what he tells himself—his "stay out of jail for now" card. Dropping his shoulders, he turns his attention to the clock, noting he'll be able to mow the lawn in just over four hours.

Melody fucking Drive.

The outlook is bleak, but his stomach still groans with an undeniable yearning for more of that luscious cherry pie.

Magic World

A silver Mercedes crawls down the street, staying well under the advised speed limit. Charlie eyes the car as it passes his house, pulling into the driveway of number thirty-seven. A middle-aged couple emerges and rushes into the house as though sunlight might turn them to dust. The third car through the gates is the Davenports'. Again, Charlie watches it, excitement and dread twisting his gut. As the black beast rolls up the driveway of number forty-three, he presses against the wall, exposing as little of himself as possible while allowing for a clear view.

The engine cuts out, and the first door opens, front passenger side. Patricia emerges and turns to get an eyeful of the street, prompting Charlie to recoil and bite down on his lip. He counts to three and takes another peek to find the tall lady making her way through the large opening doors. Veronica's next, Charlie watching as she brushes her white dress down and delicately pats at her hair. She shuts the car door and snaps her head towards Charlie's bedroom window. He recoils, heart thumping.

Three. Two. One.

Warily, he juts his head out, only to find Veronica already halfway across the road. *Shit.*

Remaining pressed against the wall, he reminds himself to breathe, his circuitry overloading with fear, dread, and chaos. His stomach flips. He thinks about shouting down his excuses to his parents but knows Veronica will hear. He even contemplates scrambling down the stairs to beg them but knows he won't make it in time. Eyes on the girl in the white dress who just got back from church, Charlie swallows hard. She's at the bottom of his driveway, little Miss Innocence with the green eyes and the big secret.

Who are they going to believe?

He grimaces just before the knock comes. And there it is, such a gentle and deceiving rap that prompts voices from downstairs, followed by the sound of the door opening.

"Charlie!" his mother sings.

He considers hiding, burying himself in the back of the closet.

"It's Veronicaaaaa!"

He thinks about locking himself in the toilet, a victim of one of those stomach bugs. He could even make those straining noises—he's done it before to get out of a visit to his Aunty Jean's house. But the thought fades fast, the wholesome smell of pancakes already giving way to bubble gum and that mysterious whatchamacallit, an irresistible concoction drawing him from the wall and to the top of the stairs. His mum twists her head towards him and offers him a wink. "Isn't that sweet, Charlie? She's brought you more of the liquorice straps."

Using the banister, Charlie creeps his way down, neither a man nor a child. Veronica smiles and holds the red liquorice towards him, sunlight enhancing the bounty in the small white bag. She leans across their threshold and places the candy on the small table underneath the mirror. "We missed you at church."

"We're not really religious," his mum answers for him.

"But who will forgive you for your sins?" Veronica retorts.

From halfway down the stairs, Charlie eyes his mum, waiting for her reaction, for her dismissal of such nonsense. But instead, she offers a half-baked smile, turns, and disappears through the archway. "I'll leave you both to it."

Veronica fixes her gaze on Charlie. "You see, Charlie. Everyone's got secrets."

Before he can say anything, the girl is gone. He descends the last few stairs and arches his neck to see her halfway across the street, on her way back to the house with the faceless child and the scale model street full of pegs. He follows, of course, snatching the bag of candy from the table on the way.

No More Than an Inch

"See you later, love," Franks says. "Are you sure you don't want me to come?"

Sheila fixes her lipstick in the hallway mirror. "I wouldn't put you through it."

"Probably best anyway. I've got the excitement of cutting our grass in t-minus four minutes and counting."

She smiles, her reflection sickening her. "Do you need anything while I'm in town?"

"Nah, think I'm good."

"Do me a favour and check on Charlie, will you? When he got back from Veronica's this morning, he looked upset. They might have had a fall out or something."

"Will do, love. We'll have a man-to-man."

"Just be sensitive, okay?"

"My middle name. Anything special you want for dinner?"

"Anytime you cook is special."

As Frank watches his wife walk to the van, his glance draws to the woman in the bedroom window opposite, one hand on her left breast and the other holding something—a hairbrush? "Go away," he mouths under his breath. "Go the fuck away." She begins running her tongue up and down the handle, her eyes not leaving his. *Fuck my life.* As the van's engine kicks into action, the woman begins sliding the end in and out of her mouth. *Oh, sweet Jesus.* Then, she brings the brush down the centre of her chest until it disappears behind the petunias.

With a stirring in his pants, Frank watches the van pull out of the driveway, half expecting it to squeal to a stop. Only as it nears the gates does he feel some relief. *Keep going. Keep going.* It disappears out of sight, and his heart rate settles. He looks back to Florence's bedroom window, hating himself for feeling disappointed that the curtain has come down on the show.

Part of him wants to march across and thrash against the door, screaming his warnings and hammering it home that it was just a mistake, reasserting it will never happen again. Instead, he steps back from the window, knowing you can't talk chaos down from a rooftop. She has control. She decides when he comes and goes.

He checks the time, feeling smaller still as he makes his way to the shed, the sound of the first lawnmower kicking into action. Fighting back the tears, he begins to work on the back lawn, drifting into autopilot until, at one point, he realises he's gone over the same patch four times. After finishing the back, he wheels the mower down the passageway, noticing Nick working on the garden of number twenty-three, a colossal pair of earphones strapped to his head. The guy lifts his gaze, offering a nod and a quick wave before getting on with the job.

Curiosity niggles as Frank goes to work on the front. A neighbourly gesture or a sordid exchange? Perhaps he's not the only one. Maybe every man and his dog—*No dogs*—has visited the lady from number twenty-three, experiencing the magic between her sheets. Shaking off the thought, he focuses on his own lawn, doing his best to match the perfect, symmetrical lines of his neighbour's grass. By the time he's finished, he's worked up quite a sweat, and as he flicks off the thrum of his mower, he realises he's the last one out there. He takes a step back, admiring his handiwork, deciding to reward himself with a shower and a beer.

The knock comes as he's towel-drying himself in the mirror, Bryan Adams in the background, singing about a summer he'd love to return to. "I'll get it, son," he shouts. He wraps the towel around his waist, wrestles his pants on, and thrusts his arms into a clean T-shirt that's too snug, all the cherry pies not helping. He dashes down the stairs to find another fresh offering on his doorstep.

"Just popping out, son. Won't be long." He waits for a reply that doesn't come.

Check on Charlie, will you?

"Charlie! Everything alright, son?"

Sensing he's plugged into the internet and that time is precious, Frank retrieves the pie and takes it to the kitchen, grabbing a spanner from the toolbox on the way out. He pokes his head outside the door to check the coast is clear and makes his move, figuring he'd be wasting his time buckling his belt.

Apple and Ginger

Charlie removes his noise-cancelling headphones, relieved to find the raucous orchestra of machinery finally at an end. He rolls to his side, wrapping his arms around a pillow for comfort, reliving the morning's events. He doesn't quite understand things, unable to get his head around an act of intimacy that leaves him feeling cold and more alone than ever. After snatching one of the raspberry liquorice straps from his bedside table, he hangs it from the corner of his mouth like a sweetened soother.

You're settling in well, Charlie. Mummy says you'll all be ready for one of her soirees soon.

He rolls over, facing away from the window, biting his lip at the image of Max and him sitting on the riverbank, throwing skimmers. *The whole street gets together; it's such a blast.* He lets out a garbled growl and turns onto his back, slamming his closed fists into the duvet on either side.

"I hate this fucking place!"

Pushing himself from the bed, he turns and makes to punch the wall but pulls out at the last minute. So many feelings, so much confusion, and nobody, nobody, there for him. He walks laps around the room, running his fingers along the walls and the edge of the bed. He rings Max, but it goes to voicemail, no doubt playing with his new best friend, showing off his new gaming system.

Call me, Max. I miss you. He deletes the text. *I need someone to talk to.*

"Fuck!" He throws it on the bed without hitting send.

Seeing the green internet light flickering on the modem should fill him with happiness, but he feels numb. Even the thought of losing himself in a different world offers little appeal, somehow feeling babyish—an immature distraction that won't put pay to the chaos of what his own life has become. He wants his old life back, a world where he was allowed to be just a child, where the only secrets stayed behind the bathroom door.

But *boys are stronger than girls.*

He takes position against the wall, gazing through his window at a street he hates, the leaves on the trees providing the only source of animation. "Hate it here. Fucking hate it." Across the way at number twenty-three, the front door opens, revealing his dad, hair matted to one side and a spanner in his right hand. Charlie can't recall the last time he saw his father holding a tool, if ever. "Better with words than his hands," his mum once said, which prompted an "Oy." He watches his father all the way across the road and listens to the footsteps up the stairs, guessing whatever he was up to must have been a dirty job, the sound of rushing water soon following.

He continues to stare out the window into the nothingness below, waiting for a text or a call from his best friend that never comes. Time passes slowly, as one would expect, with only the leaves for entertainment.

"Hate it. Hate it. Fucking *hate* it."

It's just after five when his mum pulls through the gates. He's missed her today and wants nothing more than for her to bring him close and stroke his hair the way she used to. But she's so much on her plate, what with the move and starting the new job tomorrow. He watches the van crawl down Melody Drive, but it doesn't reach their driveway. Instead, falling well short, a few doors down on the opposite side of the road. His mum exits the car, brushes herself down in a similar way to how Veronica did, and makes her way along the path to number seventeen. It's the house of the old man he saw struggling with the lawnmower earlier, the one with the combover and a face like a walnut.

Just as Charlie's about to step away, he thinks he sees Veronica staring across from her bedroom window. He leans in, his breath misting the glass as he squints into the late afternoon sun. He wipes at the pane, revealing only darkness within the pink glow.

I've seen what you do.

His stare remains drawn to the void, the portal into a magical and terrifying world he cannot tell anyone else about. Unsure how long his trance is held, he draws the blind down and makes his way downstairs on the hunt for normality, only to find his father sitting at the kitchen table, staring at the fresh-cut back lawn, muttering something incoherent. Still pursuing something normal, Charlie retreats into the lounge, switches on the television, and slumps into the couch, wrapping his arms around a cushion and waiting for his mum to pull into their driveway.

It's half an hour before she comes through the front door, loaded with four bags.

"How did you go, love?" Frank asks from the kitchen.

"Pretty good. I'm beat now, though." She straightens her hair in the mirror. "Think I'll head upstairs, get everything sorted for tomorrow. You don't mind, do you, Frank?"

"No, love. Do what you need to do."

There's still an atmosphere, Charlie can feel it. It's different, unlike the other times when his parents would throw jibes, following up with an eventual sit-down discussion and a round of insincere but tension-ending apologies. Something about the air seems heavy, stale, permanent, with no signs it may clear soon.

Sheila walks over to the couch and kisses Charlie on the forehead without smiling. "How was your day? Did you see Veronica again?"

Bringing the cushion in further still, Charlie shakes his head. "What's that smell?"

"My perfume, I think, love."

"No, on your breath."

"Oh, I stopped off to help the man down the road with some more paperwork. Would you believe someone else in the world likes apple and ginger tea?"

"Mum."

"Yes, son?"

The girl across the road isn't as innocent as she seems. It's not just pegs, bibles, and raspberry straps. She's a witch of sorts that makes me feel bad, good, and everything else in between. She has a carnival, takes my ticket, and puts me on the tallest coaster in the world. The drop is enough to make you sick, though. "That is quite unbelievable, Mum."

She smiles. "Don't go to bed too late, love. Perhaps next weekend we can do something fun together? One last shindig before school starts."

"That would be nice."

Charlie watches TV for the rest of the night, now and then glancing over to see his dad still staring out the patio doors into darkness. *Hate this place. Hate it.* Just before ten, he switches off the television and says goodnight, his dad grunting a response. He trudges up the stairs, looking in on his mum, who is either already asleep or pretending to be. He washes, brushes his teeth, and climbs into bed. There's a single message on his phone from Max: *Dunc says hi.*

The attached photograph shows them in Max's bedroom, arms around each other, pulling funny faces into the camera, the light behind giving their skin a purple tinge. Angry, envious, Charlie swipes the photo to the right, deleting it from sight.

"None of it's fair."

Sleep takes time to visit, and when it does arrive, it comes with a pink blur around the edges, giving way to an endless void of faceless children, bubble gum mountains, and a church full of peg people. He wakes just after midnight, checking his window, half expecting to see the girl's silhouette staring from her room.

All you.

It's just after four the second time he wakes, a sudden burning need to tell, to get all the poison out, but as he stands in the doorway of his parents' room, and as darkness gives way to only one shape in the bed, he figures they have enough going on.

There's no further rest for him, just stomach-churning anticipation and dread for what Monday might bring.

...brings the same. There's no childish conversation, no playing in the park, just a dream-like experience that both excites and depletes any self-worth. *Yes, you're all settling in quite well.* As Charlie crosses the road back to his house, he almost looks forward to starting school, something else to fill his mind and his time. He knows Veronica will carry on calling but thinks it might just be on the weekends. And then perhaps not at all. The thought brings relief but also a detestable notion of missing out on the ride.

The last week of the summer holidays should be fun, hanging with friends and squeezing in as many memories as possible to hold onto over the long and monotonous days at school. Still, here he is, lying on his bed in the confines of his room at the mercy of Veronica, and Melody fucking Drive. He imagines confessing his secret to Max, the boy lifting his hand for a high-five, a look of respect and awe creeping across his friend's face. But it doesn't feel like that; her hold over him makes him feel small, like a *peg* in her pouch.

The knock on their front door comes just after midday. Charlie ignores it. A few minutes later, he hears their door close, and this time he gets up to see his dad carrying the spanner across to number twenty-three. Across the way, Veronica's window shows the familiar void with the pink tinge.

Power? Control? Little church girl rebelling against her parents? He wonders why she does it and what makes her tick.

No messages on his phone, no missed calls.

After throwing himself back on the bed, Charlie closes his eyes, focussing only on the inside of his lids. The front door goes again about thirty minutes later, followed by the shower kicking into action. Time passes at once super fast and uber slow, with Charlie drifting in and out of light sleep. He feels exhausted but doesn't know why. Perhaps the heaviness of the secret or the black magic of the witch.

"Just going to get your mum from work, Charlie, and then

we're going to pick up her new car," his dad hollers from downstairs. "Charlie! Charlie, can you hear me?"

In a haze, Charlie's unsure if any acknowledgement leaves his lips.

His world continues to fade in and out until just after six when the familiar rumbling sound of their seen-better-days van spurs him from the bed. A big glossy BMW follows, offering a much more civilised hum. He watches his dad exit the van, looking older than he ever has, and his mum stepping out from her brand new car, not seeming the least bit excited.

Dinner is quiet and strained. No effort, just food for the sake of food and conversation for the sake of conversation. How was your day? The people? The office? How's the new car feel? His dad fires questions, and his mum ticks them off, neither showing genuine interest.

They follow with cherry pie, no questions asked about its origin. Stilted conversation soon turns to him, his mum kicking things off with the old faithful. "Did you see Veronica again, Charlie?"

"Yes."

"Everything okay between you two."

"Yes."

"Well, it's good that you've made a friend down the street."

"Yes."

It gets no livelier than that. Frank and Charlie do the chores while Sheila stays at the kitchen table, nursing a glass of red, responding to emails, and attending to whatever else lawyers do.

"I'm going to do some work on my book," Frank announces, taking another slice of cherry pie through to the study.

Charlie cuts a slice, too, waiting for his mum to finish, hoping they can curl up on the couch and watch some of their shows together. But less than an hour later and two glasses of wine down, she folds the laptop and offers a yawn, declaring she's going for another early night, spiciness and alcohol on her breath as she kisses the top of his head.

"Goodnight, Charlie."

"Night, Mum."

The Daily Grind

There are no surprises throughout the week. Texts from his friend Max get even less frequent. On the odd occasion when Charlie leaves the street on a chore with one of his parents, there's little sense of escape, the thought of their inevitable return through those iron gates like shackles around his hands, feet, and mind.

Veronica calls on him every morning, a bag of red liquorice straps dangling from her dainty fingers. He confines himself to his bedroom after playing at her house, waiting for the inevitable knock, the subsequent sound of the front door, and the smell of fresh pie. His mum pulls through the gates just after six each day, stopping at combover's house to help with paperwork; always that spicy smell on her breath as she kisses Charlie on the head on her way to yet another early night.

Conversation between his parents becomes more forced with each passing day, and Charlie senses the approaching storm.

Things go like clockwork, for the most part.

His visit to Veronica. His father's visit across the road, spanner in hand.

Lethargy, exhaustion, black magic, whatever you want to call it, keep him confined to his bed, where he spends his hours hugging the pillow to his chest.

Same old, same old. Until—

Charlie pushes himself from the bed and rushes towards the window to see his mum's BMW pulling through the gates. Her window down, stereo blaring, he can hear her screaming, an ear-bleeding high-pitched shrill that has curtains twitching for as far as he can see.

What the hell, Mum? Turn it off. Turn it off!

But the music only seems to get louder.

Charlie watches the BMW crawl down Melody Drive, pulling in behind the van in the driveway. The engine cuts, but still, the music spills into the street. "Turn it off. Turn it off," he mutters under his breath. *Turn the fucking music off.* He studies his mum through the windscreen, eyes wide, fingers wrapped around the steering wheel.

Please, Mum. Please.

He begins waving, frantic, trying to get her attention. In return, his mum starts beating her fists against the wheel and thumping at the horn, her screams becoming wilder, almost feral. Charlie taps on the windowpane—*It's useless!*—the ominous feeling in the pit of his stomach getting stronger still. "Oh god. Oh god." His skin tightens as his attention draws to the silhouette of Veronica in her bedroom window, surrounded by the aura of pink light.

Oh god.

A loud thud from below draws his attention to the top of his father's head. The music ceases, the car door opens, and his mum breaks into a loud, manic wail as his dad ushers her into the house, trying to avoid her flailing arms.

The storm is here.

Holding his breath, Charlie rushes to the landing, trying to pick up on the exchange, but screaming gives way to incomprehensible whimpers and sobbing. With a sensation of helplessness and fear washing over him, also a sense there is much more to come, Charlie grabs the banister and begins a stealthy creep downstairs. He thinks secrets are about to spill, but hopefully not his, because that one is his word against hers, and *boys are stronger than girls.*

We Need to Talk

"I can't do it anymore, Frank. I can't!" Sheila buries her head into her hands.

"It's okay. It's okay." Frank eases her onto one of the kitchen chairs and pours her a glass of water. "Breathe. We'll work it out." But his heart in his mouth, Frank's as sure as shit she's worked it out or that someone told her.

"We won't, Frank. We can't." Sheila trembles, mascara streaming down both cheeks. She tries to talk, but she's unable to stop herself from breaking down into a series of snivelling sobs. "I'm so—sorry."

"Love, we can get through anything. It's this place, it isn't right." Frank puts a hand against her cheek but steals it away, thinking he has no right. *It was just a mistake. Mistakes.* "Something off about it. We can work it out. We can—"

"It's over."

Desperate, he tries to blink away tears, but it's too much for him. No emotion within the four walls for so long, and now the house is spilling with it. He begins to cry, the chair creaking as he rocks back and forth.

"I told him yesterday," she says. "It will never happen again. Frank. Never. I promise you." Her words come out thick and fast, almost rolling into each other. "I promise, Frank!"

"What? What are you talking about?"

"The man from seventeen. I only ever meant to help him, but then—then—"

Frank's heart pounds, the resident knot in his stomach making itself even more at home. "Sheila, what is it?"

"He knew I was lawyer. He said he needed help." Using an arm to wipe away the excess moisture, she begins shaking her head, her face creased into deep-set wrinkles. "I'm so sorry, Frank. I don't know what came over me. I promise it was the last time. I—I—"

Dragging his chair further towards the table, Frank also begins shaking his head, trying to sift some sense from all the nonsense, noting the spicy tinge carrying on the air between them. *Ginger?* "Sheila, what's the last time? What's going on?"

"The last time we made love." She recoils at her own words. "No, not love. Not love, Frank! Just sex. Please believe me. You have to believe me!"

The guy he saw strolling across the road with a hand in the air was an old man with saggy skin, cloudy eyes, and pants up to his nipples. "This isn't funny, Sheila."

"It's just lust, Frank. I can't explain it." She expects anger, but her husband wears a face of submission and bewilderment. She studies him as his eyes dart around the room as if following a kamikaze mosquito. "It won't happen again, Frank," she pleads. "I promise. We'll move away just like you said, get away from—"

"Who told you?"

"About what?"

"Not funny, Sheila," Frank says again through gritted teeth. "I fucked up, okay. I fucked it all! And I'll be eternally sorry." He pushes from the chair and begins pacing the kitchen floor. "I was going to tell you. Honestly, I was, but what with your new job, I couldn't bring myself to do it. Fuuuuuck!"

"Tell me what?" It's her turn to be blindsided.

"Stop playing games, Sheila! The woman from the house opposite, the one who leaves the pies."

"Frank?"

Something's off, he knows it. But there's no going back now. "I fucked her." *There, it's out, and it feels better.* "More than once." *Easy, Frank.* "This is what it's all about, isn't it?" He slams a fist on the kitchen counter. "I'm weak. I'm a prick." He begins to cry, fingers clasping the counter lip. "But it's as though I'm in a—"

"Trance," Sheila mutters. It feels like her heart has missed a beat and is pumping faster, faster, trying to catch up. The room spins, an expression she thought only writers like her husband use, but she plants both palms onto the table to regain control. "Frank." She inhales but isn't ready for the words to leave. Exhale. Inhale. Exhale. Inhale. "Frank, the woman in that house. The one who leaves the pies."

"What a fucking mess!"

"Frank, that woman—"

"I'm sorry, Sheila!"

"—is eighty-two years old."

Frank turns, fingering tears from his eyes. "Please, Sheila." He marches back to the kitchen table and drops to his knees before her. "I beg you, Sheila. I'm sorry. I'm so goddamned sorry. Please tell me we can work through this."

"Frank, I need you to listen to me." She wipes more tears away and rests a hand on his shoulder. "I don't know what's happening here, but Rebecca told me the lady at number twenty-three was as frail as butterfly wings. She rarely leaves the house, Frank. The Davenports do all her shopping and mow her—"

"That must have been her daughter then because—"

"She has no children, Frank."

His mind races as he reaches towards the chair for stability, an image of Nick mowing her lawn wearing those massive fucking headphones. "Wait." Trying to process the information only adds to the exhaustion, his brain beginning to ache. "This isn't right. The woman in twenty-three... She's a goddess, a goddamn fucking movie star."

"From the sixties, maybe. Doesn't the name give it away, Frank?"

"I don't under—" To help slow the escalating chaos in his head, he focuses on a smear of syrup on the tile in front. The mere thought of what he's about to suggest twisting at his insides. "The man that came over that day." He lifts his stare to Sheila. "That's the one you're saying you slept with?"

Sheila nods. "Patrick." She sniffles as she puts her hands to her temples.

"This place. This place is fucking wrong, Sheila." He pushes himself to his feet, letting his weight fall against the kitchen counter. "That man has more loose skin than a Shar-Pei puppy. And he's got a fucking combover, for Christ's sake."

"What? No, he hasn't." The man she peels herself away from under the guise of doing his paperwork is a fucking Adonis—smooth olive skin that ripples with understated muscles. And his hair is golden, lush, and plentiful. "Frank, I don't understand."

"Sheila, it's this place, I'm telling you. The only time I'm not exhausted is when I'm with *her*. There's something off." *Something really fucking off.*

Sheila struggles to get enough air in. "What are you saying?" There's a vacuous feeling in her chest as she imagines the wrinkled, crusty hands of the old man caressing her in the way she begged to be touched. "I'm scared, Frank." The things they did, the things they said. She puts pressure on the table again, afraid the world might slip away at any second. *It can't be true. Can't be—frail as butterfly wings, Frank.*

"We're getting out of here, Sheila. Away from these fucking rules, the fucking silence of it all. And this—whatever *this* is!"

"I'm scared," she says again. She considers what Frank said—about being exhausted all the time. On her first day at work, it was all she could do to keep her eyes prised open. "I'm tired, too, Frank. All the fucking time."

"I wish you had never got the goddamn job!"

She lifts her stare to his, eyes wide, consuming cruelness that adds to the desolation. All that fighting, all the shit she had to wade through, all the toxic masculinity that almost choked her. For this. For this! "Frank, how—"

"I'm sorry." He slumps into the chair in front. "I didn't mean it, Sheila. I didn't." He throws his arms around her, bringing her in close and kissing the top of her head. "I don't know what this place is, but we're sure as hell not sticking around to find out."

"What do we do? Where do we go?"

"We'll rent if we have to. Christ, if your mother will have us, we'll go there."

"The job, though. How am I supposed to—god, this is so fucked!"

They stay like that for a while, consoling each other, wrapped in their cloud of disbelief and exhaustion, and whatever else lurks in the air down Melody Drive.

"Where's your phone?" Frank says.

"In my handbag hanging on that chair. Why? What are you going to do?"

He stands, snatching the bag from the corner of the wood. "I don't care if we lose money on this stinking place." He rifles through it, bringing out the phone. "Is her number in here? Rebecca, is it?"

"Just wait, Frank." Sheila leans over, grabbing his arm. "We're not thinking straight."

"It's this place. This fucking place!"

"Let's sleep on it. Talk about it in the morning."

"No! This place is poison. Rebecca, yeah?" *Friendly as all hell.*

"Frank, please. I can't deal with this right now. Besides, it's after—"

He lifts a hand towards her, squeezing the phone against his ear. "Rebecca?"

Sheila waits, studying her husband's drained and haggard-looking face as he brings the phone down. "What? What is it, Frank?"

He inches his head side to side. "She said to come over, she's expecting us. Fifty-seven Melody Drive."

"What? But—"

"I'll go."

"No," she says, hoping her legs will support her. "I want answers too."

Your Friendly Estate Agent

Frank swings their front door open, adrenaline coursing and heart pounding as he drums his fingers against his pockets. She's there, Florence, upstairs, framed by the last of the evening sun, naked, and reunited with her hairbrush. Discretion out the window, so to speak. *A movie star.* Pert breasts extend over the loosened bra and the arch of her back curves into the petunias. *From the sixties.*

With a contrasting yearning and sickness in his chest, Frank thinks about trying to distract his wife, but as he turns, Sheila's eyes are already wide, skin stretching thinly across her skull. "Is that Florence?" she says. "The one."

Frank nods. "What do you see?"

"An extra from *The Walking fucking Dead.*" Sheila's stomach twists, not with thoughts of her husband fondling the saggy breasts of the woman opposite or running his tongue up and down the almost translucent, wrinkled skin, but with what she got up to at number seventeen with old boy.

"Fuck this!" Frank says through gritted teeth. Hands entwined, they make their way to number fifty-seven Melody Drive, ignoring the twitching curtains, not noticing the girl with the pink glow standing in her bedroom window.

"That was quick," the estate agent says, pulling the door open before Frank can knock. But this isn't the straight pants, white blouse professional they met with over coffee, who took them around numerous houses and gushed over number twenty-four Melody Drive. "Oh, yes, you'll fit in just fine," she had said. Fit in fine. This version of Rebecca has her hair down, wearing a flowery, ruffled skirt and pink top. Almost pretty.

Incense lays at the back of their throats as they enter, noting the artwork lining the hallway. Black-and-white prints monopolise either side, each picture with a traveller at the centrepiece, dancing or holding an instrument of some kind. Folk music plays from a back room, a fast-paced melody that speeds Frank's heart rate further.

"Come through, guys."

Mustiness adds to the heaviness of incense and the ever-growing feeling of claustrophobia. The uncomfortable sensation intensifies as Frank and Sheila follow Rebecca into the large room, taking in the ceiling-high shelves packed to the brim with dog-eared books, some of the spines adorned with unfamiliar and intricate embossed lettering and symbols. A large oval golden mirror offsets a gallery wall of black-and-white photographs. "I expect you want some answers," Rebecca says, picking out a candy from the dish on her desk and easing back into the leather chair. She curls her fingers around it and blows on her hand. "Magic," she whispers, offering a childish giggle as she reveals her empty palm.

In the corner of the room, behind the chair, stands a filing cabinet, and next to that, a see-through plastic contraption containing what looks to be numbered ping pong balls. There's a tube running down to a separate and even smaller container, and within that, a further two balls with the numbers seventeen and twenty-three scrawled across in coarse handwriting.

"It's a makeshift lottery machine, Frank." She offers a smile and a wink. "Hoping I might get lucky next week."

"I want answers, Rebecca, and I want them now!"

"I prefer Miriah when I'm not at work. That okay?"

Frank edges forward, tapping his pockets even more frantically. "Whatever the fuck they call you, you better start talking."

"They're teaching me, Frank—their magic—in return for my

services. There, I said it. I don't believe in skirting around facts. Too many people do that."

"Your services?"

"Even let me have this house for next to nothing—the Davenports, that is."

Sheila feels lightheaded, disoriented, and more confused than before. It's as if she's been given the middle pieces of a jigsaw puzzle and expected to know where they go. "This is insane."

"How are the cherry pies working out for you, Frank?" Miriah leans further back in her chair. "And Sheila, you went on so much about that apple and ginger tea. Is it to your satisfaction?"

Frank doesn't realise he's clenching his fists until his nails cut into his palm. "Rebecca—Miriah—I've never hit a woman before."

"I know. I know. It's a lot," she says. "But you must understand. This is my retirement, my reward. The pie, tea, and liquorice straps are a teaser for the main course. And such powerful magic it is."

As Frank's anger builds, it takes all he has not to grab her by the neck and throw her against the wall.

"I must say, you're remarkably honest, Sheila," the woman says, rattling the candy between her teeth. "Much more honest than him."

Shelia shakes her head. "How did you—"

"The Davenports, of course. They're king and queen, Sheila. They know everything. Ev-er-y-thing."

Sheila fights the urge to cry and curl up into a ball. "Please tell us what's going on, Rebecca."

"It's Miriah." The woman sighs as though the knock on the door has really put her out. "The spell—it was cast as soon as you consumed the offering from twenty-three and seventeen, don't you see? You saw them as your perfect fantasy. And who could resist that?"

Frank notices the picture on the wall, an aerial photograph of the residents standing outside their houses.

"The spell doesn't work on photographs, Frank."

Standing underneath the baskets of number twenty-three

is a woman looking older than time—gaunt, skeletal frame with crinkled and discoloured skin suggesting decades of skin damage. No goddess, for sure, and no fucking movie star either. And then it strikes Frank that he's seen this version of Florence before—the picture hanging in the hallway of number twenty-three, the one he passed each time he buckled his pants, the one he assumed to be Florence's parents.

"Dear, dear, Florence," Miriah says. "Such a sweet old lady. Lost her husband over ten years ago, but she still has a lot of love to give. Isn't that right, Frank?"

Flashbacks invade Frank's head of hot clammy flesh, lips everywhere, hands and fingers in forbidden places. Depravity imprints on his mind, with little chance of ever being erased. He doubles over, gesturing for Sheila to pass him the wastepaper basket.

"Oh yes. Plenty of life in that old girl yet," Miriah says.

After sliding the basket to Frank with her foot, Sheila runs her finger across the photograph, stopping on the old man outside number seventeen. "No way. Uh-uh. There's just no way. No fucking way." And as Frank fills the basket with a murky sea of regurgitated cherries, Sheila retreats from the picture, repeating the same thing over and over. "It just can't be. It just can't be." She reaches the back wall and lets herself slide down, curling into a foetal position and beginning a hysterical sob "There's no way. It just can't be. Just can't—"

"Don't be like that, Sheila," Miriah says, almost a smile gracing her lips. "You'll be old one day."

"And how do you fit into all of this?" Frank says, his eyes red and raw. "Mir-iah."

"I'll give you the short version, F-rank." She waits for him to stop heaving. "The guy you know as Nick Davenport rang me out of the blue one day. Said he'd heard of my reputation as a good estate agent and had a proposal he wanted to discuss. I was dubious, I must admit, but also more than a little curious." She leans over, crunching down on the candy. "I'm good at what I do, see—learning what people like and want. Anyhow, you both know that already." She smiles. "Nick bought me a coffee, offered me a piece of candy, and I've been smitten ever since." She leans back again, sliding a file from her desk and thumbing through it. "The Davenports are wealthy, Frank. They own most of this street. Enlisted me to find good families for those homes and promised me things in return. And boy, have they delivered."

"I'm trying to remain very calm here," Frank says through clenched, puke-stained teeth.

"Bit old school, I know," Miriah says, "but this file contains everything I know about you—friends, family, acquaintances. Needn't worry, though," she adds, tapping the corner of her laptop. "Safe and sound."

"Rebecca, please," Sheila pleads.

"Miriah!" The woman's severity returns, eyebrows almost meeting in the middle. "Most of our residents are old, but they still have needs; they still want to be loved and desired. Is that so wrong?"

"You're fucked!" Frank yells. "This is twisted. And illegal."

"Oh, Frank, that's a good one. Illegal? Sex between consenting adults?" She offers a sharp laugh. "You're not the first and likely not the last to issue such threats."

"You can't do this," Sheila mutters.

"Oh, Sheila, but we do."

"Release us from the contract." Frank feels his blood boiling. "Do whatever you need to do. We'll take a loss, just get us out of here."

"I'm sorry. No can do," Miriah replies, nonchalant. "And before you kick up more of a hoo-hah, it's probably a good time to let you know I've been through your Facebook, Twitter, and Instagram accounts—built a comprehensive list of all your friends and work colleagues. And I guarantee they'll have never seen a show like this."

"Show?" Sheila says.

"We have eyes everywhere, Sheila. Cameras. In the kitchens, bathrooms, bedrooms." A wry smile forms on her lips. "And Frank, I thought I'd seen everything, but even I blushed at one stage."

Ignoring the stare from his wife, Frank does his best not to vomit again as he imagines doing those things with the pickle in the photograph. He begins pacing up and down. "I can't get my head around any of this."

"But that's the least of your worries," Miriah says, soft, soothing. "Your fate is in the hands of the Davenports now."

"You're all sick! What the fuck is wrong with you?" It becomes too much for him, and he rushes towards the desk, driving his fist into the plasterboard a couple of inches above Miriah's head.

The woman snaps her head around to inspect the damage. "You'll have to pay for that."

"Fuuuuuuuuuuuck!" Frank screams, pushing his face within an inch of hers and drawing his fist back again.

"I wouldn't do that, Frank. It's illegal, you know."

"Frank, just stop." Sheila's voice is weak, empty. "What do you want from us? What are we supposed to do?"

The leather creaks as Miriah leans forward. "Just fit in. Eat the pies, drink the tea, chew the liquorice. You're new, a novelty. Attention will die down eventually, and you'll be called on less frequently. It's a lovely street. Quiet, well kept. You'll adapt. Abide by the rules and keep the secrets." She taps the computer once again, smugness creeping across her face. "And we'll all live happily ever after."

Soiree

Charlie groans as he pushes himself to his elbows, most of the night spent staring at the ceiling without a crack. He rubs at the sleep in his eyes, wondering how the hell it got there. The yelling, the crying, the silence, none of the conversation last night sounded good. When he, at one point, heard his parents leave the house, he watched them out of sight down Melody fucking Drive, wondering where they went, who they saw, what was said, and what secrets might be uncovered. When they returned, words were few, but tears aplenty.

Fuck this place.

Tentative, he makes his way to the hallway, hoping everything will be okay, but the permanence of the knot in his chest lends a knowing.

"Mum? Dad?"

No answer.

He grimaces as the floor creaks in the still-unfamiliar places. No pancakes today. Holding his breath, he creeps towards his parent's room, the ajar door concealing relative darkness.

"Hello?"

He's just a kid, too young for the burden of Melody Drive. It's all he's experienced since setting foot in this stupid house: secrets, questions, and tears. It feels too much, as though he might just snap under the weight of it all.

The door creaks as he pushes it inwards. "Mum?"

Morning light sneaking through the curtains frames her silhouette. She's standing in the corner of the room, facing the wall.

"Mum?"

No response.

Her punishment for the music.

"Dad!"

Next time, it will be the naughty corner.

"Dad, I need you!"

Charlie pauses in the doorway, heart pounding, blood pulsing in his ears. "Dad, come here, please!" But still no sound of movement. Unsure his legs will move, Charlie takes a deep breath and edges towards his mother, who remains statuesque and unresponsive. "Mum."

Nothing.

It's just art, Charlie.

He lets out a breath, not realising he was holding it. Two feet away, he begins to feel dizzy, the softness of the bed now looking so goddamned inviting. Always so damn tired. He swallows hard and reaches towards his mother's hand, recoiling and taking a sharp breath as cold hardness greets his touch.

Three.

Two.

One.

He summons the courage to step forward to her left side, a garbled groan leaving his lips as he studies his mother's face.

"Mum!"

Wide eyes and a nose adorn the smoothness, dried streams of tears lining both cheeks. Where the mouth should be, there's only the faintest of outlines, like something a carpenter might draw before getting to work.

"Please, Mum." But only the dilation of her pupils provides animation. He pulls at her wooden arm, but there's no give. "I'll get Dad! I'll get Dad, okay!"

"Dad!" he screams, launching himself down the stairs. "Dad!"

Charlie swings into the living room to find his dad stirring on the couch. "Dad, it's Mum. There's something really wrong!" It's the worst Charlie's ever seen his father look. Dark circles, pale skin, eyes cloudy—all the sharpness gone. Just a blurry shadow. "Dad!" There's an empty bottle of wine on its side next to the couch leg.

Frank groans, his mind beginning to swim with events from the night before. "Where is she?" He swings his legs over and thrusts forward, almost tumbling as he catches the coffee table on the way past.

"Upstairs in the bedroom, but—"

"Sheila!" Frank yells, lumbering up the stairs.

"She can't talk, Dad," Charlie shouts after him. "She's in the naughty corner."

"Sheila!" Pain surges across Frank's shoulder as he catches the door frame of their room. "Sheila?" He draws level with his wife, emitting a garbled moan as he takes in her wooden, mouthless face. "The fuck?"

Charlie swings himself into the room. "Veronica said she'd end up in the naughty corner."

"What?" Frank grabs his wife's shoulder, gives a gentle shake, but she's as stiff as a board. "Sheila, can you hear me?" He tries again, but she's stuck in place, some invisible force other than gravity keeping her wooden-looking feet planted on the ground. *Magic.* "This fucking place. Sheila! SHEILA!"

"Dad, I'm scared."

Frank drops to his knees, clasping his hands around his son's shoulders. "What did you mean before—about the naughty corner?"

Charlie opens his mouth and shuts it again. *All you.* He can't breathe.

"Charlie. Look at your mum, for Christ's sake. We have to fix this."

"She said—" Charlie panics, his mind tying itself in knots. *It's all going to come out.* He's going to be in so much trouble. *Boys are stronger than girls.* He begins to shiver.

"Charlie!"

"She said the first warning was the migraine, but if she does it again, she'll be in the naughty corner." Charlie tastes the saltiness of a tear.

Frank releases his grip. "Veronica?" *The Davenports. King and queen.* "Charlie, what else do you know? Charlie, what else?"

The boy trembles as he observes his dad's face creasing in rage. "Her bedroom, the model of the street, they can hear things—conversations, the TVs, everything. I think they see things, too."

Frank takes in a few deep breaths, realising he's putting the fear of God into his son. He recalls the conversation with Rebecca—*Miriah*— and the cameras throughout the house. "I'm sorry, Charlie." The boy looks tired and pale, a shadow of his former self. "I'm sorry." He takes Charlie's hand and shuffles on his knees towards him. "What else do you know, son?"

Charlie shrugs, staring at the ground, wiping a snot bubble away from his nose with his free hand. "They can do things."

Frank replays Rebecca's words. *Eat the pies, drink the tea, chew the liquorice.* "Charlie, look at me." *Chew the liquorice. Chew the liquorice. Chew the liquorice.* "Charlie, look at me, please."

The boy, at last, lifts his gaze to his father's cloudy eyes.

"Is there anything else you want to tell me? Anything at all, son?"

Charlie looks his father in the eyes and swallows. *I want to tell you everything, Dad, but boys are stronger than girls.* He shakes his head, pursing his lips together.

"You sure, Charlie? It's really important you tell me."

Charlie nods vigorously and wipes more tears away. "What are we going to do? About Mum?"

"I'm going over."

"No, Dad, please! You can't. We're already on the watch list."

"Watch list?" Frank snaps his hand back and scrambles to his feet. "This fucking ends today."

"Please, Dad!"

"It'll be okay, son," Frank says, already thundering across the landing. "Look after your mum."

"But Dad!" Willing the statue version of his mother to move, Charlie listens to his father's feet stomping down the stairs. "I'm sorry, Mum. I'll be back. I'm sorry." He scrambles to his feet and runs down the stairs through the open door, noting Veronica staring down from her bedroom window. "Wait. They'll hurt you."

Break your back by standing on a crack.

"Dad!"

The wood's thickness soaks up any dramatic impact as Frank thumps the side of his fist against the Davenports' door. Charlie watches the vein in his father's neck throbbing, its tempo increasing as his father drives his fist harder and harder against the heavy wood.

"Can we just go back to our old house?" Charlie says. "I hate this place."

Approaching footsteps put an end to Charlie's hope that nobody will answer. "Frank and Charlie Harper," Patricia announces as she opens the door. Wearing the familiar fire-red lipstick but with her hair loose around her shoulders, Charlie thinks she looks even prettier. "Come in. Can I get you both something to drink?"

Frank pushes past. Charlie follows, ignoring the smile from Patricia on the way.

"What the fuck is going on?" Frank says, his vein still pulsing. "What have you done to my wife?"

"Sit down, Frank." Patricia's voice and demeanour is soft and inviting. Neighbourly. "If you sit, we can talk."

Making what sounds to Charlie like a snorting sound, Frank drops into the nearest couch, arms folded. "Talk!"

Charlie sits beside him, listening to the man's ever-quickening breathing as his eyes flick between the adults.

After lowering herself into the chair opposite, Patricia crosses her nylon-clad legs, and smiles. "Are you sure I can't get you gentlemen a drink?"

"Fix her," Frank says, his teeth now gritted. He leans forward in the chair. "Fix her!"

"Hello, Mister Davenport," Veronica chirps, sauntering down

the stairs in the way Charlie has become used to. There's no bun to hold her hair in place today, just long brown locks spilling over her shoulders and across the front of her colourful dress. She stops beside her mum and hands her something while whispering into her ear.

"Thanks, darling." Patricia turns to Frank. "I'll fix her, Frank. Real soon. Don't worry."

Charlie thinks he hears a growl emerge from his father's throat. He shifts position, half hoping the couch will swallow him and save him from Veronica's glare.

"I swear to God, Patricia, I'll—"

"What, Frank? What will you do?"

Frank's mind races, but he knows he's playing her game. "What the fuck do you want from us?"

"Just to live happily ever after, that's all. Let me ask you a question."

Frank grunts, his right foot tapping, tapping, tapping.

"Have you ever lived on the streets, Frank?" Patricia leans forward this time, the remainder of her smile flatlining.

Beginning to rock back and forth, Frank shakes his head. "Fix my wife." He notices the boy in the corner of the room and the embossed writing above. *The Naughty Corner.* "Fix my fucking wife."

"Home wasn't an option. Only bad things ever—"

"I don't want your fucking life story, Patricia. I want my wife back!"

"The two go together, Frank, so you better start listening."

Although delivered much softer than his father's, the words from the woman's lips tighten Charlie's skin around his skull. He lifts his glance from the floor, thinking he sees something dark flicker behind her eyes, and for a moment, her prettiness drops, unveiling something far scarier than what used to live under his bed all those years ago. This is real life, not magic world, after all.

"The things I had to endure." Patricia sniffs loudly. "Unimaginable things nobody should ever have to live through." She bites at her lip and uncrosses her legs. "Money doesn't always mean safety,

Frank. Sometimes, it means the opposite."

"Please," Frank says, his tone softer. "I just want her back."

"Home. A place supposed to be safe and secure became a living hell for me. My entire family was always consumed by greed, corruption, and control, and their inner circle monopolised by powerful men always getting what they wanted. Hell, for the right price, money could even buy a man's daughter." A solitary tear rolls down her cheek as she digs her well-manicured nails into the arms of the chair. "I had no option but to leave, Frank. I walked the streets, wondering where my next meal was coming from, while other kids my age were playing with dolls or getting crushes. And nobody cared enough to do a damn thing about it." Nick arrives at her shoulder and gives it a gentle squeeze before disappearing into the kitchen. "The police—wouldn't touch them. Fingers in too many pies. I could only dream of feeling safe. You ever had a dream, Frank?"

He wants to be a writer, wants the movie deal, the lot—would give almost anything to get it. He often fantasises about how much he'd be willing to give up. "You need help."

"I simply want to give my daughter what I didn't have, Frank. Safety." She flicks her hair behind her shoulders. "The girls found me, eventually. Gave me a home and made me feel safe again."

"The girls?" Frank shakes his head, both feet now tapping hard against the brilliant, shining wooden floor.

"Most people would refer to them as travellers. They took me from the streets and showed me their ways, things that would keep me safe. Secrets. Magic." She turns and smiles at her husband on his way back from the kitchen. "And then I met Nick. He gave me strength, and with his support, I took the mother fuckers who stole my childhood for as much as I could. Not in a million years did I think I'd grow up to be a mother, not after what I went through or saw."

"You know that feeling," Nick says, placing a tumbler of whisky on the table next to Frank, "when you meet someone you'll do anything for. I wanted Patricia shielded from further harm. To give her a chance to heal. I designed this street for her, closing it off to the outside world. We brought the girls in, their partners, too, if they had them. Payback for their kindness. Made a community of it—all safe and sound."

"You're stark raving mad," Frank mutters. "Your wife needs therapy, not a fucking fortress."

Patricia wipes away another tear, and after gracing her husband with a smile, she averts her gaze to Veronica. "There's nothing I won't do for my Veronica. She's my princess. She'll never have to endure hardship or sadness. We're just trying to provide some order in a world that's gone mad. Haven't you listened to the news lately?"

"Rule number forty-two," Nick chirps.

"It's chaos out there." Patricia offers an imperceptible shake of her head. "Everyone has lost control, out only for what they can get. The days of communities and caring, looking out for each other, are gone. But in this little slice of heaven, Melody Drive, we can ensure that never happens."

"That's one hell of a story, guys, but you just can't fucking do this. You're playing God, and besides being beyond sick, it's totally fucking illegal."

"Oh, Frank," Patricia says, apologetic eyes glancing at her daughter. "I've given you a couple of passes, but, as you know, we really don't condone swearing on Melody Drive. Rule number twenty-seven clearly states—"

"Shut the fuck up! Just shut the fuck up! Shove your stupid rules up your fucking la-di-da!" Frank swipes the tumbler from the table and thrusts himself from the chair. "You will fix my fucking—"

Charlie watches his dad put a hand to his throat. And the other. A series of rasps emerge as Frank's eyes grow wider than Charlie ever thought possible, surrounding redness colouring the previous pallid skin. "Dad!"

"It's okay," Nick says. "He's just going to sleep off his temper, Charlie."

"Leave him alone!" Charlie screams, rushing to his dad's side. "Dad! Leave him alone!"

Frank falls back onto the couch, a gurgling sound emerging as he writhes and kicks his legs in the air. "Stop!" Charlie screams, but his father's redness is becoming a shade of purple, and he can only watch as the squirming slows. "Dad! Dad! Stop this!" Helpless, he watches his father's arms fall limply to the side.

"The first week's always the hardest, Charlie," Patricia says. "Fitting in. But most people eventually come round." She holds the peg up for Charlie to see, her pale fingers pinched around the neck just above the miniature pale sweater.

"See, Charlie," Veronica says. "Told you it was a grown-up toy."

"Dad!" Charlie cries, eyes raw and watery. "Dad! Is he—is he dead?"

"Of course not," Nick says, smiling. "Just taking a time out."

"Veronica, please go and get Mrs. Harper. We must prepare."

"Sure thing, Mummy."

"It's probably best you had a little rest, too, Charlie," Patricia says. "It's going to be a late night."

Charlie watches as Patricia places the dad peg on the nest of tables and plucks the other from her palm. It's him—the peg version of Charlie—the pale blue shorts crinkling under her grip.

"No, please, don't," Charlie cries. "No!"

Lifting the smaller peg to her lips, Patricia takes a deep breath and blows. Feeling a sharp gust of wind, Charlie starts spinning backwards like an untethered astronaut hurtling into blackness. The lounge gets further away until it becomes just a pinhole of white and—

ALL TO PLAY FOR

"Charlie." The voice is tinny and distant, like from the model in Veronica's room. He hears something scraping across the floor and opens his eyes to a blur of people and a bolt of pain.

"Charlie!"

"Mum!"

"Thank god. Oh, baby, thank god. Everything is going to be okay, Charlie. You have to trust me, alright?" But it's taking all Sheila's got not to scream her lungs out, Melody Drive being as far from okay as you can get. She's already seen Patrick, sitting third from the right on the second row, as devilishly handsome as ever. She gags at what truly sits in that chair, yet some part of her still wants more. "I love you, Charlie."

"Mum, I'm scared."

Charlie's vision sharpens to reveal the audience seated in front of them, all in numbered chairs. The sea of faces conveys a whole array of emotions: fear, sadness, anxiety, and everything in between.

Patricia stands, ending the low hum of conversation. "Good evening."

Charlie also tries pushing himself to his feet, but he looks down to see his arms and legs strapped to the chair, a large number one taped across one of the legs. "Mum, I'm scared!" He snaps his head back to Sheila, who smiles weakly and nods. "I'll not let anything happen, Charlie. I promise, okay?" Dark circles around her eyes, skin taut and pale, she's not the woman he knows as Mum, and he takes no comfort from her words. Arching his neck and leaning over as best he can, Charlie sees his father sitting in chair number three, staring at the ceiling, a string of saliva hanging from his chin. "Dad!"

"Your dad was a little excitable, Charlie," Patricia says. "We gave him an extra special slice of pie for his nerves."

An inaudible rasp leaves Frank's lips as his head lollops to the right.

"Okay!" Patricia claps her hands together. "Thank you all for coming to our little soiree." Her voice is up a notch, in full-on host mode. "First things first, now that Charlie is up from his little nap, let us officially welcome our new neighbours, the Harpers, to the street."

The audience applauds—a dampened, sinister, slow clap that makes Charlie's skin crawl. His head feels unattached from his body, drifting towards the ceiling, looking down on the crowd of adults, oldies, and children. Expressions vary with age—some look bored, others excitable, and the rest on the verge of crapping themselves. Only the sight of Veronica's sickly smile as she swings her legs back and forth on the chair between her mum and dad brings him back to Earth.

All you.

"Sixty-two residents, sixty-two rules, sixty-two minutes," Patricia says. "Each time the Harpers guess a rule correctly, the corresponding number gets to leave for refreshments upstairs, or they can stay and watch. Any rules the Davenports miss, well, you know what happens, neighbours. Let's start them off on the first three together, shall we? Number one."

"No parking on the street," the audience volunteers with well-practised synchronicity.

"Number two."

"No ball games," the crowd mumble in unison.

"Number three."

"No littering."

"Harpers, you get the idea. All rules that keep our street tidy and safe. A well-oiled community."

"You said they were guidelines," Sheila says.

"Oh, I think we're past all that politeness now, Sheila, don't you?"

Charlie glances at his parents, their vulnerability causing a shudder to rattle down his spine. Part of him wants to let go and bawl like a baby, but he's needed now, and this is a game he can play. All those days spent rote-learning for French tests are about to pay off.

"Clock's ticking."

Staying focused on his mum, Charlie swallows hard. "Bubbles of five people only."

"Well done, Charlie."

From peripheral vision, Charlie sees someone stand up.

"No swearing in a public place," Charlie says. A single creak of the floor above leads him to believe they're in some sort of basement, some secret club shit.

"You're on fire, Charlie. Cursing is a sign of limited vocabulary," Patricia sings. "Feel free to go upstairs, George. There's champagne in the fridge but leave some for the rest of us."

To Charlie, it sounds as though Patricia's wetting herself with excitement—in her element. He scans the remaining audience, imagining some to have been through something similar, sitting where they are now. The thought offers no comfort at all. "No loud music when entering the street. No semi-nakedness."

Shelia clears her throat. "Mowing lawns only between three and four on a Sunday afternoon."

Charlie shuffles in his seat as best he can. "Every Sunday service at church. Vacations booked three months in advance."

"No alcohol outside," his mum says. "Patios excluded."

"The news," Frank slurs. "Lunch and evening during the weekend and at least one during the week."

Charlie watches a drop of saliva stretch and break free from his dad's chin, splashing to the floor. "No motorbikes or cars with more than two-litre engines."

"Well done, Charlie," Patricia sings again. "Many people don't get that one the first time around. You're on a roll."

The first time around. The first time around. The words throw Charlie for a second, but he tries to refocus, imagining himself sitting at his desk in his old bedroom. "No honking."

As time ticks, Charlie and his mum empty more than half the room between them. The frequency of their answers begins to slow, though, until minutes pass without an offering.

"No fireworks!"

"Ah, you've had that one already, Charlie."

"Shit! Mum! Dad!"

"Twenty-three minutes left," Patricia says.

"No caravans or boats," his dad utters, head lolloping forward. There's a bit more life behind his eyes now, though. "No police."

Patricia stands, performing a little dance that sends another shiver down Charlie's spine. "That never ends well. Sixteen to go, folks."

"No structural changes to the house," Frank says. "No washing to be hung outdoors."

"Excellent, Frank. So tacky. Less than twenty minutes."

"No bubble gum outside the house. No cats or dogs!" Charlie blurts. *But crocodiles are okay.*

He turns to his mum, who closes her eyes and bites her lip. It's down to him and his drugged-up dad. "No quarrelling in the street. No blasphemy," he says.

"House colour must be white." Frank is more alert now, managing to support his head. "No weeds."

"Nice, Frank. We have the number of a fabulous gardener, but we can hopefully talk about that upstairs."

Again, the offerings become more sporadic. Eleven people left. The same answers keep popping into Charlie's head, and he can't get any clarity. An eternity passes before his dad says, "No stickers or decals on cars or windows?"

Veronica stands but doesn't leave the room. "Indeed. So very vulgar."

Another strained silence.

Patricia begins to pace up and down the room, adding to the tension. "Six minutes left."

Charlie sees a tear running down his mum's cheek. He wants to reach for her hand. "Dad!"

"I'm trying, Charlie."

"Come on, Harpers. It's an impressive display so far. Don't fall at the last hurdle."

But time continues to pass.

"Three minutes remaining," Patricia sings.

Charlie looks at a woman in the audience who looks like she's trying to mouth something. *Shit. What's she saying? No farming bees?*

Patricia gives out a dry cough, and the woman shuts her mouth, fixing her eyes straight ahead. "For the greater good," Patricia says as a reminder of her plight.

"For the greater good," the crowd echoes.

Charlie's mind is blank. He keeps thinking about crocodiles. *Come on, Charlie! Now he's got the French word for cheese stuck in his head. Shit! Merde!*

"Two minutes."

"No bikes on lawns," Charlie yells.

"Close."

"Visible from the front. And no climbing trees!" He sees the woman in the audience smile as she leaves her seat.

"Excellent."

There's a hum of conversation from upstairs, the boards above giving out regular creaks now.

"You're doing well, Harpers," Nick offers from the side of the room.

Frank lifts his head. "Only repairmen from the recommended list."

Charlie watches another person leave.

Patricia's smiling. "One minute."

Think, Charlie, think! "No garden gnomes." Another woman leaves. Seven left. There's pressure behind his eyes, but refuses to give in. *Come on! Come on!* But he's got nothing.

"Thirty seconds."

Shit. Shit. Shit. Charlie looks across at his parents again.

"Twenty seconds."

Shut up, Patricia! Shut up! Shut up!

"Ten seconds."

Fuuuuuuck!

"That's time, people," Patricia announces, offering a single loud clap. "What a superb effort! Harpers, it pleases me to let you know you've just equalled our first-time record set by the Jones family two years ago." That sickly smile spreads across her bright red lips. "Veronica, the pegs, please."

"Here you go, Mummy."

"Rules keep us safe, keep the neighbourhood ticking, from spiralling into chaos like the world outside our gates." Patricia turns to the plant pot, brushing some soil away from the surface. "Deep breath, Harpers."

"Mum?" Charlie snaps his head around. "Mum, what's happening?"

"Inhale, Charlie. Quick!" she rasps. "It's going to be okay, I promise."

He turns his head back towards Patricia, heart pounding, watching as the lady continues scooping at the dirt. He sucks in some air but already feels the need to release.

Veronica offers him a smile. "It's only seven seconds, Charlie. See you on the other side."

Patricia drops the three pegs into the hole and begins sweeping the soil back across.

As the first bit of dirt sprinkles down the back of his neck, Charlie feels warmth run down his legs. "Mum!" But she has her eyes closed and her cheeks puffed out. He remembers what she said and inhales sharp, jolting his head back to avoid the soil beginning to cover his chin.

I don't want to die. I don't want to die. He squints into the light above, noting the almost transparency of the dangling leaf. *Oh god. Oh god.* His eyes snap shut, and blackness envelops him, not a speck of light sneaking through his eyelids and only deafening silence, albeit the blood pumping in his ears.

Already the pressure on his lungs is intense. He feels the weight of the soil pressing against every part of him and can taste the earthiness at the back of his throat.

She's killing us. He tries to move an arm, but it's pinned to his side. *Need to breathe.*

He's in the park, swinging at balls that Max is throwing. "Home run," Max squeals. And the crowd goes wild. Now all he can see is Veronica's smile.

She's out there watching me die, he thinks. Dad, please help me. It's squeezing him, making him feel like his bones will shatter at any moment. *I'm going to die. I'm going to fucking die!* He needs to breathe so bad. He can imagine the air rushing into his lungs. *Is she still smiling? This is more than seven—*

He's out, spitting the soil from his mouth and grabbing greedy mouthfuls of stale basement air.

His dad rasps. "You okay, Charlie?"

He gags, spitting only air at the floor. "I dunno. Mum, you good?"

Sheila nods, eyes streaming tiny rivers as she gulps at the air.

"Fantastic." Patricia claps her hands again. "Now we can go upstairs for champagne and canapes. Perhaps even a little bit of a jig."

Charlie watches in disbelief as the woman performs that stupid little shuffle again.

"Nick, be a good egg and unstrap them, will you, darling?" she says. "Harpers, just think of this as a reset. Three strikes, though, and you'll be down here again, but we won't make it as easy next time. Abide by the rules, and there's no reason we can't all flourish in this little slice of heaven."

Charlie's first to be released. As he stands, Veronica offers him a smile. Not a warm one, he thinks, but a knowing one.

"Oh, and Harpers, before you consider doing anything silly,"—Patricia turns and digs her fingers deep into the soil—"I'd like you to meet the Fowlers." She holds out the dirt-covered pegs in her palm. "Nice people, just not team players, if you know what I mean."

The rest of the night is a blur to Charlie. He and his parents stay close as the Davenports introduce them to others, most of whom nod and smile but don't seem truly present. "For the greater good," some say with soulless voices. Emphasising god knows how many sleepless nights down Melody Drive, their sallow skin is almost translucent, a thin veil that fails to hide the terror within. Charlie even thinks he can feel their silent scream, especially the woman with a scar running along one of her wrists.

Throughout the evening, *the girls* play their music in the corner of the room, some of them dancing. The old man with the com-bover's having a whale of a time, but Charlie doesn't like how he keeps looking at his mum.

Towards the end of the evening, Veronica taps him on the shoulder. "You did well not to tittle-tattle," she whispers into his ear. "There was a young boy called Arnold that did that once."

Even as the Harpers return to the house, the one that used to belong to the nice-but-not-team-playing family, the Fowlers, and shut the door behind them, there's little relief. They make regular tea for this evening's tipple, taking their drinks to the table outside and closing the patio doors behind them. There are tears, followed by subdued quiet as they settle into unified realisation they've just bought a piece of real estate in Hell itself, all under the guise of the Bible.

Charlie knows Princess Veronica will be back in her bedroom, basking in the pink glow, playing with her pegs, and listening to the chatter from the cells of the suburban jail. All *safe and sound*. He knows she'll knock tomorrow, a bag of liquorice straps in hand and wearing that sickly smile that matches her mother's.

There was a young boy called Arnold that did that once.

He figures the novelty will soon wear off. After all, she's the master, and he's the puppet, as are all the non-travelling residents of Melody Drive. Money, corruption, control, everything Patricia ran away from, everything she claimed made her feel unsafe—yet she's created a monster fuelled on it.

You did well not to tittle-tattle.

Add to that a dash of magic and dark secrets, and you have a street living under a permanent cloud of fear.

Exhausted, with no more tears to spill, the Harpers turn in early.

Charlie doesn't get much sleep. He spends most of the night imagining soil falling across his face and contemplating how that leaf was the last thing the poor Fowlers ever laid eyes on.

Church

An explosion of engines wakes Charlie from his restless sleep. He was playing with Max again, laughing as they ran back to the house with their stash of candy from the corner shop. He wants that back, his childhood. But this living nightmare is all he's got.

I want to go home. I want to—

The knock at his door startles him.

"Yeah?" He rubs the sleep from his eyes and pushes to his elbows.

It's his dad, at least a version of him. "Morning, son." Within the doorframe, the man appears smaller, thinner, and somewhat wooden. Peg like. The cheeky smile is nothing but a memory, and it looks like only a thin layer of pale skin covers his skull. Eyes are sunken and watery. "Time for church."

Charlie lets his head fall back; his stare again fixed on the *wrong* ceiling.

It's his birthday today, and he's pretty sure in all the drama, his parents have forgotten. Not surprising, Melody Drive being what it is. Nothing from Max either, figuring he will have had a sleepover with Dunc before all the festivities.

"Hate this fucking place."

He sees it in the eyes of the non-travelling residents—the fear, the shame, the dominance of the king and queen of Melody Street,

Nick and Patricia. *For the greater good.* And not forgetting Princess Veronica, the pretty little thing, ever smiling, ever charming.

Power. Control. Order.

"Hate it."

He swings his legs from the bed and walks towards his wardrobe, grabbing a liquorice strap from the dresser on the way past.

Who will forgive you for your sins?

THE END

Mark Towse is an English horror writer living in Australia. He would sell his soul to the devil or anyone buying if it meant he could write full-time. Alas, he left it very late to begin this journey, penning his first story since primary school at the ripe old age of forty-five. Since then, he's been published in over two hundred journals and anthologies, had his work made into full theatrical productions for shows such as The No Sleep Podcast and Tales to Terrify, and has penned fourteen novellas, including Nana, Gone to the Dogs, 3:33, and Crows. Chasing The Dragon is his debut novel.

CHAPTER ONE PREVIEW of CHASING THE DRAGON

CHAPTER ONE: I HATE JESUS
LATE OCTOBER, THURSDAY, 7:00 PM

Another shift finally comes to an end.

Iciness wraps around me as I step outside into the now lighter rain, the brightness of the moon offering only a temporary distraction from surrounding squalor and dilapidation. It's not so much the smell of fried chicken on my clothes, nor the ever-present scent of piss and liquor that makes me sick to the stomach, but the thickness of the fear in the air. It's stifling, claustrophobic, and relentless. You can almost taste it.

"Gets my fucking goat."

Safe to say, dread's bony fingers have been wrapped around this town's throat for some time, but now the place is on its knees, its death rattles soon to follow.

The dimly-lit faces of my co-workers gawp back as I slide the door closed behind me, their mouths no doubt further polluting the air with their bile and tittle-tattle. Toxic exchanges about the new guy who hardly speaks a word and does what he's paid to do instead of slacking. Only been there a week, but I'm sure they hate me already. How is that possible? I keep my head down, trying to appear as normal as possible, smiling and nodding in the right places. Yes, sir. No, sir. Yes, shove the balls in as well if you like, sir.

People tend to jump to hate at things they don't understand or that threaten the self-imposed regulations of their tiny little universe. They'll see, though. I'll open their eyes to a bigger world.

They have no idea who I am about to become.

An involuntary snicker leaves my lips, prompting an approaching elderly couple—no doubt on their way home before the unwritten curfew kicks in—to cross the road and increase their pace.

"Good evening," I say, following with a smile.

Nothing.

Residents, who once held their heads with pride, keep their stare fixed on the cracked pavement, afraid to make eye contact, scared of their own shadow. It's rare to catch them outside after seven. The poor things usually huddle together behind thick curtains and triple-bolted doors, watching the *Price is Right* and praying for just one night without harassment and a flaming bag of dog shit through their letterbox. Not too much to ask, surely?

But there's no trust around here anymore, no shared human bond.

During my time behind bars, I pledged to Mother I would do better. Bring some hope back into the world. I'm not even sure what I feel towards her anymore. Too young to understand at the time, I'm beginning to comprehend why she was always so highly strung. Pent up to the point of insanity, she just wanted the chaos to end.

"It gets my fucking goat!" she used to say, eyes wild, fingers white around her feather duster as she eyed the stranger's car parked outside our house. "Without rules, without respect, Simon, we are nothing but animals."

Yes, it's time for me to step up.

As I make my way past the boarded-up windows of once-treasured stores, my eyes draw to the house across the road, the word 'cockmuncher' sprayed across the rotten panels of the fence. A dirty, yellow streetlight shows the paint still glistening as I march across, eyeing the discarded aerosol in the overgrown lawn.

Edith, is it? Yes, Edith, the name of the woman who lives here. Mother knew her. She said the lady had a Shih Tzu that held true to its name, pebble-dashing our driveway with its little brown nuggets one morning. Eighty, if a day—the woman, not the Shih Tzu—and I suspect the old lady munches on cough drops over cocks these days.

Feeling helpless, I bend down and pick up the discarded aerosol.

"I saw who did it." The feeble voice emerges from the partially open door. "Little shit had a skateboard tucked under his arm. One of them inbred faces too."

Over the muffled sound of her TV, I hear smashing glass and howls from night walkers, accompanied by the ever-present soundtrack of thumping bass and distant sirens.

"Did you call the police?"

She offers a croaky laugh. "You're a funny bastard, aren't you? Had an incident last month, and it took two hours before the pigs showed up."

She knows as well as I do most are paid off or have given up the fight. So-called "drug lords" taking over the town, everyone in their back pocket while the place goes to shit. The sirens are just for show, an attempt to placate, but those days are long gone.

"Things are going to change around here," I say. "Mark my words."

"Some twat came to the door a few months ago promising the exact same thing," Edith says. "Shoved a leaflet in my face and told me his party would put this town back on the map. He was in the papers a week later, caught with his pants down in the disabled bogs, some hooker choking on his meat stick. You know—his love truncheon, pecker, womb ferret, purple-headed—"

"Yeah, yeah, I get it, dearie."

"Anyway, certainly not the sort of thing you want to be on the map for." She opens the door a little further, exposing a tuft of hair resembling iron wool, albeit with a blue tinge. "Do I know you?"

"Just know that things will get better."

"Why, are they dropping an effin' bomb on the place?"

"No." I clear my throat. "A saviour is coming."

She sighs, opening the door further to reveal the flickering frown across her forehead. "A bloody bible basher, I should have known. Christ, you've got some nerve, kid, touting the Lord's name around here."

"No, no, no, you've got me all wrong." Time for a change of tactic. "I despise all that stuff. In fact, I hate Jesus."

A strange, garbled croak leaves through the tiniest hole in her lips, and her eyes grow just as narrow. "You hate Jesus?" She takes an urgent step across the threshold, looks to the heavens, and makes the sign of the cross on her chest.

"Yeah, but...but"—some days you just can't win—"I mean the way you can love someone with all your heart but sometimes hate them. You know, like your parents or your partner, for example."

"My parents are worm food, and my Bernard had a coronary four years ago."

Fuck. Fuck. Fuckity-fuck.

As the woman continues her heavy wheeze, I make a mental note that saying things like, "I hate Jesus," will not necessarily win people over. Back-pedalling as fast as I can, I raise my palms in a gesture once again. "Help is coming, Edith. The caped disciple will bring order back to town."

"The caped disciple?"

Knowing I need to work on my PR skills, I offer a feeble nod and keep my mouth shut.

Shaking her head, the old lady puckers her lips again and looks up and down the street before taking a step back into darkness. "Look, son, you might mean well, but you're wasting your time around here. Even God moved out from these parts a long time ago. Found himself a nice little piece of real estate in the nice little town of *'I Don't Give a Fuck.'*"

"I'm sorry. All I'm trying to do is—"

"Just drop your leaflet and bugger off, will you? *Antiques Roadshow* is next, and I've got a casserole for one in."

Before I can respond, the door slams in my face. *Stop the chaos.* I guess she's every right to be sceptical, one empty promise after another shoved down her scraggy little throat. And questionable faith, jumping from devout to insincere at the drop of a hat, but again, I guess it's been tested many times living in this shit hole of a town. Feet together, I stiffen my posture, lift my chin, and offer a salute of sorts. "I promise to restore hope, Edith. This town will be good again. I will bring order back, you'll see."

After tossing the empty aerosol into Edith's wheelie bin, I continue on my way, contemplating just how much work is required. Suburbia's soundtrack continues around me as neon light spills onto damp streets, basking them with seediness and giving discarded fast-food wrappers a radioactive tinge. Blurry puddles offer the illusory effect of rippled portals to an underworld, the rain stinging as if tiny acidic tears of the once happy residents, each droplet loaded with a misery beyond memory.

It's chaos, Simon. Anarchy.

Even alleys are alive with moving shadows and whispers, only the desperate or foolish venturing into the darkness. The druggies are starting to come out, too, blood-stained or borrowed cash in their pockets, always on the lookout for more.

Yes, it's time. I will make a change. This town will get its hero.

I can't remember the last time I heard a bird sing around these parts. Or even the last time I heard a laugh not tainted by evil. Perhaps people can still find joy somehow, behind closed doors, their televisions providing a portal into worlds of colour and unfiltered happiness. For me, it was always the latest superhero comic—exciting tales of heroic acts in the battle of good vs. evil. A belief that things could change for the better because Christ knows we needed it. It was escapism without limits, and I guess one thing I'm thankful to my father for.

I'm close. Yeah, here we go. Not this right, but the one after. Red door, if I remember correctly, about halfway down. The house number has slipped my mind, but the address carries too much significance—*Hope Street.* What are the chances?

A shudder runs down my spine as Mother's voice catches me by surprise. *Imagine if everyone did that, Simon. A blind eye here, a blind eye there, and before you know it, we're hiding in the broom closet eating tinned peaches. It starts with the little things, Simon. You must rinse your bowl out. It's just laziness, Simon, a lack of self-respect. Rinse! Rinse! Rinse! Bastards next door parked in front of our house again. It gets my fucking goat! Crumbs on the countertop, Simon. It's chaos! How many times have I told you? And I know you're not fucking stupid. Not like your sorry excuse of a father over there, sitting in that chair while the world turns to shit. Jeff! Jeff! I'm talking to you. Someone's cat has taken a shit on our front lawn. What are you going to do about it? I'll poison the fucking thing, see if I don't.*

"Let me be, Mother. I'll uphold my pledge to you and clean up this town, but please, just let me be."

If you sit back and watch, you'll become just another casualty of the chaos, Simon. You have to set an example. You have to fight. Grow some balls. If you do nothing, you're as much to blame as the others. Don't give up like him over there, the useless sack of shit. A quitter. Always has been, always will be.

"Mama, stop!"

Look at him, just sitting on his fat arse as if nothing is happening. You have to set an example if you want people to follow. Jeff, why aren't you doing something? Jeff! Jeff! Idiots down the street playing their jungle music again. It gets my fucking goat! Go and tell them, Jeff. Jeff, can you hear me? Kids playing cricket in the street again. If that ball comes anywhere near my begonias, so help me God. Go and tell them, Jeff. Are you ignoring me, Jeff? Jeff! JEEEEEEEEEEEEEFF! Simon, for the love of God, promise you won't turn out like your weak-as-piss father or his pissant of a brother. PROMISE ME, SIMON!

And that was my childhood—witness to a relentless barrage of instructions and discipline, nervously observing from the staircase as my father absorbed most of the impact. Scared of his own shadow, he became nothing more than a shell. I hated her for it but hated my father more, especially when Mother turned her attention to me when nothing was left of him to peck at.

That's not going to be me, though. No fucking way. I'm the man who will make a difference and put this town back on the map. Just see if I don't. When the sun goes down, no more Simon Dooley. It's time to meet The Rectifier.

The Rectifier.

Rectifier.

Shit! It sounded good the first few times, but now it just sounds lame, like something to treat a breathing condition or crooked teeth. We'll call it a work in progress. After all, Rome wasn't built in a day.

CHAPTER TWO: THE LEOTARD

Behind the door, the TV blares so loudly I'm not even sure they'll hear my knock.

"Hello?"

I rap again, my attention drawn towards the flickering light behind the twitching curtains of the house next door. You see me now, but soon I'll just be a shadow, a trick of the eye, a blur on—*come on, for Christ's sake, it's pissing it down.*

RAP. RAP.

On the verge of the boggy front strip in front of the house, I notice a squished black bag, brown mush spilling onto the pavement.

Chaos, Simon. Chaos. It gets my fucking goat!

To think, all the trouble of wrapping one's fingers around your dog's steaming warm turd, then leaving the bag there, as if it's a job done.

RAP. RAP. RAP. RAP.

At last, the door opens, revealing a woman looking older than time itself, cigarette dangling loosely from the corner of her mouth. She screws up her eyes and begins to examine me.

"Is it ready?" I say.

The lines across her forehead deepen, and she takes a long, slow drag, lending thoughts of a retired detective brought in to solve a crime that's keeping the hotshots from sleep. "You what, love?"

"The costume? Is it ready?"

She's back on the case again, giving it another crack, red veins in her cheeks almost glowing in the dark. "Ah, yes. Leotard man," she says.

"It's not a leotard." It was once but shouldn't look like one now if the old codger's done her job. "It's my costume," I say, puffing my chest out. "Did you put the pockets in as I asked, and add the cape?"

"Wait there, love."

As she leaves in a puff of smoke, I snap my head to the left and inhale air less tainted with second-hand smoke or dog shit. Come on, come on, you silly old goose.

"Can you remember where I put that leotard, Alf?" I hear her say. "That weirdo's back."

"Don't let him in, for Christ's sake," a voice replies, one I assume belongs to Alf.

Arching my neck through the doorway, I can almost taste the stale warmth. Beyond the yellowing hallway, I see an ashtray overflowing with butts and a stack of empty dishes, leftover carnage from goodness knows how many TV dinners. One can hardly blame them for bunkering down, though, losing themselves in any other world than this one.

Chaos, Simon.

But it's just one cup, Mum.

CRACK. How dare you!

Sorry. I'm sorry.

It's one cup now, two tomorrow, and before you know it, you're living in a bloody shit heap, Simon. Nothing but a fucking hippy collecting your piss in empty milk bottles. Is that what you want, Simon? Is it? Because that's what's going to happen.

Sorry, Mum. Sorry.

It gets my fucking goat!

"Here we go, love."

It's less grand than I would have hoped. Lacklustre by superhero standards but better than a bin bag and tape. "Four pockets?"

"Just like you asked, pet. Two on the outside, two on the inside. It's got a zip-up back and a flowing cape."

"Eyes?"

"Red netting, just like you—"

"Wait. Where's the mouth hole?"

"Beg your pardon, love?"

"Has the weirdo gone yet, Janice?" Alf hollers from behind the discoloured wall. "You're letting all the cold air in."

"Mouth hole. A hole for the mouth," I say, trying to remain calm.

"Janice!"

"Hang on, Alf! I'm with a client."

I'm losing it, my jaw beginning to ache from clenching. "Mouth hoooooooooole."

"Just give him the leotard and tell him to eff off, will yer. Our show's starting."

She snaps her head around again. "Will you shut up, Alf? Will you? Will you just shut the fuck up?"

"And it's not a fucking leotard," I shout at the wall.

"Look, you didn't ask for a mouth hole," she says, watery eyes back on me. "If you'd have asked for one, you'd have got one."

"I just assumed you'd know to put a hole there. You know, so one can breeeeeeathe."

"Gimp suits are not my specialty," she says, folding her arms tight.

"Janice, hurry up."

"Shut up, Alf! Shut up! Shut up!"

Dropping my shoulders, I offer a resigned sigh, running my finger over the material where the mouth should be. "I just thought it would be obvious enough."

"Well, the material looks breathable for a few hours. And if you'd wanted holes, you should have—"

"Can you do it now?"

"Do what now?"

"The hole."

"The hole?"

"Now."

"Now?"

"Yes, now."

"I'm sorry, love, but I'm watching—what are we watching, Alf?"

"Fuck all at the bloody moment."

"I have a slot on Thursday morning if that suits you?"

"But it's just a hole. Can't be difficult."

"Not if you want a good job. Now, as I said, if you bring it—"

"But I need it now." I've been thinking about this moment all day; it made my skin sing. "Never mind," I say, close to tears. "It's fine. I'll take it as is."

"That'll be a hundred then." She hands over the costume and offers her crinkled palm, splayed fingers more yellow than the hallway. "Where's the party anyway?"

I lay the cash in her hand. No tip. "Party?"

"Fancy dress."

"No, you don't understand." I correct my posture, thrusting my chest out again and lifting my chin. "I'm The Rectifier."

"Come again? And what just happened to your voice?"

"The Rectifier." It still sounds strained, but I'm sure my vocal cords will get used to it. "I'm bringing hope back to town."

"Janice!"

"Okay, okay." She rolls her eyes. "That man, I tell yer. Well, I'll wish you good luck. Although I think you might be a little late, pet. This town went to the dogs long ago, and they won't give it back without a fight." She looks up and down the street before flicking the cigarette butt onto the pavement.

If everyone did that. Lack of self-respect.

I've seen so many misdemeanours today that made my blood boil, but I'm just a civilian until I'm in that costume. No power. Not long to wait now, though, and my skin prickles again at the thought.

"Well, goodnight, love," she says, now frantically rubbing at her arms. "As I said, if you need a hole for the mouth, or anywhere else for that matter, bring it back on Thursday."

Unable to tear my stare away from the smouldering butt, all I can manage is a weak, "Goodbye."

The TV kicks into action as soon as the door closes.

Chaos, Simon. Drinking your own piss.

Unable to turn a blind eye any longer, I snatch the cigarette butt from the concrete, and lift the letter box. Giggling comes from inside, somewhat reserved at first, but it soon competes with the shrill canned laughter from the TV.

"The Rectum Eater," I hear Alf say.

That's enough to send them both into hysterics, and for me to shove the butt through the door. A small step, but I guess even Spiderman struggled to cast webs at first, and I expect Superman had his fair share of crash landings and sore retinas. I stand, ready to run, but my eyes fall across the broken bag of dog shit, causing a shudder to run down my spine.

Chaos, Simon. Chaos! It's everywhere you look, spreading like mould. The pull is too powerful—my superhero senses tingling and Mother's voice screaming at me to end the chaos.

The Rectum Eater.

Am I going to do this? Am I? I'm damn sure this wouldn't fall within the superhero code of conduct. Still, until I get that suit on, I'm just a civilian.

Fuck it.

As I pick up the bag and begin forcing it through the letterbox, some of it spills onto my fingers and runs down my arm. *That's it, Simon. Get it all in. Teach them some respect.* It's all I can do not to spew, but I continue digging my fingers into the warmth, knowing becoming a superhero was never going to be an easy ride. *Get in. Get in.*

"Who the hell is that now?" Alf shouts from inside.

Ah, shit.

"It's your turn," Janice says, the blare of the TV ceasing once more.

A simultaneous groan and squeak signify the big guy is on his way. *Come on, almost there. Get in there, you fucker. Get in. Goddamn it, will you just—*

"What in the name of horseshit!" The handle turns, and the door snaps open.

"Captain Justice, at your service," I scream, wiping my shitty fingers across my thigh and making my run.

"Oy," Alf calls into the night. "Come back here, you pervy little twat."

"Small steps make climbable ladders."

"I'll stick that leotard right up your arse."

"It's not a fucking leotard!"

I see hopelessness, a town on its knees in desperate need of a hero. It's overloading my circuitry, wrongdoing wherever one looks. Someone must rise to the challenge and set an example. *Starts with you, Simon. If you don't rinse your bowl, why would you expect others to?*

Glancing over my shoulder, I see Alf still standing in the doorway. I'm not sure why I'm still running; the guy looks three hundred pounds, and that's being generous. One sudden move and Janice would be picking out an extra-large casket for him at the parlour. That said, I slow to a walk only as I turn the corner, the smell of dog shit still strong in my nostrils.

Tough beginnings.

If only they could see what I intend to do, they'd surely get behind me, perhaps even sleep more peacefully in their beds. A rookie move, letting my emotions guide my actions, and certainly not the best start to my public esteem campaign. If there is to be a change and a semblance of restored order, I need the public on my side.

Promise you won't turn out like your weak-as-piss father or his pissant of a brother, Simon.

A scene fills my head, creeping down the hallway for a midnight snack, one of my braver moments, never to be repeated. Heart in mouth, I swung myself into the kitchen, celebrating prematurely by letting out a deep exhale and offering a mini fist pump. The last thing I expected to find was a bleary-eyed and ominously skinny Uncle Rodney, his head in the fridge, a bundle of blankets hanging around his lower half but well past his arse crack. He seemed much less perturbed, lifting his head from the fridge and offering a toothless smile, blankets dropping to the floor, exposing a limp dick swinging between pasty white stilts. "Simey! Got any peanut butter in here, maaaaaaaaate?"

Mother often called Dad's brother a waste of a skeleton, and I was always inclined to agree—another victim to add to the growing tally of what was becoming a drug-fuelled town. Even Father despised him, but being *as weak as piss,* I guess he didn't have the heart to estrange himself from kin. He made me swear on my life not to tell, knowing Mother would tear him a new one if she ever found out. "Rodney occasionally sleeps things off in the shed," Father said. "It's only now and again. Better than him sleeping on the streets, don't you agree?"

No, I'll not turn out like either of those two. "I won't let you down, Mama."

Fantasising about a long, hot shower, I resume my journey home, observing the chaos. Plastic bags caught in bushes, empty bottles and cans nestled in weeds, graffiti wherever I look, and worst of all, discarded needles and condoms left in plain sight. Making a mental note of it all, I do my best to ignore the car pulling up on the opposite side of the road, taking up two spaces. *Easy, Simon, easy.* I give them the benefit of the doubt, thinking they may check their position and correct themselves, but as they exit the vehicle and slam the door shut, I'm overwhelmed and already making my way across.

You must set an example, Simon.

"Excuse me, sir."

A woman with a crew cut turns around, a white plastic bag swinging in her grip.

"My apologies," I say. "It gets dark early these days, doesn't it?"

"Is that what you wanted to tell me?"

"Actually, no. It's just... Well, you're parked over two spaces, see."

The woman looks over my shoulder and back at me again. "You don't look like a parking inspector, chicken boy."

"That's funny. Chicken boy." Mocking myself still prompts no sign of her breaking her defences. "Could you move it then, please?"

She offers a gentle shake of her head. "I'll be five minutes, tops. I'm just dropping off a food package to some of the elderlies in the high rise."

The skin tightens around my skull. "I'm guessing moving the car will only take a minute. *Tops.*"

She sighs hard, giving me another up-and-down look, eyes stopping briefly on the leotard. "Look, it's been a long day. All I want to do is take this up and then go home."

"Just move the car, then you can continue with your business."

"Five minutes, tops."

"A minute, *tops,* to move the car."

Her forehead creases. "But I'm bringing food to the elderly."

"And I'm bringing hope back to town."

"The only thing you're bringing is a migraine, chicken boy. And what's with the leotard?"

"Move the car."

"No."

"Move the car."

"No."

I feel my blood begin to boil. This woman thinks she has a free pass because she's carrying food for one of the crusties in the tower block. Words start crashing into each other in my head as I try and find a way through all this chaos. It all starts to become too much until lightning finally strikes. "I'll take the food up for you."

"No. We're not allowed to do that. They're used to seeing me, and quite frankly, you'd likely upset the poor dearies."

I hate Jesus. "It'll be fine, I like old people. Give me the food."

"No."

"Why are you being so obtuse?"

"Obtuse? It's taking all my reserve not to thump you."

"I'm not sure you should be working with elderly people."

"I'm not sure you should be breathing."

"Give me the food."

"No."

"Give me the food."

"No."

Once again, overwhelmed, I snatch at the plastic bag.

"You smell like shit," she cries.

We push, shove, twist, and dance amid a series of groans and cuss words, the cape flapping between us. Light rain begins to shower down but washes away neither our dogged pursuit for supremacy nor the shit stains down my fingers. Only as the plastic bag splits, launching the contents towards the sky, do we cease our struggle, observing as gravity comes into play, bringing the Tupperware boxes plummeting towards the ground. We watch in silence as what looks like gravy spills across the road.

The woman offers a snort as she turns to face me, the fingers of her right hand curling into a fist. "Oh, it's on now."

I take a step back. She takes a step forward. I take another step back. She takes two steps forward. I may have mishandled this situation. Perhaps I could have been more diplomatic with my approach. Still, the words in my head are unrelenting, and I know resistance is futile. "You should have moved the car."

And as predicted, the short sentence ignites a fire behind my dance partner's eyes. She offers another snort and begins her charge. Nursing my wounded ego, I turn fast and start my run, meatballs squelching underfoot.

"If I get my hands on you!"

But I'm running like the wind, beating world records. "If everyone did that, the world would—"

"I'll rip yer fucking head off!"

"I'm just trying to bring order. Why can't you just—"

"Oh, just fuck off with your self-righteous goody-goody bullshit."

"Be respectful."

"Kiss my arse."

Her voice is already growing distant, and her breathing is nothing but a wheeze. Taking the opportunity, I look over my shoulder to find her slowing, shaking a fist at the air in front. She finally stops, doubling over, sucking in the town's toxicity.

If only they knew, could see what I was trying to do. Chicken boy, she'd called me. Just like Rectum Eater, it's a name I hope doesn't stick. *Why won't anyone get on side? In this godforsaken town, why wouldn't anyone want to embrace change?* Chalking the encounter as another work in progress, I slip back into the shadows and continue home. Light has albeit faded now, bringing an even more sinister feel to town along with the familiar heaviness in the pit of my stomach.

AVAILABLE MARCH 2024

PREORDER AVAILABLE THROUGH OUR WEB STORE
EERIERIVERPUBLISHING.COM

More from Eerie River

Eerie River Publishing is a leader in independent horror, dark fantasy, and dark speculative fiction.

We are dedicated to publishing anthologies, collections, and novels from some of the best indie authors around the world. Our goal is to become a go-to resource for horror, dark fantasy and dark speculative readers, and to provide a safe space for authors to share their stories.

Interested in becoming a Patreon member?
By joining our patreon, you will be supporting our artists and authors, who work hard to produce high-quality and original content for your enjoyment. You will also get access to exclusive perks, such as early releases, behind-the-scenes updates, bonus material, and more. If you love dark fiction and want to support independent publishing, please consider becoming a patron today. Thank you for your interest and support.

www.patreon.com/EerieRiverPub.

To stay up to date with all our new releases and upcoming giveaways, follow us on Facebook, Twitter, Instagram and YouTube.

linktr.ee/eerieriver

EERIE RIVER PUBLISHING

NOVELS & COLLECTIONS
The Naughty Corner
Dead Man Walking
Devil Walks in Blood
The Darkness In The Pines
At Eternity's Gate
Beyond Sundered Seas
Path of War
In Solitudes Shadow
The Void
They Are Cursed Like You
SENTINEL
NOTHUS
Miracle Growth
Infested
Helluland
A Sword Named Sorrow
Storming Area 51

ANTHOLOGIES
AFTER: A Post-Apocalyptic Survivor Series
Elemental Cycle: Four Book Series Blood Sins
It Calls From Series
Blood Sins
Last Stop: Whiskey Pete
Elemental Series
Of Fire and Stars
From Beyond the Threshold

DRABBLE COLLECTIONS
Forgotten Ones: Drabbles of Myth and Legend
Dark Magic: Drabbles of Magic and Lore

COMING SOON

Rotten House
Chasing the Dragon
Tarot Anthology
The Earth Bleeds at Night

www.ingramcontent.com/pod-product-compliance
Lightning Source LLC
Chambersburg PA
CBHW032022310726

48972CB00002B/506